KU-531-453

THE WICKED BARON

Sarah Mallory

MILLS & BOON®

All the characters in this book have no existence outside the imagination
of the author, and have no relation whatsoever to anyone bearing the
same name or names. They are not even distantly inspired by any
individual known or unknown to the author, and all the incidents are
pure invention.

All Rights Reserved including the right of reproduction in whole or
in part in any form. This edition is published by arrangement with
Harlequin Enterprises II BV/S.à.r.l. The text of this publication or
any part thereof may not be reproduced or transmitted in any form
or by any means, electronic or mechanical, including photocopying,
recording, storage in an information retrieval system, or otherwise,
without the written permission of the publisher.

® and TM are trademarks owned and used by the trademark owner
and/or its licensee. Trademarks marked with ® are registered with the
United Kingdom Patent Office and/or the Office for Harmonisation in
the Internal Market and in other countries.

First published in Great Britain 2009
Harlequin Mills & Boon Limited,
Eton House, 18-24 Paradise Road, Richmond, Surrey TW9 1SR

© Sarah Mallory 2009

ISBN: 978 0 263 20979 2

MORAY COUNCIL
LIBRARIES &
INFO.SERVICES

20 27 38 27	
Askews	
RF	

Set in Times Roman 12¾ on 14½ pt.
08-0809-74462

Harlequin Mills & Boon policy is to use papers that are natural,
renewable and recyclable products and made from wood grown in
sustainable forests. The logging and manufacturing process conform
to the legal environmental regulations of the country of origin.

Printed and bound in Great Britain
by CPI Antony Rowe, Chippenham, Wiltshire

Sarah Mallory was born in Bristol, and now lives in an old farmhouse on the edge of the Pennines with her husband and family. She left grammar school at sixteen, to work in companies as varied as stockbrokers, marine engineers, insurance brokers, biscuit manufacturers and even a quarrying company. Her first book was published shortly after the birth of her daughter. She has published more than a dozen books under the pen-name of Melinda Hammond, winning the Reviewers' Choice Award in 2005 from Singletitles.com for *Dance for a Diamond* and the Historical Novel Society's Editors' Choice in November 2006 for *Gentlemen in Question*.

A recent novel by the same author:

MORE THAN A GOVERNESS

To jay Dixon, with thanks
for all your support and encouragement

Prologue

'Hell and confound it, Darvell, will you stop flirting with that lightskirt and give your mind to the cards!'

Luke Ainslowe, fifth Baron Darvell, gently disentangled himself from the lady's scented embrace and begged pardon. There were few amusements for the Army of Occupation in Paris, following the stunning victory at Waterloo: women and cards were two of the most popular and Luke was currently enjoying both. He looked at the eager, wine-flushed faces of the gentlemen around him and smiled. They all envied him, he knew, for he was sitting beside the most fashionable courtesan in Paris, the improbably named Angelique Pompadour. She leaned against him, her powdered head on his shoulder while he studied the cards in his hand.

Across the table, the officer of the Light Dragoons who had berated Luke made his discard and glanced up, his silver epaulettes glinting in the candlelight.

'I hear von Laage's wife is increasing again—she holds that you are the father, Darvell.'

Luke shrugged. 'Lady Sophia is air-dreaming, Denby. There are at least half a dozen men more eligible than I for that role.'

'Why, then, is the lady naming you?' demanded another of the players.

A red-faced gentlemen in grey satin laughed.

'Because Darvell is the only one von Laage would not dare to call out! Well known to be lethal with swords or pistols. Never beaten in a duel, eh, Luke?'

'Not yet, Clayman, not yet.'

'So you are telling me you were never one of Lady Sophia's lovers?' cried Major Denby.

Luke shook his head. 'We had a few preliminary skirmishes, but I never breached that particular citadel. I discovered the lady was far too free with her favours.'

Sir Neville Clayman chuckled. 'A man needs to be very rich to keep an exclusive mistress, and that is not you, eh, Darvell?'

Luke grinned. 'Devil a bit!'

There was a pause while Sir Neville considered his hand. 'But you have a title, and that is certainly an advantage. I believe le Brun's widow is hoping to become the next Lady Darvell.'

Angelique raised her head. *'Mon cher...'* she pouted and placed one white hand upon Luke's velvet sleeve *'...c'est vrai?'*

Sir Neville nodded. 'Had it from the lady herself two nights' since.'

'But you have not had it from *me*,' said Luke gently. He picked up Angelique's hand and planted a kiss in the palm before releasing it. 'The woman is an upstart. Her beauty dazzled le Brun, but there is no breeding behind that pretty face.'

'If it's breeding you want, the Tregennick chit has it through several generations,' remarked the major, 'yet you cut her dead last night. She was mad as fire.'

Luke flicked a speck of dust from his sleeve. 'Her mama insisted upon throwing her in my way at Lady Gressingham's rout. I obliged her with an evening's flirtation, that is all.'

'And you could not even recall her name the very next night.' Major Denby shook his head at him. 'By Gad, you are devil, man! No woman is safe from you.'

'Nonsense. Virtuous maidens bore me, so they have nothing to fear. And you will never find me chasing innocent little *ingénues*. But a man must have a diversion now the war is over. Mine is beautiful women.'

'Yet you'll offer none of them your heart and your hand.'

'There is no room for sentiment in marriage, Denby. When I take a wife, it will be a business contract. My father gambled away the Darvell fortune; it is up to me to restore it by marrying a well-bred heiress. But not yet.' He stared at the cards Sir Neville laid on the table and muttered a laughing curse under his breath. 'Two kings! Damnation, Clayman, your luck is running high tonight. I am out.'

Angelique smiled at him. 'Well, my lord, it was agreed if you lost at cards you would worship at my feet.' She spoke in English, a charming, provocative lilt to her words. With the light of mischief in his eyes Luke reached down, curled his fingers around one slim ankle and lifted her foot on to his knee. A murmur of anticipation ran around the room, while the lady herself leaned back on her chair and smiled.

'Well, milor'? What do you propose? What will the wicked Baron Darvell do?'

He grinned. 'I will keep my word.'

His hand moved over the pink silk stocking and she shivered delightfully when he reached the ribbon-and-lace garter at her knee. He hesitated, then his long fingers moved back to her ankle. He began to untie the strings of her pink satin slipper, calling to the waiter to bring another bottle of champagne.

'Now what are you about, Darvell?' cried Major Denby gaily. 'Do you propose to undress the lady in public?'

'Not at all, my friend. Patience and you shall see.' He pulled the little shoe free and held it aloft, the ribbons dangling over his wrist. When the waiter returned with the champagne he took the bottle from the tray. 'I wish to drink a toast to you, Angel.' He poured a little of the wine into the shoe and quickly raised it to his lips.

'You fool, Darvell, the satin won't hold it!' laughed Sir Neville.

But Luke was not listening; he had swallowed some of the champagne, the rest was seeping through the slipper and running over his hand, soaking the white ruffle around his wrist.

'It held enough,' he said. 'And witness, Angel, that none of the bubbles escaped—I drank them all.'

Angelique sat up and clapped her hands. 'Bravo, milor', I am enchanted. But we should use glasses for the rest.' She looked at him, an invitation in her dark eyes. 'Per'aps you would like to drink with me privately?'

'I regret not, Angel. I am obliged to leave you very soon.' He filled two glasses with champagne and handed one to the lady. 'I am off to England tomorrow.'

'England!' cried Major Denby, signalling for a fresh pack of cards. 'Never tell me you are going home.'

'I am indeed. Peacetime soldiering is not in my line. I have spent one winter in Paris and that is enough.'

'He's going back to Darvell Manor to become a gentleman farmer,' declared Sir Neville, smoothing the wrinkles from the sleeve of his grey silk coat.

Luke grimaced. 'Devil a bit! I plan to enjoy myself for a few more years yet. But I have a fancy to see England again. Besides, I have a commission from my brother. You may recall he was in Paris last month. He is touring Europe with his bride until the summer and wants me to make sure his new house at Malberry is ready for his return.'

'Ah, the fortunate James,' nodded Sir Nicholas. 'He married his heiress.'

'Fortunate indeed,' agreed Luke. 'Not only is she rich, but pretty and agreeable, too.'

'Perhaps you should try marriage, Darvell,' suggested the major.

'I think not, my friend. It would take a paragon indeed to make me give up my freedom.'

Angelique drew a finger gently along his cheek. 'Milor', it is not necessary that you should give up *everything*.'

For a moment he looked serious. 'Oh, yes, it is. Only a deep, long-lasting devotion could tempt me into matrimony.'

'And what would tempt the lady, his prowess in the bedroom, perhaps?' quipped an officer in scarlet regimentals.

'That and his title,' responded another.

Luke joined in the general laughter. 'Aye, that would have to do it, gentlemen, since there's no fortune to speak of.'

Angelique held up her glass. 'Then you will come back to Paris, *mon cher*?'

'Perhaps.' He handed her the wet satin slipper. 'It is past midnight: I must take my leave.'

Chapter One

The atmosphere in the morning room of Broxted House was decidedly tense. Carlotta stared at her uncle, her chin raised and a hint of defiance in her dark eyes. Lord Broxted met her look with a frown of exasperation.

'Carlotta, you are no ordinary débutante. It is no matter that your mother is the daughter of an earl; twenty years ago she eloped with a penniless Italian artist.' He paused and a faint look of distaste flickered across his aristocratic features. 'They both of them…*paint*…to earn their living.'

Carlotta clasped her hands even more tightly in her lap. 'I am not ashamed of my parents, Uncle.'

Lady Broxted, sitting beside Carlotta on the elegant little sofa, reached over to pat her hands. 'No, of course you are not, my dear, and no one is suggesting that you should disown them, only…'

'Only what, Aunt?'

Lady Broxted avoided Carlotta's eyes and fluttered her fan nervously. 'Tonight we attend Lady Prestbury's rout—your very first *ton* party. It is what we have been working for, is it not, ever since we carried you off from Malberry last June and installed you in Miss Currier's extremely select seminary? Not that I think it was necessary to send you there; no one would know you were brought up in Rome, for the English governess your mama employed gave you an excellent education, and all that was needed was a little polish—but there, your uncle was adamant.'

'I was, madam, but I fear we are straying from the point,' put in the earl, frowning at his wife.

'Yes, of course, my dear. Carlotta, now we are in London and…that is, I think it might be best if…'

Lady Broxted twisted her hands together, looking very uncomfortable.

Carlotta prompted her gently. 'If what, Aunt?'

'Well, as you know, we decided at the outset that you should take the family name of Rivington—so much simpler for us all, my love, and *quite* usual when one is taken up by relatives—but perhaps also it would be as well if we did not mention your parents. Broxted thinks it best if we merely say they live retired in the country, should anyone ask.'

'And is it the fact that my mother eloped or my father's occupation that would be most unacceptable?' retorted Carlotta, bridling.

'Well, you will admit that either of those things would set tongues wagging,' came the frank reply. 'Any hint of gossip could be quite *ruinous* to your chances of making a good match. Not that I want you to lie,' added Lady Broxted hastily. 'That would never do. Merely that you do not *offer* the information.'

'Should a gentleman show a marked interest in you, then of course it would be necessary for him to know the truth,' put in Lord Broxted. 'And if he is fond of you, then I am sure it will make no difference.'

Carlotta bit her tongue to prevent herself from saying she did not care what anyone said of her. After the kindness she had been shown by her aunt and uncle over the past year, it would be churlish in the extreme to admit how little she cared for anyone's good opinion. Part of her wished she could return to her parents, but they had been so happy to think of her going into society and making a good marriage. It was what she must do to repay all their goodness to her.

She had been in London with Lord and Lady Broxted since the beginning of May; a flurry of shopping trips and visits to my lady's dressmaker had filled her days and at last she was ready to attend her first ball. She only wished she could summon up more enthusiasm for it, but her depression was always there, just below the surface. A sadness she had tried to hard to overcome, but even now, after almost twelve months, her dreams were still haunted by a tall, handsome man with laughing, wicked eyes. Determination kept her smiling, made her hide her bleakness from her aunt and uncle. Lady Broxted was patting her hands.

'I cannot tell you how much I am looking forward to launching you into society, my love. It has been a constant sadness to Broxted and me that we did not have children and so it is doubly delightful that I have you with me now.'

Lady Broxted began hunting for her handkerchief. Lord Broxted drew out his own and handed it to her, saying as he did so, 'We are indeed delighted to take you up, Carlotta. It is the least I can do for your poor mother. When my father disinherited her upon her marriage I was shocked, but powerless to help. Then, of course, we lost touch for so many years, but now, I believe it is in my power to reinstate you into your proper place in the world.'

In the face of such kindness Carlotta's anger died away as quickly as it had come. Impulsively she hugged her aunt.

'There, there, Aunt, pray do not cry—if it is your wish, then of course I shall tell no one about my parents. Let us go upstairs and you can advise me which one of my new gowns I should wear this evening.'

In an effort to give her aunt's thoughts a more cheerful turn,

Carlotta accompanied her aunt up to her bedchamber where the maid quickly brought out several of Carlotta's new gowns for inspection. Lady Broxted discarded the pink muslin with apple-green acanthus leaves embroidered around the hem, declaring that almost every other young lady would be wearing pink. Her hand hovered over the lemon satin before settling on the white sprigged muslin.

'This is perfect for your first appearance,' she said. 'You have too much of the Italian in you to appear as a typical English rose, but we must turn that to our advantage—the white muslin will accentuate your olive skin. Thank goodness you have such a flawless complexion, my love, for that means we can leave your lovely shoulders bare. My own woman shall have the dressing of your hair; when it is brushed it glows like polished mahogany and you shall have tiny white rosebuds amongst your curls. It is early for roses, I know, but the cost will be worth it and I shall have a small posy made up for your corsage, too. What do you say?'

Carlotta could not deny a small *frisson* of excitement at the picture her aunt had drawn. When she had been a child growing up in Rome she had never dreamed that one day she would be staying in one of the largest houses in Berkeley Square, preparing to attend a fashionable ball. The gown her aunt was holding up to her was of the finest muslin, embroidered all over with tiny exquisite white rosebuds. The tiny puff sleeves were gathered and fastened with satin ribbons and a wider satin band ran around the high waist. Little Carlotta running barefoot in her father's studio had never imagined owning white satin slippers with leather soles so fine that they would be worn through after one outing, but such a pair was now lying in a drawer, wrapped in several layers of tissue paper. Carlotta smiled at her aunt.

'I will look like a fairy princess,' she murmured.

Lady Broxted handed the gown to her maid and caught Carlotta to her in a warm, scented embrace.

'You will indeed, my love,' she murmured, her voice breaking. 'You will make us all so very proud of you.'

Luke glanced up at the imposing entrance of Prestbury House. Flambeaux burned on each side of the double doors and liveried servants were on hand to assist the ladies from their carriages and escort them up the shallow steps to the grand entrance hall with its soaring marbled pillars. Letitia Prestbury was a formidable hostess and invitations to her fashionable parties were jealously guarded. Luke had no gilt-edged card nestling in his pocket, but he was confident he would not be turned away. Giving his coat sleeves an infinitesimal tug, he joined the long line of guests processing up the grand staircase. From the reception rooms above came the sound of many voices intermingled with the scraping notes of several violins. No lone fiddler or squeaky quartet for Lady Prestbury—her guests would dance to the best musicians money could buy.

As he reached the top of the stairs he found his hostess waiting for him, smiling.

'Well, Cousin, we are honoured to have you attend our little party.'

He bowed over her hand. 'I promised you I would come.'

'But you are so often enticed away by more exciting pleasures, are you not?' She laughed at him. 'I did not send you an invitation because I thought my society gatherings far too staid for the Wicked Baron!'

He grinned at her. 'Perhaps I have reformed. It is not impossible, Letty.'

She twinkled up at him. 'True, Luke, but it is highly unlikely! I know just what it is that has brought you here.'

'You do?'

'Aye, 'tis curiosity, to see the latest heiress.'

He looked down so that she would not read the truth in his eyes. 'Oh?' he said lightly, brushing an invisible speck from his coat. 'And who might that be, my lady?'

'You know very well,' she said, tapping his arm with her closed fan. 'Broxted's niece, Miss Rivington. We were all agog when we heard he was bringing her to town, and he has settled ten thousand pounds on the chit! If that wasn't enough to make her a target for every young man in town, the girl is a positive beauty. But be warned, Luke, she is not for you: I have it from the countess herself that Broxted has great plans for his niece. He will be looking higher than a mere baron.'

'And so he should, but that is no reason why I should not make her acquaintance.'

'Very well, go on in with you.' Lady Prestbury waved him away. 'But you are wasting your time, Cousin.'

With another graceful bow Luke moved on. So it was already decided that the beautiful Miss Rivington was not for him; well, perhaps society's latest débutante might think differently. He walked into the ballroom and paused near the doorway, looking around him. Lounging against one wall were several callow youths standing with their mouths open as they watched the couples go down the dance and Luke saw that their eyes were following one dainty figure in particular.

Miss Rivington, he presumed.

His heart missed a beat: he had to admit she was entrancing. Her hair was curled artlessly about her head, adorned with white rosebuds that looked like stars against the night sky of her dark hair. Her white muslin dress flowed around her as she danced, showing her slender figure to great advantage. She was laughing, her huge dark eyes positively twinkling with merriment. No matter the pain it had cost him to ride away from Malberry last September, he knew now he had been right to do so. This was where she belonged, taking her rightful place in society where everyone could admire her beauty. And she looked so happy, smiling and chattering with the other young people as the music ended. He stifled a sigh. He had told himself that she would soon forget him and so it seemed. She looked so natural here, as though she had never known any other life. He was glad for her, truly. He must give her no cause to think he wished it otherwise.

Carlotta's confidence was growing with every dance. Her new sprigged muslin gown was light as air and the admiration of her dance partners was exhilarating. The ballroom was ablaze with light from the gleaming chandeliers. It bounced off the cream-and-blue walls and caused the gold-leaf decoration on the ceiling to glow like the setting sun. With the exception of the occasional blue or scarlet jacket of an officer, the men were dressed in dark coats, but the ladies presented a dazzling picture in an array of colourful gowns, from the bronze and emerald satins of the matrons to the paler shades deemed suitable for débutantes. Carlotta smoothed her hands down over the white muslin and realised what a good choice it had been. Not that she had any opportunity to tell her aunt so, for she had been on the dance floor almost constantly since her arrival.

After a few initial nerves she found that the dance steps came quite naturally and she was even able to take time to glance at the huge gilt-framed mirrors that adorned the walls of the ballroom. She saw herself reflected there, dancing with a series of attentive partners. Carlotta could hardly believe that she was the slender, dark-haired girl reflected in the mirrors, but so it was, and she was content to give herself up to the enjoyment of the moment.

She was so much at her ease that when Lady Broxted brought forward a lanky young man whom she introduced as Viscount

Fairbridge, Carlotta gave him a friendly smile. She thought his expression rather vacuous, but she encouraged him to talk to her and soon they were on the best of terms. Truly, she thought, as he led her from the dance floor, it was impossible to be gloomy on such a happy occasion.

During a break in the music she was conversing with a group of lively young people when she heard her aunt's voice behind her.

'Ah, there you are, my love. Do allow me to present Lord Darvell to you.'

And the world stopped for Carlotta. The laughing, chattering crowds were forgotten. She had known this moment would come, had rehearsed it a thousand times, but still she was not prepared for the stomach-wrenching spasm that threatened to render her senseless when she heard that name. Of course, she had only known him as Major Ainslowe, but she had not been living in her aunt's household for many weeks before she learned his full title. Gathering all her strength, she turned and dragged her eyes up from the white satin waistcoat and dazzling neckcloth to the face above. The faint hope that it might all be a mistake withered. The gentleman standing before her was achingly familiar. She did not need to cast more than a fleeting glance at his lean, handsome face—it was etched on her soul. As he bowed over her hand, she looked at the waving brown hair that curled over his collar. She recalled the silky feel of it beneath her fingers, tried desperately not to remember the touch of his lips, not on her glove, but on her own mouth, caressing, demanding—she thrust such thoughts away. They had no place in her life now. *He* had no place in her life now.

She forced herself to look at him. Could he have forgotten her? No, his glance told her he knew her, but there was no sign of uncertainty in his hazel eyes as he smiled. He was so sure of his welcome. How could he be so complacent—did he not know what he had done to her? But of course he did; she was aware of his reputation now. It was rumoured that France was littered with women whose hearts he had broken. A bitter wave of anger and unhappiness swept over her, but her training had been very good; she buried those feelings and presented him with a bland, polite mask. Lady Broxted was not aware of their previous meetings, and Carlotta would not have it known now. She withdrew her hand from his grasp, saying coolly, 'My lord.'

'Miss Rivington.' His self-assurance made her seethe. He was laughing at her! 'Your aunt tells me you are not engaged for the next dance. I would be honoured if you would allow me to partner you.'

Luke observed the upright little figure before him. By heaven, she was even more beautiful than he remembered: those large dark eyes—just one flashing look sent his heart soaring again—and the soft red lips that had tasted so sweet against his own. Even as his blood stirred Carlotta lowered her gaze and the dark lashes veiled her thoughts from him. She inclined her head, accepting his invitation with every appearance of maidenly modesty and with a polite bow he turned away. This was the game they must play, of course. No one must know that they had met before.

As he walked away from Carlotta, Luke allowed himself to indulge in the pleasant memory of his very first visit to Malberry twelve months earlier. He had not expected to delay his journey to Darvell Manor by more than a few nights, and he had certainly not expected to find such an angel looking down at him from top of the scaffolding that filled the entrance portico.

He had been running up the steps to the main entrance when a soft, musical voice had stopped him in his tracks.

'Excuse me, but you cannot come in here.' The voice had come from above.

'Oh? And why may I not come in?' Luke spoke to the air.

'It is private. This house belongs to a gentleman.'

Luke spread his hands. 'And am I not a gentleman?' A slight movement on the platform close to the ceiling caught his eye and he observed a slight, boyish figure staring down at him.

'Are you the owner?'

'No,' said Luke, 'but I am come on his behalf.'

'Oh. Mr Kemble is not here.'

'So I can see. Where is he?'

'They have all gone to the inn. It is mid-day and they are always hungry by mid-day.'

'But not you?'

'No, I must finish the fresco while the plaster is still wet.'

Luke shielded his eyes, trying to get a better view of the shadowy figure so high above him. 'Are you not a little young?'

'I am eighteen.' The voice grew a shade deeper.

'Come down and let me look at you,' said Luke, intrigued.

'No, sir. I cannot leave my painting.'

'Then I shall come up to you.' Luke put his foot on the ladder and heard a squeak from above. 'Well? Will you come down now?'

'I will, but only for a moment.'

Luke stood back and watched as the figure scrambled onto the top ladder and began to climb down. He grinned. The upper body was shrouded in a loose shirt, but the tight-fitting breeches left nothing to his admittedly rather wild imagination—the figure descending from the scaffolding was most definitely *not* a boy!

Moments later she stood before him, her eyes, large and dark, regarding him with a mixture of defiance and apprehension. She was very petite with a mass of gleaming near-black hair, constrained at the back of her long, slender neck by a poppy-red ribbon. A paint-spattered shirt billowed from her shoulders, but could not disguise the gentle swell of her breasts, and the tight-fitting breeches were worn with a nonchalance that would have done credit to any actress at Drury Lane. He bit back an appreciative smile.

'Well, does my brother know he has hired a lady to decorate his house?'

'You are Mr Ainslowe's brother?'

'I am. And who are you, what is your name?'

'I am Carlotta Durini.' She clasped her hands together. 'Perhaps I should explain.'

'Please do.'

'My—my father is the artist commissioned to paint Malberry Court, but he has broken his leg and—and I am finishing the last frescoes for him, so that the house will be ready on time. Please, sir, you must not think that there is any plot to deceive, but there was no one else to do it, and, if it is not finished in time, Papa will not be paid the full amount, and then Mama cannot have her maid—and it is only this one ceiling—'

Laughing, he reached out and caught her hands.

'Peace, peace, Miss Durini! Do not upset yourself.'

Her hands were very small and soft within his grasp. Smiling, he let his thumbs gently stroke her wrists, just above the palm, and he felt her agitated fingers grow still. Her lustrous dark eyes were still wary, but he detected the beginnings of a shy smile curving her mouth. Luke found himself wondering what it would be like to kiss those soft red lips. His smile deepened; he opened his mouth to charm her with a few well-chosen words, but they were never uttered. The sound of voices drifted in on the still air. He looked out across the park and saw a group of figures emerging from the trees. Something very like disappointment passed over him.

'I think this must be the others returning now. I will talk to Kemble.'

Those dark eyes regarded him anxiously. 'You will not turn me off?'

'I have no power to do so. But if your work is not up to the standard…'

To his surprise, the worried look left the girl's face.

'It will be, sir. I have been well taught.' She stepped back, gently pulling her hands free. 'If you will excuse me, I must go back to my painting; if the plaster becomes too dry, the fresco will be ruined.'

Without another word she scrambled up the ladder and was soon lost to sight. With a sigh, Luke turned to meet the man who was hurrying towards him.

It was natural that Kemble, Mr James Ainslowe's clerk of works, should want to show his employer's brother all the renovations that had been carried out, and to assure him that the work was proceeding as scheduled. However, at length Luke could contain himself no longer.

'Is it now the fashion, Mr Kemble, to employ female painters?'

There was an uncomfortable silence.

'You refer, my lord, to Signor Durini's daughter.' Luke maintained a polite silence, and soon Kemble continued. 'I believe she has been running wild in the *signor*'s workshop since she was a babe, and learned all his techniques. Howsoever that may be, when the *signor*'s apprentice loped off back to Italy, there was no one to take over, and with the master due back in less than three weeks, the *signor* was desperate for his frescoes to be finished. I admit I was not very happy at first, having the chit here, but the *signor* assures me she can paint, sir.'

'But is she not…distracting?'

Mr Kemble grinned.

'I confess I had to give a couple o' the lads a clout 'round the ear for staring…'

* * *

Now, in the overheated confines of Lady Prestbury's ballroom, Luke thought that Kemble himself might stare if he could see Signor Durini's daughter outshining every other young woman in the room.

Carlotta watched Luke walk away from her, then stumbled to one of the cushioned benches that lined the walls of the ballroom and sank down. She was shaking. She put her hands to her temples, trying to stop the memories, but it was no good. She was back at Malberry, climbing down from the scaffolding after completing that first fresco. Even now she could remember her satisfaction at a job well done, feel the warm sun on her back…

'So you have come down at last.'

Carlotta jumped. With one hand still clutching the scaffolding, she looked around to see Luke sitting on the stone steps, leaning against the base of one of the pillars. His lazy smile made her tingle, right down to her toes.

'Mr…Ainslowe.'

He grinned. 'Yes, I suppose I am.' He jumped to his feet. 'I was taking a stroll through the park and realised you were still here. Do you always work this late?'

'Sometimes later.' Carlotta eyed him warily. The workmen had all gone back to the village, and even Mr Kemble would be in his lodge behind the stable block. Luke was smiling at her now, the twinkle in his hazel eyes making it hard for her not to smile back at him.

'I think I should escort you home.'

'Oh. I mean, um, I—I have first to clean out my brushes,' she said, backing away.

'Of course.' He nodded gravely. 'Go along, then. I shall wait here for you.'

* * *

She expected him to be gone by the time she had finished putting away her paints and tidying the little paint store, but he was still sitting on the steps as she came around the side of the house, and, with a little spurt of surprise, Carlotta realised that she would have been disappointed to find him gone. He rose to his feet.

'I was beginning to think you had run away from me.'

Carlotta's cheeks grew hot; she *had* considered avoiding him and going around the far side of the house. He held out his arm, but she gave a tiny shake of her head and began to walk down the drive, keeping a good distance between them. Safe. Sensible. Yet the truth was she did not *feel* sensible. She felt exhilarated in his company, aware of him walking beside her, matching his step to hers. She was sorely tempted to reach out her hand and take his arm, to draw closer to him. She did not understand why she should feel like this. It was all very confusing.

'Kemble tells me your father's apprentice ran away, and that is why you must finish the ceiling for him.'

'It is only two of the minor scenes. Papa has completed all the major work.'

'Yes, I was looking at the murals in the house. They are spectacular.'

'Papa is a much respected artist in Rome.'

'You must be very proud of him.'

'I am.'

'And is that what you want to do, paint life-size murals?'

She laughed. 'No, it would be thought improper.' She flushed, and glanced across at him. 'Not that my work is not perfectly good. My father would never have consented to my finishing the ceiling if he thought there would be cause for complaint.'

'You need not worry; I have seen nothing that would make me say any such thing.'

They walked together across the grass towards the edge of the park. Through the trees a short distance away the roofs of the houses at the edge of the village could be seen. Carlotta was aware of a faint disappointment that their walk would soon be over.

The sun had set and the early summer twilight was muting the colours of the park. Once they were amongst the trees the shadows deepened. When they reached the stile he vaulted over, then turned and held out his hand. After a brief hesitation, Carlotta took it. His touch disconcerted her; as she stepped down, she stumbled and would have fallen if he had not caught her in his arms. Laughing at her own clumsiness, Carlotta looked up and found his face very close. The laughter caught in her throat as she looked into his eyes. They were no longer twinkling with humour but dark and mysterious. Her heart began to pound against her ribs. No man had ever held her, let alone like this before. Her hands were resting against him; she could feel his chest, smooth and hard beneath the silk waistcoat. Even as she was wondering what to say, his arms tightened and he was kissing her.

Carlotta was at first too shocked to react. His lips fastened on hers, and there was fluttering excitement deep within her, as if her insides were dissolving. A confusion of fear and exhilaration filled her mind, making sober thought impossible. She responded to his kiss; with none of society's restraints holding her back, it seemed the most natural thing in the world to relax against him, her senses revelling in the feel of his arms about her. He encompassed her, mentally and physically. She was aware of his very male strength, crushing her against him. It was frightening, exciting, but there was something else awakening within her—a dark, dangerous attraction such as she had never known before. Carlotta had just decided that they should not be doing this when Luke raised his head and released her. She felt unaccountably bereft.

'I beg your pardon,' he said contritely. 'I did not mean to frighten you, but you looked so dashed irresistible.'

She swallowed hard, trying to regain her composure. She wondered if the world would ever be the same again.

'You did not frighten me, sir.' Her heart was thumping so loud she thought he must surely hear it. 'I…um…I must get home now.'

'Will you not take my arm?'

She shook her head, her cheeks hot with embarrassment. Until that moment she had not considered how she must look, dressed in boy's clothes, smelling of paint and resin. Mama had told her she should wrap herself in a cloak when going out, but Carlotta had always laughed at her, asking what could possibly happen to her on the short journey between Malberry Court and her home? Now she knew.

'No. No. I think I will go on alone from here, if you please.'

He seemed to tower over her, a black shadow in the gloom. Her heart flipped as she thought he might try to kiss her again— she doubted she was strong enough to resist him and was shocked to realise that she did not *want* to resist him. She did not know whether she was most disappointed or relieved when he stepped away from her.

'Of course, if that is what you wish.'

He climbed up on to the stile and sat there, smiling at her, his teeth very white in the dim light. 'Well,' he said as she hesitated, 'go along with you.'

Carlotta began to walk away, her spine tingling as she imagined his eyes raking her back. As soon as a bend in the lane hid the stile from sight, she took to her heels and ran the final few yards to her home.

* * *

'Carlotta, are you quite well?'

Carlotta blinked and looked around the crowded ballroom. Her aunt was at her side, regarding her with some concern.

'Pray do not tell me you have the headache, when everything is going so very well. Come, child, your next dance partner will be looking for you. I am so pleased for you—all but two dances taken this evening! It can be a little difficult when one is new to town, but I knew that as soon as the gentlemen saw how well you dance they would come begging to be presented to you.'

'And did Lord—Lord Darvell ask to be presented, Aunt?' Carlotta tried to keep her voice casual.

'Oh, yes. He came straight up to me and begged for an introduction.' She dropped her voice to say confidentially, 'Carlotta, Darvell is a very wild young man.'

'I know that, Aunt. The Wicked Baron. I have heard all about him.'

'Oh, well, I should not call him *wicked*, exactly,' temporised Lady Broxted, determined to be fair. 'Indeed, no one has heard *anything* of him for the past twelve months, but his conduct before that, when he was still in the army—well, it is not fitting that I should tell you everything, but you are best to beware of him, my love.'

'If he is so very dangerous, I am surprised that you should introduce him to me!'

Lady Broxted sighed. 'I know, but Broxted is well acquainted with the family and it would be very difficult not to acknowledge the connection. I think it a great pity that Darvell sold out. Mayhap he thinks to settle down.' She tapped Carlotta's arm with her fan. 'He may be looking out for a rich wife, for I believe he has not a penny to his name. If so, then he may set out to charm you, Carlotta, but your uncle would not wish for a liaison *there*, my love.'

Carlotta gave a brittle laugh. 'You need have no fears in that direction, Aunt!'

'Good. However, one cannot deny that he is very engaging and will make you a handsome dance partner. By the bye, his brother James owns Malberry Court. I tell you this so that you are forewarned; we must not let slip your family's connection with the house, must we?'

By the time Lord Darvell returned to claim his dance, Carlotta had decided she would be cool and aloof. She would treat his lordship as if they had never met. However, when he took her hand in his own firm grasp, she was not prepared for the surge of emotion that seared through her. She had closed her mind to those first long months after she had left Malberry, the lonely nights when she had cried herself to sleep. Now with one touch he had brought it all rushing back, the longing, the desire and the sheer, blinding agony of finding he had gone.

Carlotta bit on her lip; even now she could not bring herself to think too much of those dark, empty days, afraid that if she did not keep it locked away, her grief would grow and consume her. It was better to concentrate on her anger. He had betrayed her and she wanted to hurt him as he had hurt her. She set her mind to consider how best to do it. Eyes glittering, she answered his attempts to converse with monosyllables, earning a frowning look from her partner. When he suggested they should sit out the second dance she silently acquiesced and accompanied him to a quiet alcove. He smiled at her as they sat down together.

'You are looking very well, Carlotta. I hardly recognise you.'

She unfurled her fan. 'La, I am glad of that, my lord! I vow I was such a gauche little thing when we first met.'

'You were charming.'

Carlotta had not wasted her time at Miss Currier's seminary.

She summoned up memories of a certain rich, spoiled, young lady she had met there, and with the sole aim of distancing herself from him as soon as politely possible, she gave a very creditable titter.

'Oh, dear me, I was utterly innocent then, and ready to make any number of mistakes. Thank heaven my uncle the earl found me when he did.'

'Do you think so?'

'O lord, yes! I had no polish at all, and no possibility of making a great match, but my uncle the earl says that now, with his backing, I can look *very high indeed* for a husband.' *Heavens,* she thought, *how vulgar that sounds!*

'And is that why you are in town?'

He was looking at her now with a shadow of doubt in his eyes. She summoned a dazzling smile, feeling as brittle as glass inside.

'But of course. I am looking about me, but am in no hurry; I can take my time until the right man, and the right fortune, comes along.' She reached out and placed one gloved hand on his sleeve. 'Forgive me for speaking to you in this way, my lord, but I feel we are old friends.'

With bitter satisfaction she observed how he almost recoiled from her. He said stiffly, 'You will be wondering perhaps why I did not come to see you, as I had promised, at Malberry.'

Panic flared. She dare not let him near that raw nerve. She waved her fan slowly. *It is too late for explanations*, she told herself. *The damage is done, Carlotta. Do not let him see how much he hurt you.*

'I had quite forgotten about that,' she said brightly. 'When my uncle came to carry me away, it drove all other thoughts completely from my head!'

'Thus you come to town to find a husband.'

Smile, Carlotta. A smug, self-satisfied, superior smile. Put him in his place.

'Yes, indeed. My uncle has several eligible men in mind for me. All of them *extremely* rich,' she added.

He looked at her, a tiny crease in his brows. 'You have changed, Carlotta.'

She lifted her shoulders to give a slight shrug. 'I am merely being practical, my lord.'

'I thought you were above such mercenary concerns.'

'La, only a fool would claim such a thing. I know the value of a fortune, my lord. Nothing else will do for me.'

She held her breath, forcing herself to meet his gaze with a look of arrogant unconcern. After a moment he looked away.

'Then I wish you luck in your quest, Miss Rivington,' he said quietly.

He rose and, with a little bow, turned and walked away. Carlotta's expression did not change as she watched his retreating form, but inside she felt sick to her core.

Luke stormed out of the ballroom, his jaw clenched to curb his anger. He had expected to find Carlotta altered, but he had not thought she would turn into such a heartless fortune-hunter. A year living with the Broxteds had destroyed the innocent charm that had attracted him to her. Now she was no different from all the other females with their arch smiles and false laughter. He made his way down the stairs and out into the street, where he jammed his hat on his head and began to stride back towards Piccadilly. What had changed her, or had he been mistaken all along? Perhaps he had missed something when he had seen her at Malberry Court, some clue that she was not as sweet and innocent as he had thought. He remembered trying to draw her out during one of their many picnics that summer on the lawn at Malberry.

* * *

'You are an enigma, Miss Carlotta Durini. You say you were born in Italy, and have only been here for a few years, yet your English is faultless.'

'Mama is English.' Her glance was pure mischief. 'She is the daughter of a great nobleman.'

'Oh? You intrigue me. Who?'

She laughed and shook her head. 'I shall not tell you. Mama met my father when she was touring Italy with her family. They ran away together. Mama says it was love at first sight.' She wrinkled her brow. 'Do you think that possible, Major Ainslowe? Can one fall in love so quickly?'

Luke had certainly thought so. Carlotta had stolen his heart within a week of their first meeting. Now as he strode away from Prestbury House he wondered if he had been mistaken in her. Perhaps there had never been anything more than a cold, calculating mind behind her sweet face.

Chapter Two

Carlotta gave herself a mental shake. This was her first ball; it would not do to cry. She put up her chin. She would not give Luke the satisfaction of seeing how close she was to dissolving into tears. Instead she summoned up her brightest smile to greet her next partner. She had already danced with Mr Woollatt earlier in the evening, and on first acquaintance she had found him rather pompous. However, his blatant admiration was balm to her wounded spirits and she treated him to an excess of charm as they danced together. After that she spent the rest of the evening dancing and laughing as though she had not a care in the world. It was only as she was waiting for her cloak that she discovered Luke had left early and had not witnessed her vivacious behaviour.

'Well, it really does not matter,' she told herself as she climbed into the carriage. 'We have met, the sky did not fall and I know now that we have nothing to say to one another. I can forget all about the odious Lord Darvell.'

'I beg your pardon, my love, did you speak?'

Lady Broxted's gentle enquiry made her jump and she hastily disclaimed. Pulling her cloak about her, she subsided into one corner and stared disconsolately out of the window. She was determined not to think of Luke Ainslowe, but his image was as persistent as the man himself; she recalled how he had come to Malberry Court, armed with a picnic basket, and insisted that she take luncheon with him. She had refused at first, but she could still hear his voice, deep and seductive, persuading her to leave her painting and eat with him.

She was very conscious of her boy's attire as she seated herself on the very edge of the rug, but Luke never mentioned it as he fed her tidbits of cheese and bread and fruit. She explained how his brother James had sought out her father and commissioned him to paint Malberry Court. Luke responded by telling her something of his life in the army and of the great battle that had taken place at Waterloo. Sitting out in the sunshine with the soaring white pillars of the house at their backs and the calm waters of the lake spread out before them, she soon lost her shyness. He was very easy to talk to. She liked to make him laugh and see the merry glint in his hazel eyes. It seemed quite natural to accept Luke's invitation to join him again the next day, and the next. She was so comfortable in his company, talking of everything and nothing. They understood each other so well. Or so she had thought, until the day he had ridden out of her life forever.

With everything so new and exciting, Carlotta found much in London to divert her. Lady Broxted was determined that she should enjoy her first Season and spared no pains to keep her entertained. There were rides in the park, shopping with her aunt, promenades and balls, assemblies, masquerades and parties. Carlotta threw herself into such a round of enjoyment that she declared to her aunt she did not have a moment to think. It was not true—there was too much time to think. Even two weeks after the Prestbury ball, when she was out riding with her friends, it was so easy to allow the chatter to flow over her and to lose herself in her own thoughts, remembering how attentive Luke had been at Malberry, bringing food to share, escorting her home in the evenings—it had been an idyllic, happy interlude. She had felt safe with Luke. He had not attempted to kiss her again, even though she knew she wanted him to do so. She remembered that she had been very close to kissing *him*, the day he had climbed the scaffolding. She had peered over the edge of the platform to find him grinning up at her...

'Good morning, Major—or is it past noon now?'

He made a great show of getting out his watch, saying severely, 'It is gone three, madam. Are you so caught up in your work that you do not know the time?'

A laugh trembled on her lips but she tried to frown. 'I am very busy, sir. Pray do not disturb me.'

'Can you not come down?'

'No, sir, I cannot. What are you doing?' She laughed. 'You cannot come up *here*.'

'I can, and I will,' he said, setting his foot on the first ladder. 'I want to see you in your eyrie.'

She felt the platform shake as he began to climb and she quickly collected up her palette and brushes out of the way.

'So this is where you work.' He crawled onto the platform. 'Good God, how do you manage?'

'It is a little cramped, to be sure. There is no room to stand and one has to work crouching or lying down. But it is easier for me, because I am so much shorter than you.'

He pointed to the large roundel in the centre of the ceiling. 'Is that your father's work?'

'Yes.' She giggled as she watched him twisting his long frame around, trying to look at the fresco. 'It is easier if you lie on your back, only you must not, of course. You will make your coat dirty.'

Ignoring her warning, he stretched himself out on the platform. 'Ah, yes, I can see it much better now. A god and his attendants.' He shifted his position. 'And the other roundel, the smaller one at the far end?'

She slid down beside him and gazed up at the ceiling. 'I painted that one. You are still too close to see it all properly; it will look so much better from the ground.'

'It looks wonderful to me now,' he said. 'I am impressed.' He rolled over and propped his head on his hand, smiling at her. 'Now, when will you come down?'

The frescoes were forgotten. His face was only inches from her own. What if she was to reach out to him, to take his face in her hands and pull him down to her, to kiss *him*? The urge to do just that had been so strong she shivered. Such wicked thoughts!

'Carlotta.'

She jumped. No longer was she lying beside Luke Ainslowe on the high scaffold at Malberry; she was ambling through Hyde Park on her docile little pony. The rest of her riding party had moved ahead and, to her dismay, she found Lord Darvell was beside her on a sleek, long-legged bay. Her cheeks grew hot—had she conjured him with her musings?

She had not expected him to seek her out after her performance at Prestbury House. She thought she had made her feelings perfectly clear, but here he was, smiling at her and causing her heart to flutter in the most foolish way imaginable.

'We had no opportunity to talk, the other night.'

'There is nothing I want to say to you, my lord.'

She urged her mount to a trot, wanting to catch up with her party, but Luke's hand shot out and caught her bridle.

'Not yet, Carlotta. Allow me to enjoy your company for a little while.'

She stiffened. 'I did not give you leave to use my name.'

'No? I told you I would do so. At Malberry, do you remember?'

She hunched a shoulder. 'I have no wish to remember Malberry.'

'No?' he said again, his slow smile slicing through her defences. 'Why should you not—did you not enjoy our time together there? Have you forgotten that I commissioned you to paint me?'

She stared ahead of her. Of course she remembered. She remembered every word he had spoken to her. She realised she would very much like to paint him, not posing statesman-like in a studio, but as he had been at Malberry Court, relaxed and reclining on the grass. For his brown hair she would use a base of raw umber and add fine brushstrokes to represent the blond sun-streaks—mixing in a little Indian yellow, perhaps. And his eyes—it would not be difficult to recreate their colour, like polished hazelnuts, but could she capture the smile that lurked in their depths, or the way his mouth quirked into a smile?

Carlotta looked away suddenly. This was too dangerous a game—she was only a memory away from crying. She assumed a haughty look and raised her brows at him.

'You would commission me, my lord? But it is well known you have no money.'

'That will not always be the case.'

She curled her lip at him. 'But it is irrelevant, since I shall not be painting you. Indeed, I have no need to do anything, now.'

'Perhaps not, but I thought painting was your passion.'

She managed a tinkling laugh. 'Oh dear me, no. How unlady-like that would be.'

She noted with satisfaction that his hand on her rein tightened, and the little mare side-stepped nervously.

'What has happened to you, Carlotta? At Malberry you were…different.'

He was watching her intently. Carlotta knew she would have to look at him, but she would die rather than show him her true feelings. He was a rake, everyone told her so. He had been her first love—her only love—and he had broken her fragile young heart. But that was what rakes did; he could not change his nature. It had taken her months to rebuild her life—only the knowledge of how dear she was to her parents and to her aunt and uncle had given her the will to carry on. She could not let him hurt her again. She raised her chin and fixed him with cold, indifferent eyes.

'At Malberry, my lord, I was a child, ignorant of the world. I thought fortune was not important. Now I know better.'

She forced herself not to look away, praying that he would not see past her icy, supercilious stare to the raw pain in her heart. For a long, treacherous moment he held her eyes; not by the flicker of an eyelid did she betray the anguish that was ripping her apart. She watched as his puzzlement turned to contempt. She had not thought she could feel any more miserable, but the disdain she now read in his eyes was almost unbearable. Almost.

He released her bridle and gathered up his own reins, saying curtly, 'Then I shall leave you to your fortune-hunting, Miss Rivington. Good day to you.'

Luke dug his heels into the bay's sides and cantered away, ignoring the stares and frowns of those who considered it unseemly to move at more than a snail's pace. Damn the chit. When he had first seen her at Malberry he had intended nothing more than a little flirtation to pass the time. By heaven, the girl had given him his own again! He scowled; it was his own fault, for he had told her of his financial problems. They had been sitting on the lawns at Malberry on one of those hot, sunny afternoons when he had persuaded her to come down from her high perch for a little while. He had been curious to know why her father was so anxious to have the frescoes finished.

* * *

'It is most important that my father fulfils his obligations, you see,' said Carlotta, stretching out on the grass and putting her hands behind her head. He tried not to stare at the way her paint-stained shirt settled over the gentle curves of her breast. 'He must be paid on time.'

'And why is that?'

'Because there are bills outstanding, expenses to be met... As a gentleman, perhaps you would not understand.'

He grinned at that. 'I understand only too well about debts; I have an abundance of them.'

Carlotta wrinkled her brow. 'It must be very unpleasant to be under such an obligation, I think.'

'But it is unavoidable,' he said lightly. 'Any gentleman living in town will tell you that his expenses are very high. There's one's house and stable to be maintained, not to mention one's tailor.'

'But surely you could cut back, economise...' She bit her lip. 'I can see that I have made you angry, I beg your pardon. The way you live is none of my business.'

'No.' He had not meant to sound so cold and he saw the sudden, anxious look Carlotta threw at him. When she did not speak, he said gently, 'What, Mistress Durini? Have you no riposte for me?' She shook her head, and looked surprised when he laughed. 'At last I have found a woman who does not want the last word!'

Carlotta sat up. She said angrily, 'I think you are making May-game of me, sir.'

'No, no, pray, Miss Durini, forgive my incivility. I was jesting when I talked of the expense of town life; I have only recently returned from Paris and I *have* no town house to maintain—and to the best of my knowledge neither do I owe my tailor a penny. The debts I do have relate to my estate, and I plan to address that problem very soon. There, will you cry peace with me now?'

* * *

His hand tightened on the reins and the bay skittered, throwing up his head. Damnation, he had never owned as much to any woman before and what good had it done him? He had given her a stick to beat him with. A short, bitter laugh escaped him. He had been within an ace of offering for her—thank Providence it had come to nothing! What a lucky escape—he had no wish to be married to such a shallow, mercenary female.

He brought his horse to a sudden stop.

The only trouble was, he could not bear the thought of anyone else marrying her.

During the following weeks it was inevitable that Carlotta and Lord Darvell would meet frequently, but a polite, distant nod was their only acknowledgement.

'I am surprised that Darvell does not pay you more attention,' remarked Lady Broxted, when they saw him in Mrs Price's drawing room one evening. 'He is generally very appreciative of a pretty young lady…a little *too* appreciative in some cases,' she added reflectively. 'He is an incorrigible flirt.'

Carlotta glanced across the room. Luke was enjoying a lively dialogue with a very pretty blonde matron and she quickly looked away again.

'I do not think I am quite to his taste, Aunt. I doubt I am pretty enough to tempt his lordship.'

'Nonsense, I have received any number of compliments for you, my love,' replied Lady Broxted. 'But I suppose we should be thankful for Darvell's lack of interest; your uncle has settled a generous dowry upon you, and he hopes you will contract an alliance with a gentleman of means.'

Carlotta raised her chin. 'You need have no fear, Aunt; I shall not throw myself away upon an impoverished fortune-hunter like the Wicked Baron.'

Lady Broxted looked at her closely. 'Oh dear, what has Lord Darvell done to deserve such vehemence? Perhaps it is his lack of attention that has piqued you. After all, you cannot deny he is very attractive. However, if you showed a partiality for him, I have no doubt Broxted—'

'Dear ma'am, I have *no* partiality for him!' cried Carlotta, an angry flush warming her cheeks. 'I am quite *thankful* that he does not notice me.'

'Well, then, there is no more to be said on the matter.' reasoned Lady Broxted. 'You are a very sensible little thing, Carlotta. I have no doubt we can achieve a very creditable match for you. Fairbridge seems to have taken a shine to you.'

Carlotta followed her aunt's gaze to observe the tall, fair-haired young man standing on the far side of the room.

'I think the viscount is more interested in our host's daughter, ma'am. Do you see how he hovers about Miss Price, and how she blushes when he speaks to her?'

'Perhaps you are right.' Lady Broxted sighed. 'Pity, for he would make you an ideal partner. His mama is well disposed towards you, too. Her late husband was a great friend of Broxted's and I think she would like to strengthen the connection.'

'Dear ma'am, is it not a little early to be contemplating marriage?'

'It is never too early,' said my lady firmly. 'I am determined to see you well established. However, we must not repine. There is time yet.'

'I hope so, ma'am,' replied Carlotta, her eyes twinkling. 'We have been in town for little more than a month!'

At that moment a young gentleman approached to claim her hand for the next set and she went off, still smiling.

The ballroom grew hotter and more crowded as the evening progressed, and in between dances Carlotta was glad to stand by one of the open windows to cool her heated cheeks. She thought with longing of her parents' cottage in Malberry village: her mother's last letter had been full of trifles such as her success in the herb garden and the diligence of the new maid, as well as news of her latest commission and her father's progress at Malberry Court. He was now decorating the little temples that littered the gardens. Carlotta wished she could be with them, but it was not possible. She was fanning herself gently when Julia Price came to join her. Carlotta said in her open, friendly way, 'Your mama must be very pleased with the success of her party, Miss Price.'

'Yes, I think she is. It is always a concern that no one will come, for there are so many concerts and entertainments.'

'Well, I think you need have no worries, your rooms are full to overflowing. Is this what they call a sad crush?' Carlotta asked. 'I believe that means it is a great success.'

She must remember to put it all into her next letter to her parents; Mama enjoyed reading about the parties and entertainments.

'Yes.' Miss Price was smiling at her. 'We are very fortunate tonight, I think. Is this your first Season, Miss Rivington?'

'It is. My aunt and uncle have been kind enough to sponsor me.' Carlotta sighed. 'They are very good, but it is all so new and there is so much to remember: I am in constant dread that I shall embarrass them!'

Miss Price was quick to disclaim, 'No, no, that could not be—you always look so calm and at ease.'

'Thank you, but I am in a perpetual quake, I assure you, Miss Price.'

'Do, please, call me Julia.'

'Very well, if you will call me Carlotta.'

'That is a very pretty name.'

'Thank you. It is—' Carlotta became aware of someone approaching and broke off, turning to see Viscount Fairbridge at her side, his pale blue eyes fixed upon Julia. He bowed.

'Miss Price, you p-promised me the next dance, I think…that is, if I am not interrupting…'

Carlotta smiled at him. 'Pray, my lord, do take your partner.'

'You shall not object if I leave you?' asked Julia, looking anxious.

'Not at all. Off you go and enjoy yourself.'

Carlotta stepped back, smiling, as Julia put her fingers on Lord Fairbridge's sleeve for him to lead her away. Too late did she see Lord Darvell standing behind the viscount's lanky form. They were only feet apart. He checked as he saw her, a slight frown in his eyes. He was already turning away when their host's jovial voice boomed out.

'Now, now, how fortunate is this, my lord!' Mr Price put his hand on Darvell's arm. 'The next set is forming and here is Miss Rivington without a partner.'

Mortification swept over Carlotta. A glance at Lord Darvell showed her that he felt very much as she did, and for a brief moment she wondered if he would walk off, but Mr Price was clapping him on the shoulder, crying, 'Well, go to it, man!'

Carlotta opened her mouth to protest, but she could not speak. Lord Darvell stepped forward, stony-faced. He held out his hand.

'Will you do me the honour, Miss Rivington?'

There was no escape. To refuse would be to embarrass them all. Tentatively she put her fingers on his sleeve.

'You are too good, my lord.'

Damnation. Luke swore under his breath. However much he tried to avoid Carlotta, it seemed she forced herself upon his notice. No, he must be honest with himself, it was not her fault. He remembered his efforts at Malberry Court, when he had realised that he was in danger of falling in love with the bewitching little sprite in her shirt and breeches. He had done his best then to keep away from her, finishing his business with the clerk of works late one afternoon and planning to set off for Darvell Manor the following morning without returning to the Court. But when he left Kemble's lodge he found the heavy storm clouds had brought an early dusk and lightning was already splitting the sky. He saw the faint glow flickering from the windows of the house and rushed in, expecting to find flames licking at the newly painted walls. Instead he had found Carlotta.

'What the devil are you doing in here?'

His voice, edged with irritation, vibrated against the empty walls of the drawing room.

'I might ask you the same, sir, when you have not been near the house for days.'

Heaven and earth, the chit was challenging him!

'I have been at the lodge with Kemble, discussing plans for moving in the furniture. I saw the light in the windows as I was about to leave and came up to see what was amiss.'

'I am sorry, then, if you thought it was intruders.'

'I was more concerned that the lightning had started a fire. Why are you not at home?' he barked the question at her, frowning.

'I wanted to have one last look at my father's work. I beg your pardon; I never meant to disturb anyone. I will go now.'

'Oh, no, you will not.'

She blinked.

He took off his hat and shook it, sending off tiny droplets of water that sparkled in the candlelight. 'I mean the storm is too violent. It is not safe.'

'Oh.'

That one little word, spoken so softly, was his undoing. His heart went out to her; she looked so vulnerable, holding aloft the candlestick with one shaking hand. He said gently, 'You need not worry, you are perfectly safe here.' He stepped forward and took the candlestick from her. 'Let us look at your father's work together.'

They wandered through the empty rooms until they found themselves in the salon, which occupied one end of the house. There was only one painted panel, set between the two marble fireplaces. The other three walls were taken up with long windows, designed to allow in maximum light, although now they only gleamed blackly as the rain spattered against the glass. Luke crossed the room, raising the candles higher as he studied the mural.

'Your father is a great artist, Carlotta. This is really very good.'

'Thank you. May I show you something?' She took his arm and led him to the far corner of the panel. 'There,' she pointed. 'Look closely at the decoration on the lady's sandal.'

He peered closer. 'A tiny snail.'

'Yes, a *lumaca*.' She laughed. 'It sounds so much prettier in Italian. It is Papa's signature. He does not tell many people, but it is very important to him. When he was in Rome he would often paint copies of the great masters for the foreign visitors to take home and put in their grand houses. He insisted that as long as he signed them then there was no harm in it; he was not trying to trick anyone.'

'I am honoured you should share it with me.'

He looked down at her and Carlotta smiled back at him briefly before she looked away, suddenly shy and awkward. As if to distract him, she pointed up at the chandeliers.

'When all those candles are alight this room will glow. Can you imagine how elegant it will look, with all the ladies in their finest gowns?' She sighed. 'I wish I could see it.'

'Perhaps you will.'

She laughed. 'Perhaps! I will creep up to the windows and press my nose against the glass one night.'

The thought made him angry. 'That is not what I meant,' he growled. 'You should be in here, dancing with all the other young ladies.'

'Do not frown, sir. I do not want you to pity me.'

'No, of course not, but I am determined you shall dance here.' He put down the candlestick and opened his arms to her. 'Come.'

'You are nonsensical!' She laughed, but did not resist as he took her hand and began to lead her around the room, humming a tune.

'Do you waltz, Miss Durini?'

'No, sir. I have never learned.'

'Well, the gentleman holds the lady like this.' He drew her towards him, pushed her cloak off her shoulders until it hung like a train behind her and slid one hand beneath it to rest on her back. Immediately her body tensed. A tremor ran through him as her breasts pressed again him, separated from his skin by only a few thin layers of silk and linen.

'I have been told the waltz is considered by some to be improper,' she remarked. 'It certainly feels very daring, to be standing so close.'

She looked up at him, smiling shyly, and suddenly he could not breathe.

'Well, sir, what next?'

'This.'

He placed his fingers beneath her chin, tilted up her face and kissed her, very gently. She gave a faint sigh when he lifted his head, but did not move away. Tension crackled between them. Carlotta leaned against him, a tiny movement, but it was enough. With something very like a groan he swooped down on her again and his kiss this time was much more urgent. She responded, her lips parting in surrender to his demands and her body melting against him. His arms tightened. He nibbled gently at her lip and in response she put her arms around his neck.

Together they sank to their knees and he lowered Carlotta

to the floor. She clung to him as he stretched out beside her, his mouth moving slowly, sensuously, over her lips while one hand slid to her breast. Luke felt her tremble, her back arched. A pulsing wave of desire swamped him. His fingers tore at her shirt, pulling it free from those soft, clinging breeches, then his hand was on skin, caressing the gentle curve of her waist. He ran his fingers over her stomach and she drew it in, gasping. He covered her face with kisses, drinking in the sweet taste of her, a taste of summer flowers and new-mown hay. His senses reeled. He had known many women, but never had the urge to possess and protect been so strong. She moaned softly and his touch faltered. He was overwhelmed with tenderness. She was such an innocent, it was important not to hurt her, not to frighten her. He knew the heady heights that love-making could achieve, but for her it would be new, strange and bewildering. Suddenly he was aware of their surroundings, lying on the cold, hard floor. By God it was not even his house!

He raised his head and stared down at her. Carlotta gazed up at him so trustingly and with a sudden, startling clarity he knew it would not do. This was not how he would show his love to Carlotta.

'This has gone far enough,' he muttered, almost to himself. He got to his feet and held out his hand. Her brows contracted and she looked at him with bewildered, frightened eyes.

'What is it?' she whispered. 'Have I done something wrong?'

His smile was strained as he pulled her to her feet.

'Not you, sweetheart.' He brushed his lips against her mouth in a fleeting, butterfly kiss. 'You are everything I could wish for, but this is not right, not here, on the bare floor of an empty house. You deserve so much more than that.' He looked towards the window. 'I think the rain has stopped. We must get you home.'

There was an uncomfortable silence. Carlotta did not move.

'I thought you were going to teach me to waltz.'

She sounded so lost that he had to stifle the temptation to take her in his arms again. He reached out to pull her cloak back over her shoulders.

'I am no saint, Carlotta.' He bent to pick up the candlestick.

'You are not angry with me?'

He lifted her hand, pressing a kiss into the palm. 'No, love. I am not angry with you.'

No, he had not been angry with her then, but now, as he led Carlotta on to the crowded dance floor, it occurred to him that he had been wrong about her; even then she had been trying to catch herself a rich husband.

With all the pleasure of someone walking to the scaffold, Carlotta accompanied Lord Darvell onto the dance floor. His hand beneath her arm was stiff; indeed, she thought his whole body was rigid with disapproval. She summoned up all her courage to help her through this ordeal. Anger came to her aid. What right had he to disapprove of her? When they took their places in the set she put up her chin and gazed steadily at some point over his shoulder. The music began; they held hands, moved forward until they were almost touching, the delicate flowers of her corsage trembling within an inch of his waist-coat. She must concentrate on her steps and forget her partner. There was no need for them to talk, after all. However, she soon discovered that Luke had other ideas.

'Why did you change your name to Rivington?' he asked her suddenly.

'It is in deference to my aunt and uncle. They have been very good to me.'

'And perhaps you are ashamed of your origins.'

'I am not! It is not unusual to take the name of one's benefactor.' She almost snatched her hand away as the dance parted them. Insufferable man! He was determined to think badly of her. Carlotta's head came up: she would not court his good opinion.

Luke fought down his anger. Damnation, one could not have an argument in the middle of a ballroom. The movement of the dance took him past his partner and he almost laughed aloud at the fury of her look. One had to admit those dark eyes flashed magnificently when she was angry. It seemed she planned to ignore him for the duration of the dance, but he would have none of it. The chit should learn that she must at least show him society manners.

'How are you enjoying London, Miss Rivington?'

'Very well, I thank you.'

He waited, and when she did not continue he raised his brows. 'Is that all? Have you no praises to heap upon the entertainments and the shopping to be had in town?'

'If I did so, you would write me down as a thoughtless, frippery creature.'

'You would prefer me to think you sullen, and above being pleased.'

'I do not care what you think of me,' she told him in a low voice.

Luke growled with frustration. Blast it, why should the chit anger him so? He gave a harsh laugh. 'Be careful with your scowls, Carlotta,' he hissed as they parted again. 'The wind may change and you will never smile again.'

Carlotta reined in her irritation. All around her the dancers were laughing and enjoying themselves. It would not do to let the world see she was arguing with her partner. As they came back together she said sweetly, 'Thank you for the timely reminder, my lord. Because *you* cannot help your temper, it is no reason for me to lose mine.'

His smile was as false as her own, but his eyes glittered dangerously. She sought for something commonplace to say.

'We are very fortunate with the weather, are we not? It is

warm enough to make fires unnecessary, yet still cool enough to make dancing a pleasure.' He did not reply. She thought he looked very much as if he was grinding his teeth. Carlotta raised her brows. 'Come, my lord. When I go to such trouble to converse, surely you can make the effort to respond.'

'Since we are now at the end of the dance I am spared the necessity.'

She put her fingers on his arm and allowed him to lead her off the floor. 'We are both spared,' she muttered. 'We need no longer be polite to one another.'

'I noticed no politeness, Miss Rivington.'

Carlotta's eyes narrowed, but there was no opportunity to reply, since they had reached Lady Broxted, who was deep in conversation with her hostess. Lord Darvell left them without a word, but to Carlotta's relief her aunt did not appear to notice. Instead she caught Carlotta's hand and pulled her closer.

'My dear, we are discussing the most delightful scheme. Mrs Price informs me that Madame Saqui is performing at Vauxhall next week and we are minded to get up a party—what do you think of that?'

'Madame Saqui?'

'She is a rope walker,' explained Mrs Price. 'Quite a sensation. She first performed at Vauxhall last year and was so successful that she had been retained.'

'Well, Carlotta, would you like to see her?'

'Very much, Aunt, thank you.'

Mrs Price clapped her hands.

'Then it is settled. We shall all go together. And I shall find two young gentlemen to accompany us, for I am sure you and Julia will enjoy yourselves much more if you each have a handsome escort.' A commotion at the door caused her to look up. 'Now, who is this come in at this late hour? I had not expected anyone else to turn up—good heavens, it is Ainslowe and his new wife!'

As Mrs Price hurried away, Carlotta stood on tiptoe to see the couple at the door. Even from a distance she recognised James Ainslowe. He was not quite as tall as his brother, but he had the same nut-brown hair and an ease of manner that expressed itself in the charming smile he now bent upon his hostess. Carlotta could imagine him apologising for his late arrival, treating Mrs Price to the same glinting smile that Luke had shown her when they had been together at Malberry. The memory gave her an empty, hollow feeling inside. She instantly quashed it and turned her attention to Mrs James Ainslowe. She was a lively brunette with a generous figure that was shown to advantage in a low-cut gown of bronze *broché* silk and a matching jockey cap over her glossy curls. A gold tassel on the cap swung to and fro as she carried on an animated conversation with her hostess. Carlotta heard Lady Broxted's smothered exclamation.

'Is anything wrong, Aunt?'

'I could wish they had stayed in Berkshire a little longer,' muttered Lady Broxted. 'What if they should recognise you?'

Carlotta laughed at that. 'That is not possible! They were on the Continent when I was at Malberry.'

'You must be very careful, Carlotta, not to disclose your real name.'

'I thought we had already agreed that, ma'am.' She hesitated. 'Would it be so very dreadful, Aunt, if it were known that my father was an artist?'

'It would be embarrassing for your uncle, my dear, and for me. So much better that no one asks about your parents.'

Carlotta felt a little tremor of unease. 'Perhaps then it would be best if we lived a little more retired. Surely there is no need for you to puff me off quite so much.'

Lady Broxted stared at her. 'Do you not *wish* to go about, my love?'

Carlotta hesitated. Looking into her aunt's anxious face, she realised that her aunt's pleasure in the balls and parties they attended was more than equal to her own and she could not disappoint her.

'Yes, of course I do, Aunt, but I would not embarrass you for the world. Perhaps we could avoid Mr and Mrs Ainslowe…'

'No, I am afraid that is impossible; they will be seen everywhere and you must be seen everywhere, too.' My lady drew herself up to her full, if diminutive, height. 'We must hope that your identity is not discovered, at least until we have you safely married. There is no reason why we should not carry it off. After all, there is no one here who knows you, is there?'

Carlotta knew that this was the moment to confess the truth, but she remained silent. She watched Lord Darvell cross the room to greet the new arrivals and her heart sank. It was clear that Luke was on very good terms with his brother and sister-in-law; doubtless he would tell them all about his dalliance with the painter's daughter. It seemed very likely that by the end of the evening all Lady Broxted's hopes for her would be at an end.

Luke gripped his brother's hand. 'James! When did you arrive in town?'

'This morning. Adele was desperate to buy new gowns.'

'Nonsense!' cried his wife, turning from Mrs Price. 'You were just as anxious to get to town. Luke, my dear, how are you? As handsome as ever, I see.'

'And you are even more enchanting,' replied Luke, kissing her hand. 'How did you find the Court?'

'It is beautiful; thank you for your efforts. Kemble told us you were at Malberry for weeks.'

'Yes, thank you,' said James. 'I really did not expect you to do more than look in on the place once or twice.'

'Poor Luke,' said Adele. 'Was it very tedious for you?'

Luke wanted to say that, surprisingly, it had been some of the happiest weeks of his life, but that would invite questions, and Adele was damnably perceptive. He dared not risk it.

'I endured it as long as I could,' he replied coolly. 'However, I thought you would stay there longer.'

Adele shook her head, sighing. 'We have had nothing but each other's company for the best part of a month.'

'An ideal arrangement,' murmured Luke, grinning, and earned for himself a sharp tap on the arm from Adele's fan.

'You may stop those knowing looks at once! James and I are very much in need of company before we murder one another.'

'Aye.' Her loving husband smiled. 'So we thought we would come to town for a few weeks, then take a party back to the Court with us for the summer.'

'You will come, won't you, Luke?'

'Of course, Adele. That is, unless anything better comes along.'

She gave a gurgle of laughter. 'How I have missed your teasing! We have been abroad for so long, and everyone there was so serious.' She tucked her hand in his arm. 'Come, we have not seen you since Paris. One can never say everything properly in a letter, so you must tell me all you have been doing and then we will arrange for you to accompany me to Bond Street.'

'Surely that is your husband's duty.'

She waved one gloved hand. 'Alas, James has no eye for colour.'

Luke began to back away. 'I regret, Adele, that I have a great many engagements—'

'Nonsense, you cannot be too busy to take me shopping.'

He cast a despairing look at James, who merely laughed.

'No use appealing to me, Luke. I've come to town for my own amusement. You are always at your ease with the ladies, you will enjoy yourself!'

Chapter Three

Lady Broxted emerged from the milliner's shop and stopped, blinking in the sunlight. 'Well, Carlotta, where shall we go now?'

Following her aunt out on to the flag way, Carlotta gave a little sigh. 'Must we go anywhere else, Aunt? We have bought so many gloves and shoes and hats that I dare not think what my uncle will say.'

'Tush, child, what should he say? Broxted knows how it is in town. One's gloves soon become soiled and the dirty streets quite ruin one's shoes.'

'And the bonnets, ma'am?' asked Carlotta, regarding the hatboxes carried by a wooden-faced footman.

'One can never have too many hats,' opined Lady Broxted firmly. 'Now, let us go in here, for, having seen how well you look in green, I am determined that you shall have a new silk dress for the evenings.'

'Pray, ma'am, do not go in,' begged Carlotta. 'I have been sized up, measured and pulled this way and that until I am quite exhausted with it—' She broke off, realising that Lady Broxted was not listening.

Following her aunt's intent gaze, she saw Mrs Adele Ainslowe approaching. However, when she observed Adele's escort she was aware of a sudden feeling of breathlessness— her heart seemed to be fighting to escape her body.

'Dear me,' muttered Lady Broxted, 'how did she persuade Darvell to come shopping with her? Mrs Ainslowe, Lord Darvell, how do you do?'

Adele stopped and gave them her wide smile. 'Good day to you, Lady Broxted, and this must be your pretty niece that everyone is talking of. Pray won't you introduce us? I heard that you were at the Prices' assembly, Miss Rivington,' she continued once this office had been performed. 'I am ashamed to admit that James and I came in very late, and there was not time to meet everyone.'

Carlotta answered as best she could. She was very much aware of Luke standing behind his sister-in-law. She was also a little overawed by Mrs Ainslowe's vivacity. She had thought her very good-natured when she had first seen her and now, at such close proximity, her impression was confirmed; she could see the humour twinkling in her green eyes. Adele was looking past her, taking in the parcels piled up in the arms of Lady Broxted's hapless footmen.

'So,' she continued, 'we are on the same errand, I collect. We have been shopping all morning. Poor Darvell is quite out of patience with me. Tell me, is that little Frenchwoman still trading at the end of the street? Madame Beaufaire, the milliner. I was always able to find something I liked there, but last Season she was talking of returning to Paris, now the war is over.'

'Yes, yes, Madame Beaufaire is still there,' replied Lady Broxted, adding with a triumphant little smile, 'we have just purchased a new bonnet of leghorn straw from her for Carlotta…'

Mrs Ainslowe laughed gaily. 'Then you will be all the rage, my dear, and we shall all be looking daggers at you when you wear it! But this is your first time in London, is it not, Miss Rivington? Tell me how you find Bond Street.'

'Exhausting,' Lady Broxted answered before Carlotta could

speak. 'My poor niece is crying quits before we have completed even one side of the street, which is a great shame, because I did so want to visit the silk mercers of Covent Garden.'

Carlotta gave a rueful smile. 'I am sure one soon grows accustomed, but it is all so new to me. You must forgive me; my senses are quite overcome by so many shops, so many wonderful things displayed. I am very much afraid that if I have to make one more purchase, I shall be completely undone.'

'Well, then, I have the very thing,' cried Mrs Ainslowe. 'We shall change partners. Lady Broxted and I will finish our shopping together while Darvell escorts Miss Rivington back to Berkeley Square.'

'Oh, no, ma'am!' cried Carlotta, appalled. 'Truly I am not tired, I was merely funning.'

Luke bent a frowning look upon his sister-in-law. 'Pray, Adele, do not be so overbearing.'

She gave him a mischievous smile, but turned to address Carlotta. 'My dear Miss Rivington, I can see that you are quite done up. You must accept this opportunity to rest. Let Darvell take you home; he dislikes shopping as much as you and has been wishing himself elsewhere for the past hour. Your aunt and I can enjoy ourselves for a while longer, then we shall follow you. What do you say, Lady Broxted?'

'You *are* looking a little tired, Carlotta.'

'No, really, I couldn't leave you, Aunt—'

Mrs Ainslowe raised her hand. 'Do not think we are putting ourselves out for you, Miss Rivington. This arrangement will suit us all. And you need not fear any impropriety; one of Lady Broxted's footmen shall walk behind you.'

'Well, if Lord Darvell does not object to taking my niece home…'

Carlotta could see that her aunt was weakening. 'No, really, I could not impose upon Lord Darvell!'

She was ignored. Lord Darvell was bowing.

'Nothing would give me greater pleasure, ma'am.' He spoke with studied indifference and Carlotta cringed. 'Well, Miss Rivington, shall we leave these ladies to their hedonistic pursuits?'

She was trapped. There was nothing she could say that would not sound churlish and ungrateful.

'There, now!' cried Mrs Ainslowe, beaming. 'Take good care of her, Luke. Tell James I shall send for the carriage later to collect me from Broxted House.'

The two parties went their separate ways. Carlotta stared ahead of her. At Malberry she had wanted nothing more than to be alone with Luke but here, even with Lady Broxted's footman walking a few paces behind, she felt very tense. It was as though she was walking beside a wild beast. A tiger, perhaps, that might pounce on her at any moment. However, when he spoke, Luke's tone was perfectly polite.

'My new sister is a minx,' he remarked. 'She likes to organise everyone her own way. I must apologise for her.'

'Not at all,' murmured Carlotta cautiously. 'I like her; she is very…very refreshing.'

He laughed. 'When you have known her a little longer, you will call her exhausting. She has so much energy to expend on her friends, especially when it comes to matchmaking. Tell Adele your requirements, Miss Rivington, and she will have you fixed up with a rich husband before you can blink an eye.'

Hellfire! Luke swore under his breath. What had made him say that? He had been surprised at the lightness of spirit he felt at the prospect of having Carlotta to himself for the short walk to Berkeley Square. She looked so pretty with that straw bonnet framing her face, the dark brown ribbons matching her eyes. He wanted to put their quarrel behind them, but his joking remark had come too soon. He sensed her drawing away from him.

'I beg your pardon, I—'

She waved her hand, saying airily, 'Pray do not apologise, my lord, it is an excellent notion. I am sure Mrs Ainslowe must know all the most eligible gentlemen in town. And she will not be shocked by my ambition—after all, your brother married her for her fortune, did he not?'

Luke ground his teeth. 'I'll have you know that James is very much in love with his wife!'

'I am sure he is,' came the honey-sweet reply. 'But I'd wager the fortune does not detract from their happiness. Perhaps we could ask him, for he is even now approaching us.'

'We shall do no such thing,' he retorted as James hailed them from across the street.

'Luke, well met!'

James tossed a coin to the crossing sweeper and came up to them, a look of enquiry upon his features. Luke performed the introduction almost reluctantly and Carlotta held out her hand.

'Mr Ainslowe, how do you do, sir? I was speaking to your wife but ten minutes since.'

Luke glanced down at the little figure beside him. She was smiling shyly up at James, showing no sign of the scheming minx he knew her to be. James, damn him, was beaming back at her, obviously enchanted.

'Were you, by Gad? I thought she had prevailed upon Luke here to take her shopping.'

'She did, but she has met a kindred spirit in Lady Broxted,' explained Luke. 'Miss Rivington, however, has made her purchases and I am escorting her back to Broxted House. Where are you going, brother? I did not know you would be coming out today or I would have let you escort your own wife.'

'It wasn't my plan to come this way, but I was at Brooks's last evening with a party of friends, and I am now off to collect my winnings from Sir Gilbert Mattingwood. Quite rolled up, he is. Poor Gil, almost lost his boots last night and did not have the means to pay me, so he told me to call on him today at his lodgings in Dean Street, which is where I am going now.' He took out his watch and studied it. 'By Jove, is that the time? I had best get on; there is a house sale in Curzon Street later today and I thought I might give it a look. I fancy there are one or two nice pieces of Sèvres that would look very well at Malberry Court. So—your servant, Miss Rivington; good day to you, Luke.'

James strode away and Luke set off again. He was aware that Carlotta was watching him and said irritably, 'Very well, I will admit that James could not be fitting out his house in such grand style if Adele had not brought a fortune with her. But there is a very strong affection between them.'

'I am sure there is,' was all she would say, but her soothing tones made his fingers itch to strangle her.

He took his leave of her at the door of Lord Broxted's residence, but as he bowed over her hand, a thought struck him. 'Tell me, Miss Rivington, once you have married your fortune, how do you propose to enjoy it, if you are so ill disposed to shop?'

There was a flash of anger in her eyes but it was gone in a moment. She said haughtily, 'It is the proximity of all those other shoppers that disgusts me, my lord. When I have my fortune, then the merchants will come to *me*.'

As the door closed behind her, Carlotta felt an immediate surge of remorse that her antipathy for Lord Darvell had prompted her to utter such an ill-bred comment. She ran up to her room, trying to shut out the look of surprised contempt that she had seen in his face at her words. It was the second time she had seen that look in his eyes and it hurt, even though she knew she deserved it. She sat before her mirror and tried to tidy her curls, which had been sadly flattened by her bonnet.

'What if he does think me mercenary?' she asked her reflection. 'I do not care a fig for his opinion!'

Nevertheless, the feeling of guilt persisted, even though she tempered it with anger at Darvell for being so easily persuaded to think ill of her. Had he learned nothing of her character in those weeks at Malberry Court? It was bad enough that he should consider her capable of chasing a rich husband, unforgivable that he should think that she, with so little herself, should be disdainful of others.

Such reflections made Carlotta more conscious of her behaviour, so that when Mrs Price sent a note to inform them of her plans for their visit to Vauxhall Gardens she was careful not to utter one word of dissent.

'There are to be eight of us,' remarked Lady Broxted, scanning the letter. 'That will be a squeeze at supper, but we shall manage.'

'Who is going, Aunt?'

'Let me see… Mr and Mrs Price, naturally, and Mrs Price depends upon my bringing Broxted. I shall have to work on him, for in general he is not fond of such entertainments, which is why it is such a joy for me to have you here, my love, to share in my pleasure. Then there is Julia, and you…oh, and she has engaged Lord Fairbridge and Mr Woollatt to join us. Splendid. How merry we shall be.'

'Yes, splendid.'

Carlotta smiled and tried to sound enthusiastic. Mr and Mrs Price's boisterous spirits would more than compensate for her uncle's retiring nature. She suspected that Julia and Lord Fairbridge would wish for nothing better than to spend an evening together, and Mr Woollatt might be a little dull, but he was perfectly respectable. Besides, there would be Madame

Saqui and the fireworks to entertain them all. She told herself it would indeed be a splendid party.

An unseasonably cold spell of weather on the appointed day persuaded Lady Broxted to advise Carlotta to wear her new round gown of blue bombazine with a matching pelisse.

'I had thought it would not be needed until much later in the year, but it will not do for you to catch a chill, my love.' Lady Broxted watched her niece putting the final touches to her dress. 'And you should wear your new kid boots, too, for the rain has left the ground very wet underfoot.' She went to the door. 'Mrs Price says we are to take the water to Vauxhall rather than the new bridge—will that not be a treat?'

Carlotta agreed and hurried downstairs to join her aunt and uncle in the carriage that would take them to the river. They found the rest of the party waiting from them on the quay and they all set off in high good humour for Vauxhall.

'This is your first visit to the gardens, Miss Rivington?' asked Mr Woollatt as they alighted on the far side of the river.

'Yes, sir.'

'Then I think you will enjoy the spectacle. The Grove, you see, is before us—that large rectangle, enclosed by trees and colonnades. Mr Price has hired a supper box for us on the far side, I believe, from where you will be able to watch and listen to the orchestra while we eat. Before that, of course, there is the cascade to be seen, and later, we have the funambulist.' He smiled at her look of surprise. 'Madame Saqui, the tight-rope walker—more properly called a funambulist.'

'Oh,' said Carlotta.

His smile widened. 'You see, Miss Rivington,' he continued, 'I will endeavour to fill your evening with education as well as entertainment.'

'Oh,' she said again.

'For example, did you know that there are over one hundred supper boxes in these gardens?'

'Yes, so shall we find ours?' put in Mrs Price, coming up. 'It is far too bright yet to see the walks at their best. Instead, we shall all enjoy a cup of arrack punch.'

Carlotta made haste to agree, thinking she would need something if she was to endure Mr Woollatt's rather pompous lectures for the whole evening.

Once they had discovered their supper box, the little party passed the time watching the crowds while they sipped at their punch. Carlotta was not sure that she liked the taste of the thick, pungent drink or the way it burned in her chest when she swallowed it, but she struggled on, and had finished the whole cupful when Lady Broxted remarked that it was almost time for the cascade to be revealed.

'Pho, plenty of time yet, it is barely eight o'clock,' said her husband, consulting his watch. 'There is nearly an hour to wait.'

Lady Broxted fidgeted with her fan.

'But the cascade is only on display for fifteen minutes, my dear, and there is always such a crush. If one is late, it is difficult to see anything.'

The earl looked a little contemptuous. 'I have already experienced the spectacle, several times,' he announced. 'I shall stay here.'

'Very true, my lord,' agreed Mrs Price. 'Having seen the cascade on several occasions, I too should much prefer to remain here. No doubt you are the same, Lady Broxted, but the girls must not miss it.' She smiled at Lord Fairbridge and Mr Woollatt. 'Perhaps, sirs, you would like to escort them?'

'Indeed we would!' exclaimed the viscount, jumping up. 'That is, I can't speak for Woollatt, of course, but I should very much like to—I mean...' He trailed off in confusion, a flush darkening his fair cheek.

Mr Woollatt rose to his feet and said smoothly, 'We would be delighted to escort Miss Rivington and Miss Price to the cascade, my lady. That is, if you think you can trust us to take such precious treasures through the gardens.'

Mrs Price laughed gaily and spread her fan.

'Mr Woollatt, how charmingly you compliment our young ladies. Of course we trust you, do we not, Lady Broxted?'

'Indeed we do, my dear sir. Off you go now. You will be able to secure a good view of the cascade, and when you return we shall go together to see Madame Saqui performing.'

Carlotta regarded her aunt with a little surprise, but a moment's reflection made her realise that Lady Broxted con- sidered both gentlemen worthy suitors and she was eager to promote them. She wondered what her aunt would say if she expressed a desire to remain in the supper box, but Julia was already standing up and the viscount was tenderly placing her paisley shawl about her shoulders. Carlotta could only ac- quiesce with a good grace.

With plenty of time to spare, Mr Woollatt led them all on a cir- cuitous route through the gardens, pointing out the various statues and grottoes on their way. His tone was very much that of a man instructing a child. Julia and Lord Fairbridge were so engrossed in each other that they did not notice, but Carlotta found herself trying to think of something outrageous to say to shock him out of his complacency. Just when she thought she could no longer endure making polite conversation a bell rang out, summoning the crowds to the cascade and the wide path quickly filled up.

'Now you see how wise we were to get here early, Miss Rivington?' murmured Mr Woollatt, drawing her forward. 'We are not quite at the front of the crowd, but I think we shall have a capital view from here.'

With a fanfare, the curtain was drawn back to reveal the display; Julia laughed and clapped enthusiastically, but Carlotta was aware of a little disappointment. The metal representation of a stream and miller's wheel was ingenious, but it clanked noisily, and her artist's eye found the garish setting and lurid colours a little childish. However, as they strolled back to their box, Julia was so enthusiastic about what they had seen that Carlotta suppressed her criticism. Remembering her resolution to be charitable, she even found a few words of praise for the spectacle when they returned to the supper box and her aunt asked her for her opinion. Satisfied that she had acquitted herself well, Carlotta settled down beside Lady Broxted to enjoy a light supper of paper-thin ham, followed by fruit tarts and syllabub laced with wine, while they watched the crowds parading through the Grove.

'Goodness, I vow there are an extraordinary number of gentlemen here tonight,' remarked Mrs Price, her bright eyes surveying the throng.

Lady Broxted nodded. 'More than one usually sees here, certainly.'

'Well, that is to be expected,' said Mr Price. 'A lady performing on a rope high in the air—they have come to watch her, hoping to glimpse more than a pretty ankle, what?' He laughed loudly at his own wit. Lord Broxted, Carlotta noted, gave only a tight little smile.

Mrs Price nodded towards the latest group of gentlemen to appear in the Grove. 'We are certainly acquainted with some of them. Look.' She began to wave to attract their attention.

Like a flock of starlings the noisy crowd changed direction and headed towards their box. To a man they were dressed in the height of fashion with their cut-away coats and light-coloured trousers.

'Heavens,' murmured Julia, moving a little closer to the viscount. 'So many of them.'

'But we know them, my love,' cried her mama, still waving. 'Look, there is Mr Eastleigh, and Sir Gilbert Mattingwood… Sir Peter Ottwood…oh, and Lord Darvell, too! Good evening, my lord, gentlemen. My goodness, the gaming houses will be quite empty tonight.'

'We can always go back to 'em later, ma'am,' cried a fair-haired gentleman with florid cheeks and a twinkle in his blue eyes. He bowed over Mrs Price's hand. 'Thought we should take a peek at the incomparable Saqui.'

Luke followed his friends towards the supper box where Mrs Price was waving and smiling at them all. He had not really wanted to accompany his friends to Vauxhall, but when he saw Carlotta in the box his spirits lifted. He felt the usual tug of attraction as he watched at her. She had discarded her enshrouding domino and looked enticing in her gown of blue satin. The deep colour enhanced the creamy tones of her flawless skin. Her dark hair was curled artlessly around her head, providing a charming frame for her pale face and those huge dark eyes. The anger he had felt at their last meeting was forgotten. He moved forward, ready to smile, to speak to her warmly, but Sir Gilbert was there before him, turning from Mrs Price to fix his eyes upon Carlotta. By God, thought Luke irritably, the man's almost drooling.

'Talking of incomparable,' murmured Sir Gilbert, 'won't you introduce me, Mrs P.?'

Luke noted that Lady Broxted was tutting with disapproval at this forward approach, but Mrs Price merely laughed.

'Of course! Miss Carlotta Rivington, may I present to you Sir Gilbert Mattingwood?'

It was as much as Luke could do not to scowl with frustration as Carlotta gazed up at Mattingwood, a shy smile curving her lips.

'Your servant, Miss Rivington.' Sir Gilbert fixed his laughing blue gaze upon her face. 'Now, why have I not seen you before?'

'I have not long been in town, sir.' Still smiling, she looked past him to meet Luke's eyes for a fleeting moment. Luke knew he was frowning and he saw her smile falter, until Sir Gilbert's next words recaptured her wandering attention.

'Your first visit here, is it, Miss Rivington?'

'Yes, sir, and for Miss Price, too,' answered Carlotta. 'We are mightily impressed.'

'We have been to see the cascade,' offered Julia in her soft voice.

'And did it please you, Miss Price?' asked Luke, determined to say something, however inane.

Julia clasped her hands, a beatific smile upon her face. 'Oh, very much, my lord. It was magical—such a colourful spectacle!'

He smiled and nodded, but from the corner of his eye he could see Carlotta laughing at something Mattingwood was whispering to her. Hell and damnation, could she not see Sir Gilbert for the flirt he really was? He turned to her.

'And what of you, Miss Rivington?' he said. 'What thought you of the spectacle—did the colours suit you?'

'It is very ingenious,' she answered him carefully but her wariness only fuelled his anger.

'But not to your taste, which is for a more…classical form of art.'

Her eyes flew to his face, he could see she thought he was about to denounce her. He would never do that—did she not know him yet? He wanted to say something reassuring, but Sir Gilbert was speaking again.

'Everyone should see the tin cascade,' he remarked with a laugh. 'But only the once!' He leaned a little closer to Carlotta. 'I would be honoured to show you some of the *other* attractions of Vauxhall, Miss Rivington.'

Mr Woollatt stepped forward. 'If Miss Rivington wishes to see anything, then it will be my pleasure to escort her,' he said, his rather heavy chin jutting out belligerently.

Sir Gilbert straightened, still smiling. 'Alas, then, I feel my loss most acutely.'

Carlotta smiled. She was aware of the compliment the gentlemen were paying her and would have been more than human if she had not felt a little tremor of excitement at their gallantry. She nodded at Mr Woollatt, then turned to give Sir Gilbert an apologetic smile. 'I am sorry to disappoint you, sir.'

He inclined his head. 'Madam, you could never disappoint me.'

Her smile grew. She was very happy to indulge in this mild flirtation, conducted from the safety of the supper box where she had the protection of her aunt and uncle. It was also a refreshing change from Mr Woollat's dull lecturing. When she looked at Lord Darvell, however, his disapproving stare somewhat dimmed her enjoyment of the moment. As the group moved away, Mr Price shook his head.

'Scapegraces, the lot of 'em,' he said. 'I hear Mattingwood is done up—could not pay his gambling debts at Brooks's the other night. 'Tis a poor show when a man cannot pay his way.'

'Actually, he did pay up,' put in Lord Broxted, scrupulously fair. 'I was there myself, heard him tell Ainslowe he would settle with him the next morning.'

'Ah,' said Mr Price, winking at Mr Woollatt, 'we've all heard that one before, I dare say.'

'No doubt,' continued the earl, 'but in this case he honoured his commitment. Gave Ainslowe a painting to cover his debt.'

'A painting!'

'Aye,' said the earl. 'A Tiepolo. His father brought it back from the Grand Tour.'

'And is it genuine?' asked Mr Price. 'Has he had it valued?'

Lord Broxted looked affronted. 'Ainslowe doesn't need to do that; he has Mattingwood's word, as a gentleman.'

'Never mind that now.' Lady Broxted rose. 'Madame Saqui will be performing soon; I would like us to have a good view of it.'

They joined the crowd congregating around the fifty-foot mast erected for Madame Saqui's celebrated rope walk. Mr and Mrs Price led their party to a good viewing spot. Carlotta was not sure whether it was by accident or design that they found themselves again in the proximity of the group of young bloods that included Sir Gilbert Mattingwood. With a little skilful manoeuvring, Mrs Price managed to place herself next to Sir Gilbert and engaged him in a rather flirtatious conversation while they waited for Madame Saqui to ascend the rope. Carlotta had taken Mr Woollatt's arm and now stood patiently while he explained to her in excessive detail the number of appearances the lady had made in England. Her mind was beginning to wander when she heard a familiar voice in her ear.

'Your escort is a veritable *encyclopaedia*, Miss Rivington.'

She froze. Luke was standing behind her, pressed so close by the crowd around them that they were almost touching. Her nerves tingled along the length of her spine and she shrank closer to Mr Woollatt. Her escort patted her arm.

'These crowds are a little frightening, are they not?' he said. 'No need to be alarmed, Miss Rivington. I shall not let you go.'

'Fortune favours Woollatt in all ways.'

These next words were merely a whisper; she could almost have imagined them except that she could feel Luke's breath, warm on her cheek. Carlotta found herself trembling. She closed her lips tightly; she would not respond to his teasing. The crowd's applause alerted her to the fact that Madame Saqui had appeared. Carlotta tried to concentrate on the stocky little woman ascending the rope, but she was too aware of Darvell standing so close behind her; if she leaned back just a little, she would be resting against him. The temptation to do just that was so strong it frightened her. Her senses reeled, the blood was singing in her veins. She dare not turn to look at him, but half-expected to feel his hand on her back, or her neck. Anticipation sizzled through her—the thought of his fingers stealing around her waist, pulling her back against him, the touch of his lips on her cheek where a moment ago she had felt his warm breath… It shook her to realise how much she wanted it to happen. She wanted to scream with frustration.

Mr Woollatt was directing her attention upwards, explaining how taut the rope must be, telling her of the special slippers Madame wore to grip the rope.

'It is rumoured she is being paid one hundred guineas a week to perform here,' he said, gazing up in rapt attention at the little figure above him.

'That is nothing to a man of Woollatt's fortune,' Luke murmured in her ear. 'You will be able to command your own private performance when you are his wife—ouch!'

Carlotta smiled. Her heel encased in its soft kid boot had connected very neatly with Luke's shin. It was a small victory, but it eased some of her tension.

Mr Woollatt looked round. 'Oh, is that you, Darvell? Demmed crush, ain't it?'

Carlotta kept her eyes resolutely upon Madame Saqui. She heard Woollatt saying, 'Pray do not crowd the lady, there's a good fellow. Ah, look, Saqui's turning. Bravo, ma'am!'

Carlotta joined in the general applause as Madame Saqui turned gracefully on her high perch. She jumped as a loud cannonade commenced, and a noisy display of fireworks lit up the sky. Madame Saqui moved easily to and fro on the rope, and began a graceful descent. The crowd cheered and roared for more and Carlotta risked a look behind her. Luke had gone.

Chapter Four

'Well, well, how exciting!' exclaimed Lady Broxted. 'Did you not think so, Carlotta?'

'Yes indeed, Aunt. Even my uncle looked to be enjoying it. Is that not so, sir?'

Lord Broxted allowed himself a small smile. 'It was very unusual. I have not seen her before, but I believe she has performed at Drury Lane. A most enterprising female.'

'But she was not very pretty,' uttered Julia. 'I thought she would be dainty, fairy-like.'

'No, she was quite mannish,' agreed Carlotta. 'But very accomplished for all that. Shall we return to our supper box now, Aunt?'

Lady Broxted tucked her hand into her husband's arm. 'Oh, I think we should take a stroll around the gardens first. The lamps look so pretty now it is dark. But there is no need for us all to stay together. Mrs Price, would you object if we allowed the younger ones to go off by themselves?'

'Not in the least, ma'am!'

Carlotta's heart sank a little. 'But surely there is no need for us to go separately. I am sure you will know the most attractive walks, Aunt.'

'But we will want to take a much more leisurely pace. No,

my dear, let the viscount and Mr Woollatt take you about. There can be no harm in it, when there are so many people here.'

'Yes, you can chaperon each other,' cried Mrs Price, almost bustling them away.

Carlotta turned to Julia for support, but her friend was looking positively starry-eyed at the prospect of walking through the gardens with Viscount Fairbridge, and Carlotta did not have the heart to spoil her evening. She resigned herself to accompanying Mr Woollatt and began to search for some topic of conversation. There was no lack, but since Mr Woollatt liked to turn everything into an educational lecture she soon found her mind wandering.

'...of course, the dark walks were once notorious for salacious behaviour,' Mr Woollatt remarked as he led her through one tree-lined avenue. 'You can imagine that the little recesses you see at intervals along here were black as pitch before they put up the lamps on the main walk. The gardens have been forced to shut on more than one occasion, due to complaints of licentiousness...'

Carlotta sighed and thought to herself that there was no possibility of her partner behaving licentiously. She had no idea what had happened to Julia and the viscount. They had disappeared, but she guessed they would be having a much more enjoyable time of it. 'The gardens were actually closed for a while and the proprietors were ordered to put lamps here. I think you will agree that the colourful illuminations now make it much more pleasant, although the recesses are still far too dark.'

'I think it would be very exciting to walk through here in the dark with a lover,' Carlotta said, a mood of rebellion growing within her, but her words were uttered so quietly that Mr Woollatt was not discomposed by them. She was disgusted at her cowardice. Why could she not shout at him and make him recoil at her vulgar behaviour? With an inward sigh she realised her strict upbringing did not allow her to behave in such an un-ladylike way. As they turned into another narrow alley, she saw a familiar figure coming towards her. Thanks to the compulsory lighting in what Mr Woollatt informed her had been a notorious trysting place, she was able to recognise Lord Darvell while he was still some distance away. He was arm in arm with a female who was displaying her ample charms very freely. In one glance Carlotta took in the improbably black curls, painted cheeks and vividly carmined mouth. Her own lips curled in distaste as she watched the woman leaning against her partner, laughing immoderately at something he said. As they drew nearer Carlotta realised she did not want Darvell to know she had seen him. She clung a little closer to Mr Woollatt and turned her face up to him.

'Do you not think it romantic here, under the trees?' she remarked. She knew Luke and his—she sought for a word to describe the wanton creature, but nothing ladylike seemed appropriate—his *woman* would be very close by now, and kept her eyes resolutely upon her companion.

Mr Woollatt regarded her with a rather startled expression. 'I—I beg your pardon, ma'am, what was that?'

Out of the corner of her eye she realised that they were about to pass Luke and his partner. There could be no doubting that he had seen her. She snuggled even closer to Mr Woollatt.

'I think this is *such* a romantic setting. The coloured lamps, the wind whispering through the leaves.' She gave an artistic sigh. 'It makes one long to be able to burst into song, or—or to write verse.'

Even as she said it, the thought of Mr Woollatt turning poet almost made her laugh, but she maintained her soulful pose, turning towards him even more, so that she could peep over his shoulder. She was rewarded for her efforts by the sight of Luke looking back at them, a heavy frown creasing his brow.

'I—um—I have never thought of it in those terms,' said Mr Woollatt, 'but now you have suggested it, I can see how some might find these coloured lights inspiring.' He smiled down at her. 'I had no idea you were such a sensitive little thing, Miss Rivington.'

With Luke now safely out of sight, Carlotta felt it was safe to draw away from Mr Woollatt, but he was holding tightly to her arm.

'Damme if I don't think you are right, m'dear—there *is* something enticing about these lamplit walks.' He nodded slowly. 'Yes, 'fore Gad I think you have made my heart beat a little quicker, Miss Rivington, I—oh—'

He stopped suddenly and released her, clamping one hand to his chest.

'Mr Woollatt, is something wrong? What is the matter?' Carlotta stared at him in concern. He was bent forward a little, his face contorted with pain. A vein on his right temple bulged alarmingly.

'Can't—quite—seem to get m'breath,' he gasped.

Carlotta looked about her, wishing that her aunt or someone she knew was at hand. There were but one couple in view and they had eyes only for each other. She took his arm.

'You must sit down, Mr Woollatt.' She guided him towards the nearest recess and was relieved to find that it was empty. 'Come along, sir. Sit down here in this little bower for a few moments.'

Mr Woollatt staggered to the rustic bench and collapsed on to it, breathing noisily. His hands were tugging at his neckcloth.

'Can't breath,' he gasped again.

Carlotta stripped off her gloves and fumbled with the knotted linen at his throat. It was too dark to see clearly, but at length she managed to untie the cravat and loosen the shirt around his neck. She glanced down at the waistcoat strained across his chest.

'If you will excuse me, sir, I will unbutton your waistcoat

too, for I think you will feel more comfortable without that constriction.'

'Yes, yes, thank you, that *is* better,' he muttered. The waist-coat fell away from his chest and he took a deep breath. His frilled shirt billowed out, gleaming palely in the dim light.

Carlotta sat down beside him. His chest was rising and falling with his huge, noisy gasps for air.

'What should I do, sir?' she asked him anxiously. 'Would you like me to fetch someone?'

He reached across and patted her hand, saying wheezily, 'No, no need for that. I think if I rest here for a moment, I shall be well again.'

Carlotta sat beside him, listening to his laboured breathing and thinking miserably that if he died now it would be her fault for exciting him with her flirtatious behaviour. A little tear slipped down her cheek. Aunt Broxted would be horrified to learn how badly she had behaved. She would most likely pack her off back to her parents. At that moment Carlotta thought that she would like nothing better than to return to the little cottage in Malberry, to live in obscurity. She looked again at Mr Woollatt, slumped on the bench beside her. His breathing was much more normal now, but his eyes were closed.

'Mr Woollatt?' Her tentative call made him open one eye.

'Ah, my apologies, Miss Rivington,' he murmured. 'I seem to have been a little overcome. Pray allow me to rest for a few moments more, then I shall return you to your family. I regret this most heartily; I assure you it has never happened to me before.'

'You must not worry yourself, sir,' she replied, relieved that he was showing signs of recovery. 'Rest as long as you wish.'

He patted her hand again, closed his eyes and put back his head. A few moments later he began to snore gently. Carlotta did not know whether she was most indignant or relieved by this. She hoped Mr Woollatt would not sleep for too long, for her aunt and uncle would be growing anxious, but she did not think that she should leave him and go back through the gardens alone. It was growing late and she was aware of the sounds of raucous laughter and coarse jests coming from the adjoining walks. Occasionally she heard footsteps on the gravel path and held her breath, praying no one would look in and see her in the shadowy arbour. As the evening wore on and they remained undisturbed she began to relax, the tedium of sitting quietly in the darkness beginning to steal over her. She thought that she should put on her gloves again and was looking for them when a voice close at hand made her jump.

'Miss Rivington. What a pleasant surprise.'

Lord Darvell was leaning against the pillar at the edge of the recess, arms folded across his chest. As the lamps that lined the walk were behind him, his face was in shadow, but Carlotta thought his stance was decidedly insolent. His tone certainly indicated no pleasure at this meeting. She jumped up and went across to him, putting a finger to her lips.

'Please, Mr Woollatt is sleeping. Do not wake him.' She tried to keep her voice to a whisper.

His lip curled contemptuously. 'Exhausted your lover, have you?'

Carlotta stopped. She had been about to explain everything, but his words suddenly made her realise how the situation must look, Mr Woollatt with his clothes in disarray and her gloves lying discarded at his feet. Her cheeks flamed and she felt hot with embarrassment. 'It is not what you think.'

'No?'

He pushed himself off the pillar and stepped towards her. He towered over her, a huge, menacing black shape. Carlotta could feel the anger emanating from him and had to force herself not to retreat; something of her old spirit reasserted itself. She would not give him the satisfaction of seeing her distress.

'Woollatt looks well satisfied.' His insolent tone flayed her. 'Did you learn those skills at your fashionable academy, or does it come naturally to you?'

Carlotta gasped. Any explanation she had planned vanished from her mind. Even before he had finished speaking her hand swept up towards his face, but he was too quick for her and caught her wrist. Outraged, she tried to pull away, but with a savage laugh he captured both her hands and pinned them behind her. This brought them closer, her bosom pressed against the hard rock of his chest. Shock rippled through her. Carlotta found herself staring at the diamond pin nestled into the snowy folds of his neckcloth. She felt an overwhelming desire to subside against him and burst into tears. She drew on her anger to support her, threw back her head and gave him a scorching look.

For a long moment they stared at one another. The poor light cast deep shadows across Luke's face and Carlotta had never seen him look so menacing. She realised that he, too, was breathing heavily, far more so than the exertion of their little tussle warranted. Pressed against him, she could feel his heart hammering in his chest as fast as her own. She was taut as Madame Saqui's high rope, heart pounding, nerve-ends tingling with excitement even while she berated herself for the way her body betrayed her. Standing so close reminded her of their dancing together at Malberry. She remembered how safe she had felt in his arms. *Then* he had been smiling and gentle. Now, as he crushed her to him, she could see only anger in his eyes. Panic threatened to engulf her. She fought it down. She would not give in.

'Release me at once,' she hissed, to be rewarded with a wolfish grin.

'Why? Do you not like being in a man's arms?'

'Not in yours!' she flashed.

His hold tightened. He lowered his head and murmured, 'You enjoyed it once, do you not remember?'

Dear heaven, why did he have to remind her! Carlotta sought to control her wayward emotions. She dared not look into his eyes and instead fixed her gaze upon his mouth, but the sight of his lips, parted slightly to reveal his strong white teeth made her recall his kisses, the way he had grazed her bottom lip, the delicious excitement he had roused within her. The urge to turn her face up to his and invite him to kiss her again was almost irresistible. Desperately she dragged her eyes away. If he did not release her soon, she feared she would give in. Or she would scream.

'I thought you such an innocent at Malberry, Carlotta.'

She managed a bitter laugh. 'You said yourself I have learned a great deal since then.'

His eyes flickered back to the sleeping Mr Woollatt. 'Enough to snare a rich husband?'

She resorted to summoning up images of the haughty girls she had known at school and said with what she hoped to be a fine air of cool arrogance, 'Oh, yes, I think so.'

She forced herself to look at him. The contempt in his eyes cut her like a knife and it took all her resolve to maintain her haughty pose, knowing it was her only defence. He stepped back suddenly, but Carlotta could not move. She was like an animal, unexpectedly released and paralysed with fear. She rubbed her bruised wrists.

'Why did you come here?' she asked him.

He looked down, smoothing his sleeves as if brushing away all signs of their contact. 'I was passing your box and saw that you had not returned. I was concerned. Foolish, is it not?'

'Extremely foolish. And the…female you had on your arm?' She could not resist the question.

'Just that. A female looking to make a few shillings from any gentleman wandering alone in these gardens. Unfortunately for her I have no interest in her charms and she has gone off in search of more lucrative company. She offers her body to the highest bidder.' He paused. 'Very much like yourself.'

This time he made no move to stop her and her open palm slammed onto his cheek with a force that made her fingers sting. She stepped back, holding up her head.

'Your opinion of me is now quite clear,' she said, her voice low and shaking with anger. 'You can have nothing more to say to me.' She turned away from him.

'What?' His jeering voice followed her. 'Do you have no response for me? Are you not going to rip my character to shreds, Miss Carlotta Rivington?'

She closed her eyes, forcing back the tears. Her shoulders slumped a little, but she managed to speak with scarcely a tremor in her voice. 'Goodbye, Lord Darvell.'

He did not reply, and after a few moments she heard the scrunch of his hasty footsteps on the gravel as he walked away.

Carlotta went back to the bench. Mr Woollatt showed no signs of waking up, so she put her head in her hands. How had it come to this? That Luke should think her capable of—she shuddered. Only one man had ever held her, had ever kissed her. There had been a violent storm at Malberry last summer, so violent that she had gone inside the house to wait until the thunder and lightning had passed before making her way home. Luke had seen the light from her candles and come to the house to make sure all was safe. She remembered how they had danced in the empty salon, how he had taken her in his arms and kissed her so long and so thoroughly that she had never wanted it to end. When eventually he had put her away from him she had been afraid that she had erred in some way and he had been at pains to assure her that he was not angry.

But he was angry now, here in one of Vauxhall's famed dark

walks. She had seen it in his eyes when he looked at her, when he accused her of having a lover. He despised her. And who could blame him?

In the darkened arbour with only the sound of Mr Woollatt's stertorous breathing to break the silence, Carlotta thought she could never be more despondent, but she was wrong.

When Mr Woollatt awoke and was well enough to escort her back to their supper box, they were greeted by Lord and Lady Broxted with a mixture of anxiety and relief. Mr Woollatt quickly explained that he had suffered a little dizziness and been obliged to rest for a while. Carlotta was relieved that her aunt and uncle accepted this explanation, but the knowing looks and smirking comments from Mr and Mrs Price made her cringe, and it was an ordeal for her to maintain her composure for the remainder of the evening.

A grey dawn was already lighting the sky as Carlotta fell into bed, and she felt little refreshed when she sat up to drink her hot chocolate later the following morning. She contemplated pleading a headache and remaining in her bed for the day, but common sense told her she could not hide for ever and she thought it better to face any criticism as soon as possible. She dressed with care and made her way to the breakfast room, where she found her aunt and uncle already at the table. It was not long before the subject of Vauxhall was broached. Madame Saqui's exploits on the high wire had to be exclaimed over, Lord Fairbridge's marked attentions to Julia Price discussed and Carlotta waited with a sinking heart for the inevitable comments on her own behaviour. She was surprised, therefore, when Lady Broxted merely remarked that she thought her niece had made a hit.

'Yes,' said Lord Broxted with ponderous humour, 'if I had not known Woollatt for so many years I would suspect him of dalliance last night, keeping you to himself for so long.'

Carlotta was not tempted to smile.

'He was suddenly taken with a shortness of breath, Uncle. I was very worried for him; he could barely walk and we were forced to sit down for a considerable time. If he had not recovered when he did, I should have been obliged to seek help.'

Lady Broxted leaned across to pat her hand.

'You did very well, my dear. Mr Woollatt was most complimentary about you. He was very impressed with your concern for him.'

Remembering that it was her outrageous attempt to flirt that had brought on his malady, Carlotta thought this could be no more than flattery and dreaded seeing Mr Woollatt again. She was relieved, therefore, when they met some days later, to find that he treated her with the same polite courtesy he had always shown her. Mr and Mrs Price only mentioned the incident once and, as Carlotta made a supreme effort to conceal her embarrassment, the matter was allowed to drop. She saw no sign of Lord Darvell during the ensuing week and Carlotta began to hope that the episode at Vauxhall Gardens would soon be forgotten.

Lord Darvell was making every effort to blot out the disgraceful scenes at Vauxhall. Never had he felt such overwhelming jealousy as he had that night, seeing Carlotta with that prosy bore Woollatt. If she was determined to marry a fortune, then let her do so—it was none of his concern. But the demon in his head told him it *was* his concern, that if he could only break through the brittle, society maiden she had become, he might find the sweet, innocent Carlotta he had known at Malberry.

'Don't be a fool, man,' he told himself impatiently. 'She is changed. She is the same as every other woman in town, desperate to make a good match. You have seen her with your own eyes, making up to Mattingwood and flirting outrageously with Woollatt. Let her go.'

He would do just that. They must meet, of course, but he

would be no more than civil to her. Carlotta had made it perfectly plain that she wanted nothing more to do with him. So be it. It was over.

Chapter Five

By an unlucky chance, Lord Broxted's party arrived at Lady Yatebury's rout at the same moment that Lord Darvell walked into the entrance hall of the magnificent Yatebury town house. Carlotta's heart sank as Lord Broxted, knowing nothing of the contretemps at Vauxhall, hailed Lord Darvell pleasantly and Luke returned the greeting with a courteous word. As he turned to Carlotta, however, Luke's eyes hardened and his bow was a calculated insult. Her cheeks flamed. How dare he treat her thus! She chose to ignore him and followed her aunt and uncle up the stairs. But despite her brave intentions she was painfully aware of him, her spine prickling with the knowledge that he was but a few steps behind her. Their hostess was standing at the top of the stairs and already calling down excitedly to Lady Broxted.

'My dear, so pleased you could come—it is a veritable crush! But I am so disappointed, the new orangery is not in use yet! I had hoped to have it ready for this evening, but they were still working on it this morning, and my plantsman has let me down and will not be bringing the flowers until next week. It cannot be helped, however, and you must come again as soon as it is ready, for I am burning to show it to you, since you are my *particular* friend.'

They had reached the landing by this time and Lady Yatebury

touched her cheek to Lady Broxted's while keeping up a constant flow of chatter. She turned to greet Carlotta, exclaiming at her beauty and cupping her face in her hands while she examined her.

'Such perfect skin! I am sick with envy, my dear, for the smallpox ruined my complexion years ago, which is why I am obliged to wear these patches upon my cheek, but you are in blooming health.' She turned to smile at Lady Broxted. 'She is so pretty I vow she will have every gentleman at her feet, Celia. But you must take care of your heart, little Carlotta,' she continued, her kind eyes twinkling. 'Have a care that you do not take a liking to a rascal such as Darvell here. We would not have you losing your heart to the Wicked Baron—that would never do!'

Carlotta blushed, but said nothing; Luke was beside her, bowing over Lady Yatebury's hand.

'Miss Rivington has nothing to fear from me.'

She winced: his indifferent tone was like a blade slicing into her heart. Pride came to her aid. A half-smile, a haughty look and she murmured, 'Lord Darvell is too kind.'

They moved on to the crowded reception rooms and did not speak again. Carlotta dreaded the coming evening. Heartache, anger and nerves combined; by the time dinner was announced, she felt quite sick and unable to eat anything from the numerous dishes spread on the dining table. She drank her wine in nervous sips and accepted another glass—or was it two? She could not be sure.

However, with so many young people present it was impossible not to be in infected by their high spirits and after dinner Carlotta began to relax a little. When the gentlemen joined the ladies in the drawing room, the conversation became much more animated and Carlotta even began to enjoy herself. She tried not to think of Luke, or the fact that he had spent most of the evening with Mrs Leonora Daniels, a young married lady who was quite clearly throwing out lures to him. She watched him now, bending low over her chair, his brown hair almost touching the matron's blonde curls as he listened to her. She hunched one white shoulder. She was sure she did not care; there were gentlemen enough paying her extravagant compliments and she was minded to enjoy a little flirtation. In fact, she was feeling quite light-headed. Possibly the effect of the wine, she thought hazily. The younger members of the group congregated around the pianoforte where several of them were persuaded to sing or play.

Carlotta joined Sir Gilbert Mattingwood in one duet, but refused to perform another, despite numerous compliments on their performance. She was sorting through the music to find a piece for Julia Price when from the corner of her eye she saw Luke approaching with Mrs Daniels on his arm. She concentrated on the music sheets, but she need not have feared, for Luke did not once look her way. Mrs Daniels addressed Julia as they drew closer.

'Miss Price, I saw you at Almack's last night. Did you not think it very flat?'

Carlotta had been there too and had found it incredibly dull, although when she observed the dashing matron in her fashionable gold robe and matching turban, hanging on to Luke's arm in the most possessive way, nothing would have persuaded her to agree with the lady on any point. She remembered that Julia had spent most of the evening with Viscount Fairbridge, so she was not surprised when Julia declared herself very well satisfied with Almack's.

'Well, I doubt I shall go there again for some time,' Mrs Daniels purred, 'Unless, my lord, I know that *you* will be there.'

'That you will not do,' returned Luke with a smile.

'Darvell never goes to Almack's,' declared Sir Gilbert.

One of the other gentlemen laughed heartily, saying, 'Good thing, too, or he would cut us all out with the ladies.'

Luke bowed. 'Anything to oblige you, Elmwood.'

'Lord Darvell rates his charms very highly,' muttered Carlotta. Immediately all eyes were turned on her.

'No, no,' Luke reproved her gently, 'you do me an injustice, madam. I do not rate myself above the average.'

'Aye,' cried Sir Gilbert merrily. 'It is the *ladies* who value his attentions. They are all ready to swoon at his feet.'

'Not all of them,' retorted Carlotta. Her head was bent over the music, but the words came out louder than she had intended. Mrs Daniels left her partner and moved forward a little.

'Oho,' she said softly, 'Darvell, here is a woman immune to your charms. How can this be, Miss Rivington?'

'It would be a very sad world if we all liked the same thing,' returned Carlotta, her cheeks hot. She was beginning to regret her rash words and wished someone would turn the conversation to safer channels.

'Indeed, but there are some things we must all value, and Lord Darvell has them in abundance.' Mrs Daniels was watching Carlotta, a small, contemptuous smile playing around her mouth. 'Pray, Miss Rivington, tell us what *you* find attractive in a man?'

'Yes, Miss Rivington.' Luke came forward until the candlelight was reflected in his eyes, like little dancing devils. 'Tell us what qualities you admire?'

Carlotta looked around the little group: they were all watching her, but for once she was not put out by this. She felt a little reckless and looked up fearlessly to meet the challenge in Luke's eyes.

'Honesty, integrity, a sense of honour,' she ticked them off on her fingers.

Mrs Daniels laughed; Carlotta watched her throw back her

head, giving everyone the opportunity to admire her fine neck
and shoulders.

'My dear, those are the attributes of every gentleman.'

'But are they the attributes of every lord?' flashed Carlotta.

A ripple of amusement ran around the group.

'Now you intrigue me, Miss Rivington,' murmured Mrs
Daniels. 'Darvell, is this aimed at you? What scandalous things
can she know of you? Pray, Miss Rivington, do tell us.'

Carlotta gave another of her haughty looks. Really, she was
growing quite adept at this. 'No more or less than anyone has
heard of the Wicked Baron.'

Luke was watching her. He said softly, 'Come, Miss Rivington,
will you not give me the opportunity to defend myself?'

She put her closed fan to her lips and modestly cast down her
eyes. 'A lady does not indulge in idle gossip, my lord.'

With a smile she left the group. She had not intended to be
so outspoken, but it had been worth it to see the startled look
upon Luke's face, to hear the whispered murmurs of those
around her. She heard Julia begin her piano piece; with
everyone's attention upon the music, she slipped away. The
sensation of having rocked Luke from his indifference elated
her and she wanted a little solitude to savour the sensation. All
the reception rooms were crowded, but in one corner of the
main salon, behind a silk screen, she spotted a small door. It
was covered in the same Chinese paper as the walls and she
would not have noticed it if it had not been ajar. Most likely it
was a servants' passage, or perhaps another way to the stairs.

Desperate for a little cool air, Carlotta slipped through the
door. The light from the salon illuminated the opening, but
beyond that the corridor was black, the dark panelling on the
walls adding to its gloom. She slipped into the darkness and
took a few steps into the cool passage. In the distance she could
discern a glimmer of light, but it was at the far end of the

passage and Carlotta decided she should go back. As she turned to retrace her steps she saw a figure in the corridor behind her. She could see nothing but the black outline of the man, but she knew immediately it was Luke. He had followed her through the rooms! Blind, unreasoning panic overtook her. Carlotta picked up her skirts and ran.

She made for the patch of light in the distance. It was a doorway, opening into a bare, moonlit room. Carlotta ran in, glad to be out of the cloying darkness. The moonlight flooded in through long windows that filled three of the walls and showed that the room was completely empty. This must be Lady Yatebury's new orangery, she thought as she breathed in the familiar smells of fresh plaster and new paint. Her buoyant mood was fading fast; she was tired and her head was aching. After the noisy, overheated ballroom the conservatory was blessedly cool and peaceful. She listened carefully. There was no sound from the corridor so she walked over to the window. As she gazed out on to the walled garden, she wondered what madness had possessed her to challenge Luke; surely it was better to ignore him, even to avoid him, until this pain in her heart had diminished to a manageable ache. With a sigh she rested her forehead on the cold glass.

'So, the vixen shows her teeth.'

Carlotta jumped. Lithe as a cat, Luke had come silently into the room. She swung round to face him. Words of apology sprang to her lips, but she bit them back; his face in the moonlight was as hard and cold as marble. It was too late for soft words. She lifted her chin to gaze at him defiantly. 'I said nothing untoward.'

'But you implied much,' he said, coming towards her.

She curled her lip. 'You are called the Wicked Baron; much is expected of you.'

He came closer and Carlotta stepped back until she felt the window pressing against her shoulders.

'Then I am afraid I must disappoint you,' he murmured.

He was less than arm's length from her and Carlotta forced herself not to move.

'I am not afraid of you.'

She was rigid with nerves, and her voice shook a little. Luke's teeth gleamed, but she could discern no humour in his look, no softening of those harsh features.

'Well, you should be. You should be very afraid.'

He reached out and placed his fingers on her shoulder, then drew them down along the embroidered neckline of her dress. Carlotta's nerves were stretched to breaking. At his touch her breasts tightened and rose. Against her will they were inviting his caresses. She clenched her hands, digging the nails into the palms. She wanted to run, but some instinct told her that such an action would inflame an already dangerous situation.

'If—if you try to kiss me, I shall scream.'

He came even closer. Carlotta fought down the urge of her wayward body to close the gap, to lean forward and press herself against him. His eyes held hers and she knew he would see her fear reflected in them. She could not breathe; Luke, too, was taut as a bowstring, the atmosphere between them so brittle only one wrong word could shatter their control and that, she knew, would be disastrous. They gazed at one another, Luke towering over her, dark and menacing. Carlotta's lips parted as he leaned towards her. Her head tilted; unable to prevent it, she was offering him her mouth to kiss. Then, when it seemed inevitable, when her very being was screaming to feel his mouth against hers, he stepped back and gave a little laugh.

'Oh, no, Carlotta, you shall not have the pleasure of my embraces again: that time is past.' His words, the cold tone, hit her like icy water. She leaned back against the window, the cold glass on her skin the only link with reality as he continued. 'But I shall watch your progress, my dear, and if you *should* manage to catch a rich husband, perhaps I shall disclose what delights await him. And you *were* delightful, my dear, that one time at Malberry.'

She ran her tongue across her dry lips. 'W-we did nothing wrong.'

His smile grew, but it was as cold as the moonlight. 'You were alone, at night, in an empty house with the Wicked Baron—do you think any man would believe I did nothing more than kiss you?' He took her chin between his thumb and fingers and forced her to look at him. 'You know I am right, my dear.'

Angrily she knocked his hand away. 'I know nothing of the sort!'

'Believe that if you want to, Carlotta, but I know enough about you to ruin your chances of making a good match.'

'Then you are wicked indeed, my lord.'

He merely laughed, turned on his heel and walked away. Shivering uncontrollably, Carlotta sank down against the window and wrapped her arms about her.

Luke strode back through the corridor, wondering what had come over him. He had grown used to jesting and teasing during his years in the army, so why had Carlotta's little barbs cut so deeply? He had loved and lost other women in the past and it had never been difficult to put them behind him, to see them again without a flicker of remorse. He had thought he could do the same with Carlotta, once he realised that she was intent upon finding herself a rich husband. And he had resolved to stay away from her, a resolve that had lasted only until their very next meeting! As he stepped back into the crowded reception room, he swore fluently under his breath. He would never forget the look of haughty disdain on her face the first time they had met in town, her taunts regarding his lack of fortune, but even that had not killed his feeling for her. It was seeing her at

Vauxhall, behaving like any wanton in that darkened arbour with Daniel Woollatt that finally convinced him she was not the sweet innocent child he had left at Malberry.

Her behaviour this evening had been calculated to anger him, like the bitter reaction of a spurned woman, but that did not make sense—*she* had spurned *him*, telling him he was not remotely rich enough to be a contender for her hand. Yet her jibes were like a gauntlet thrown down between them. He knew he should have ignored her challenge and allowed himself to enjoy the charms of Mrs Daniels, but he could not. He had followed Carlotta through the crowded rooms and out into that bare, moon-soaked room.

His anger flared again as he remembered her standing before him, haughty and defiant. When he had moved close to her, smelled the familiar, flowery perfume, he had found her hard to resist. He saw again her face turned up to his, the dainty features so perfect, the mouth so kissable. He had been tempted. She was enticing, bewitching, almost irresistible. His muttered 'excuse me' as he pushed through the dancers was very nearly a snarl and earned for him several angry looks, but it mattered not as long as they moved out of his way. He had to get out; he needed peace and quiet to regain his self-control and work out just what it was about Carlotta that roused him to such fury.

And after that, he needed to decide just what he was going to do about it.

Chapter Six

The confrontation with Luke unnerved Carlotta and she pleaded a slight chill for the next few days until she could face the world again. Lady Broxted was very understanding.

'Poor lamb, but it is not unexpected,' she said, visiting Carlotta's bedchamber. 'We have been very busy of late, and a number of our friends remarked that you seemed pale and distracted when they were taking their leave of you at Lady Yatebury's. You shall keep to your bed for a little while.' She smiled, patting Carlotta's hand as it lay upon the bedcovers. 'I shall cancel our engagements for this week; you must be well for our little soirée.'

But as the day drew nearer it became clear to Carlotta that Lady Broxted's 'little soirée' was going to be a major event. On the eve of the party she went to find her aunt, to offer her some assistance. She found her in the morning room, surrounded by papers and making her final arrangements.

'But, Aunt, you cannot possibly wish to invite all these people,' objected Carlotta, gazing in awe at a list of guests that ran over several sheets of paper. 'You said we were to have a snug little evening—how will you find room for so many?'

'Dear child, this is only half the guests!' Lady Broxted

twitched the papers from her fingers and looked at them with satisfaction. 'I think we can be sure that most of them will come; I am renowned for my parties, you know. We shall open up both the saloons and set out supper in the dining room. And if it stays dry, we shall also be able to open up the long doors to the terrace and hang lanterns around the garden. We shall have to bring in extra staff for the kitchens, of course, and we shall need more link boys in the square…'

Carlotta was not listening. One of the sheets had floated to the floor and she scooped it up, her smile dying away as she scanned the names. 'Dear ma'am, surely there is no need to invite Lord Darvell.'

'Of course he must be invited. It is unlikely that he will come, however, for he is a great favourite in town and always in great demand. And since he has shown no inclination to fix his interest with you, he may well consider my little gathering far too tame.'

Carlotta clung on to that thought. There must be far more exciting things for a wild young baron to do in London. Besides, he had made it perfectly clear that he despised her.

No, she decided it was most unlikely that he would come.

'I am beyond doubt the most contrary young woman in the world!'

Carlotta gazed at her reflection gloomily. She had no wish to set eyes on Luke Ainslowe ever again, but she had a great desire that he should see her now that she was looking her best. The thought that he might not attend her aunt's soirée was just too galling.

Jarvis, Lady Broxted's dresser, had spent a great deal of time arranging Carlotta's hair and the result was very pleasing. Tiny apricot-coloured rosebuds nestled amongst her dark curls and matched the roses embroidered around the flounced hem of her rich cream satin evening gown. An overdress of fine white net gave an ethereal, shimmering quality to her skirts and she executed a few dance steps before her mirror, watching the effect.

'Very pretty, miss, I'm sure,' said Jarvis, surveying her with a professional eye. 'We could wish that your complexion was whiter—perhaps a little powder…'

'No, no powder, thank you, Jarvis, I am quite happy with my colour. I inherited it from my Italian father.'

Jarvis tutted.

'Hush, Miss Carlotta,' she said, bending to straighten the hem of Carlotta's gown. 'You know her ladyship does not want you to be saying such things, especially tonight.'

'No.' Carlotta sighed. 'She wants everyone to think me a very English young lady.'

'Aye, she does, and English young ladies do not jig about in front of the mirror! Now, pray you keep still, miss, while I tuck away this stray curl… There, that's better. Off you go and join her ladyship, for your guests will be arriving any moment.'

Carlotta picked up her fan and ran down the stairs to join her aunt. She found her on the landing, at the top of the curling staircase that led up from the entrance hall. She glowed with pleasure when Lady Broxted exclaimed how well she looked, and took her place beside her as the first of their guests was announced. At first Carlotta found it exciting, watching the ladies come in, arrayed in satins, silks and muslins, their tassels and ostrich plumes nodding as they made their way up the stairs. The gentlemen were dressed more soberly, mostly in coats of black or dark blue with knee breeches or pantaloons, but there was an occasional splash of colour as a military man made his appearance in his regimentals. A few of the guests she had met already, such as Mr and Mrs Price and their daughter, but many were strangers, and her head was soon buzzing with names and faces that she feared she would not remember. Mr Woollatt arrived just as the orchestra was tuning up. He immediately launched into an apology.

'My dear Lady Broxted, I would have been here sooner, but my steward has arrived from the country and I was obliged to see him.' He bowed low over Lady Broxted's gloved hand. 'As a matter of fact, I wanted to be one of your first guests,' he continued, bowing gallantly to Carlotta, 'to make sure of the first two dances with Miss Rivington.'

Carlotta blushed and began to repeat the argument she had already used for several other gentlemen that evening. 'You are very kind, sir, but I shall not be dancing for some time. As you see, I must greet our guests—'

Lady Broxted interrupted her. 'Nonsense, child. All but a very few stragglers are here now. You have done your duty, no one expects you to stay here for ever.' She gave Carlotta a beaming smile. 'Take her away, Mr Woollatt. Carlotta's first two dances are free, so you shall be her reward for showing such patience.'

Reading the triumph in her aunt's smile Carlotta suspected that she had planned this. There was nothing for it but to accompany Mr Woollatt and take her place amongst the dancers.

Luke arrived at Broxted House with his brother and sister-in-law just as the first set of dances was ending. Lady Broxted had left her post at the head of the stairs, but as they entered the saloon she hurried across to greet them.

'Apologies for being late, ma'am,' said James, bowing over her hand. 'If Adele had not taken so long choosing her gown, we would have been here a good hour since.'

Adele gave him a playful tap with her fan. 'You will not blame it all upon me, James—admit that you could not tie your neckcloth!'

He grinned. 'I will admit nothing, especially in front of my brother here.'

Luke managed a faint smile. He wished he had not agreed to come, but Lady Broxted was smiling at him, holding out her hand and welcoming him. There was no escape now.

'Since you are all three acquainted with my niece, then you have missed nothing.' She smiled and added with a touch of pride, 'Except, gentlemen, that I quite fear that she is engaged for every dance.'

Luke looked across the room at Carlotta, who was at the centre of a laughing, chattering crowd of young people.

'That is definitely a severe loss, ma'am,' he said politely.

He resisted Lady Broxted's attempts to introduce him to any other young lady, and when Adele went off with her hostess the two brothers retired to a quiet corner. Luke tried to ignore James's quizzical glance, but his brother took his arm.

'Out with it, Luke—what is the meaning of this long face you are showing the world? You have been quite distracted recently, refused several invitations to dine with us—why, man you have all but given up gambling! If I did not know you so well I'd think you were in love.'

Luke felt the flush mantling his cheeks. 'Nothing so foolish!' he growled.

James gave a crack of laughter. 'Oho! So it *is* a woman,' he exclaimed. 'What happened, did she turn you down? That must be a new experience for you.'

'Go soak your head, James! Just because you are head over heels in love with Adele, pray do not think it happens to everyone.'

'Well, it should. I have never been so happy, which makes me want you to be happy, too. So tell me what is the matter.'

Not for the world could Luke tell his younger brother about Carlotta. He was not about to admit that any woman could fill his thoughts night and day.

'I have been looking at the accounts for Darvell Manor.'

'Depressing, are they?'

'Damnably so.'

'My offer of a loan still stands, brother—'

'No, it is not as bad as that. Not yet. I wish, though, that our father had told me the true state of affairs, I could have helped him.'

'He was too proud to admit that he had spent your inheritance, Luke. He always thought he could win it all back at the gaming tables.'

'Instead of which he lost even more.' Luke sighed. 'When Father died, I should have sold out, taken control of the estate, looked after you—'

James put a hand on his shoulder. 'It was too daunting a task for a young man of one-and-twenty. No one blamed you for going back to what you knew, to the army. And you found enough money to make me a generous allowance—we should not forget that.'

'But if I had begun the improvements then, five years ago, I could have been a wealthy man by now—or at least comfortable!'

'Aye, but would you have been happy, working your land while your comrades faced Bonaparte without you?'

Luke sighed. 'No, you are right, James. I would not have missed Waterloo for the world. I could not have forgiven myself. But now—'

'Now you need to take charge of your affairs, Luke. Send that rascally agent of yours to the right about.'

'I already have. In fact, I have put in motion a number of improvements at the Manor and must go back there soon.'

'Go where?' asked Adele, coming up at that moment.

'To Darvell. My estates need proper management.'

'But you are not going immediately?' She laid a hand on his arm. 'You promised to come back to Malberry with us.'

He gave her a wry smile. 'Yes, I did. And I shall come with you, you have my word.'

'Good, you will be able to see my new Tiepolo,' murmured James.

'The one Mattingwood gave you in payment of his gambling debts?'

'That's right. I sent a man down with it yesterday. I'm going to hang it in the library.'

'And we are gathering any number of people to join us at Malberry for the summer,' added Adele.

'Aye, well, make sure there are some uncommonly pretty ladies amongst the guests, my love,' said James, grinning. 'We need to provide my brother with plenty of distraction, for I think he is nursing a broken heart!'

The rooms were crowded and noisy. A sign, thought Carlotta, that the party would be deemed a success. Once it was realised that Miss Rivington was no longer busy greeting her guests, a flattering number of gentlemen began vying for her attention. Carlotta had no illusions about the attraction; her uncle had made no secret of the fact that he would make a generous settlement upon her marriage, and most of her dance partners were single gentlemen like Sir Gilbert Mattingwood, eager to improve their acquaintance with Lord Broxted's protégée. She was amused, therefore, when Lord Fairbridge claimed his dance with her. She saw his eyes following Julia, who was further down the line, partnered by a handsome soldier with bushy side-whiskers. After a half-dance of stilted attempts at conversation she was prompted to protest.

'My lord, would you not rather be dancing with Miss Price? Pray tell me truthfully,' she said, her eyes twinkling, 'I promise you I shall not be offended.'

The viscount looked at her, alarmed, but her smile reassured him. He gave her an apologetic grin.

'She has promised me another dance after supper,' he confessed. 'To be seen dancing together more often would give rise to gossip.'

'It would indeed,' she agreed cordially. 'And so you must dance with all the other young ladies in the meantime.'

'Yes.'

His affirmation was so wistful that Carlotta almost burst out laughing. As the dance ended she gave him a speculative look.

'If you would prefer, we could sit out this next dance, my lord.'

'Could we?' he gazed at her hopefully.

Stifling a giggle, Carlotta took his hand and led him to the edge of the room and out through one of the long windows to the terrace.

'So many people and so much chatter, it is not conducive to conversation,' she told him as they stepped out into the lamp-lit garden. 'So, have you made an offer for Julia?'

Her direct question made him stutter.

'N-no. M-my mother thought it w-would be best if we waited until the end of the Season.'

Carlotta remembered being presented to Lady Fairbridge earlier in the evening—a colourless little woman with a small, rosebud mouth and arching eyebrows that gave her a look of permanent surprise. She had been very gracious, but in the manner of one bestowing a great honour, and Carlotta thought it unlikely that the viscountess would consider a mere Miss Price to be a suitable bride for her son.

'And what do Julia's parents say?'

'I—um—have not yet spoken to Mr Price, but Mama is sure he would agree.'

Carlotta considered it much more likely that Julia's father would want to draw up the marriage settlements immediately and make sure of such a prize, but she decided it would be unkind to say so.

'And does Julia know how you feel?' she asked him.

'Oh, yes. That is, she would do nothing without her parents' approval, of course, but I cannot think there will be any obstacle.'

'Except your mother.'

Carlotta wished the words unsaid, but the viscount was not offended.

'It is not what she would wish,' he agreed, considering the matter. 'Julia—Miss Price—does not have a large fortune, but she is in every other way perfectly suitable.'

'She is not exactly a pauper,' retorted Carlotta.

'True, but Mama was hoping I might find someone a little nearer my own station,' he said, twisting his hands together in some anxiety.

'Hmm, someone from a noble family, do you mean? That would be more difficult, I think. I have only been in town a few weeks, but it seems to me there are very few young ladies—' She saw his anguished glance and clapped her hands to her mouth. 'Oh—you mean me? Because I am Earl Broxted's niece?' She went off into a peal of laughter. 'I beg your pardon,' she said, wiping her eyes. 'I think if your mama knew me better, she would agree that Julia is a far more suitable bride for you!'

They walked the length of the terrace and back again in an amicable silence, but as they approached the long windows Carlotta said, 'Come, the music has finished so we had best return; my next partner will be looking for me.'

They made their way back to the saloon so much at ease with each other that when Carlotta spotted a patch of dust upon the shoulder of his coat she did not hesitate to mention it.

'My lord, you have pollen on your shoulder from the bushes.'

Smiling, she was reaching up to brush it away as they walked back through one of the long windows. Then the viscount stopped suddenly and she looked up to see Lord Darvell blocking their way.

Carlotta felt the blood draining from her face. Her hand was still on the viscount's shoulder and as he stopped she was obliged to lean against him to correct her balance. Luke stood before her, his face stony. Carlotta gathered her courage. She must be strong; he could not hurt her here, in front of all these people. She stepped away from the viscount, smiling.

'Thank you, my lord. I must find my next partner…'

He bowed and turned away. Luke's hand shot out and gripped her arm.

'My dance, I think.'

Carlotta glared at him. A young man came up, saying shyly, 'Miss Rivington, I believe you are engaged to dance this gavotte with me—'

He put out his hand, but Luke was already pushing past him, dragging Carlotta on to the dance floor. The young man looked confused.

'Miss Rivington—'

'Go to the devil!' snarled Luke.

Carlotta tried to pull her hand away, but Luke's grip was inflexible as iron. He almost flung her into position on his right, his stormy gaze daring her to run away. Carlotta ran her tongue nervously over her lips and glanced around her. Everyone was intent on taking their places for the gavotte. She must not draw attention to herself; it would not do to cause a scene. She dragged her head up. One dance, that was all. She would get through it. She knew the steps, but faltered a little when she turned to face her partner. His eyes bored into her, no longer a laughing hazel, but cold and hard as polished stone. The tense line of his jaw revealed his anger.

'What were you doing on the terrace with Fairbridge?'

Her brows rose. A tiny spark of an idea nudged at her brain. Could his anger be caused by *jealousy*? Not that she cared a jot for him, of course. She gave him as haughty a look as she could manage.

'I do not see that I need discuss such things with you, my lord.'

'Do you think he would even look at you if he knew your real name?'

His voice was low so that no one else could hear him. Knowing that the viscount had set his heart on Julia Price, Carlotta was able give him a glittering smile.

'Oh, I do not think it would make one jot of difference to him. But, naturally it is more advantageous to use Lord Broxted's family name. It confers an added dignity.' They turned away from each other, and as they came back together she added, 'Especially when one is looking for a husband.'

She noted his scowl with savage satisfaction as she completed the move.

'And has all this *added dignity* produced a suitor worthy of your consideration?' he asked.

'Several.'

His grip on her fingers tightened painfully, but she would not complain.

'No doubt they will be delighted to know the extra skills you will bring with you, just think of the savings—no expensive Chinese silks for your walls, my dear, you will have original paintings, all your own work. No doubt you will devise something…suitable for the bedroom.'

Her eyes narrowed. 'Your wit, my lord, is better suited to a tavern than a *ton* party!'

'And how would you know that, unless you were born in one?' he threw back at her. 'An Italian tavern, no doubt.'

She bit her lip, anxious that the other couples should not hear their bickering. She made her swift pirouette and the dance continued, everyone laughing and chattering as they executed the gavotte steps. Carlotta smiled until her cheeks ached. She looked up at Luke, who seemed to be smiling quite naturally, yet when they came close he snarled at her through clenched teeth, 'By God, you deserve that I should expose your deception.'

Carlotta grew cold. For herself she did not care, but her aunt and uncle—they were so anxious to conceal her history, she must do all she could to avoid embarrassing them. 'You could not be so cruel.'

He was standing behind her, their hands held high. He muttered savagely into her ear, 'Oh, I can be much worse than this, my dear. I intend to let you carry on with your little charade, but remember, I know the truth about you—I can bring it to an end whenever I wish.'

He turned her around and she glared at him, her palm itching to slap his smiling face, but he held tightly to her hands. 'Smile, Carlotta, the gentlemen like to see a happy face.'

Her eyes glittered. Mechanically she performed her steps, forcing herself to sink into the final, graceful curtsy to her partner. He bowed, then removed the white rose from his buttonhole and handed it to her.

'A token, Miss Rivington, that you may remember this dance.'

Mechanically she put out her hand, but kept her eyes fixed on his face. He looked so cold, so merciless that her fingers clenched, closing around the stem until the sharp stab of a thorn brought her to her senses. She must face the truth—it was not jealousy that made him act so. He hated her, and she had given him every inducement to do so by acting as a heartless fortune hunter. Tears burned her eyelids and she blinked them away. No one should see her misery.

Still smiling, Luke took her arm and led her off the dance floor. Angrily Carlotta pulled away. Giving him one last, scorching look, she dropped the rose, turned on her heel and walked quickly towards Lady Broxted, who was talking with Mr Price. With his long stride, Luke had no difficulty keeping pace with her; as they approached, Mr Price beamed at them.

'There, sir, I was watching you go down the dance. Capital entertainment, eh, my lord? Miss Rivington makes an excellent partner, does she not?'

Carlotta seethed as Luke bowed and smiled at her.

'Indeed, sir, I have rarely enjoyed a dance more. She is a true artist.'

Stifling her indignation Carlotta turned away. Behind them a console table held a dish of confits and she hovered near it on the pretext of choosing a sweetmeat.

'Let me recommend the marzipan.' She heard Lord Darvell's voice in her ear. 'I believe it is an *Italian* delicacy.'

'I wish you would leave me alone,' she muttered.

'Now why should I do that, when there is such good sport to be had?'

Carlotta hunched a shoulder. She began to fan herself rapidly. So, the battle lines were drawn. At every opportunity Lord Darvell would taunt her. It seemed cruel, when he was the one who had deserted her—even now the memory of those halcyon days at Malberry still had the power to hurt her. But she would never admit that; pride would not allow it.

She suddenly felt desperately weary, longing to leave this crowded, busy life where she could not relax and be herself. In a mood of deep depression she thought of asking her aunt to take her away from London. The words hovered on her tongue.

'My dear child, you are very flushed.' Lady Broxted regarded her anxiously. 'Are you unwell, are you not enjoying yourself?'

Her resolve wavered—how could she be so ungrateful when her aunt had gone to so much trouble on her behalf?

'I am enjoying myself very much, Aunt, thank you. I am just a little warm.'

'Aye, town is grown white hot,' agreed Mr Price. 'But I have good news for you, I have just been talking with your aunt— you will not object if I tell Miss Rivington what is decided, ma'am? We are all to go away for the summer! There, you will like that, I am sure.'

'Go away?' Carlotta offered up a prayer of thankfulness. 'Aunt, that is splendid news! Where are we going, and how soon?

Lady Broxted laughed and put up her hands. 'Good heavens, my dear, how eager you are to be away from here.'

Carlotta flushed. 'Forgive me, I mean nothing against Broxted House, dear aunt, but Mr Price is right—London is growing so very warm.'

Mr Price nodded at her. 'Aye, my dear, we are all feeling it. Poor Julia suffers dreadfully. This invitation has come just in time.'

'So?' Carlotta was eager to find out more. The idea of leaving town was too tempting. 'Where are we going, Aunt—is it Brighton? Worthing? Mr Price, will you not tell me?'

Mr Price beamed at her. 'Mrs Ainslowe has invited us all to Malberry Court for the summer!'

Carlotta stared. Her dreams of escaping her tormentor crumbled away to dust. Behind her, she heard Luke laugh softly.

Chapter Seven

'Malberry Court?' Carlotta shot a swift, questioning glance at her aunt.

'Your uncle has already agreed everything,' said Lady Broxted, a hint of reproach in her voice. 'We are to travel to Malberry at the end of the month.'

'Aye,' cried Mr Price. 'And a merry party we shall make of it, eh, ma'am? If you will excuse me, now, I see my dear wife is beckoning to me, so I shall go and see what she wants.' He beamed at them again. 'I shall leave you ladies to talk about the treat in store for you!'

Carlotta knew that a crowded room was no place to discuss the forthcoming visit to Malberry Court and, by the time the last of the guests had left, Lady Broxted wanted nothing more than to retire to her room. Carlotta was obliged to wait until the morning to express her anxiety.

When she learned at breakfast that her aunt was keeping to her room after the rigours of the party, she would not be put off any longer. She found her aunt sitting up in bed, sipping at her hot chocolate.

'Aunt, do I disturb you? I need to talk to you.'

Lady Broxted waved away her maid. 'Of course you do not

disturb me, child. Come, sit on the edge of the bed and tell me what is making you look so anxious.'

'Dear ma'am, surely you have guessed? The visit to Malberry Court—is it wise for us to go, do you think? I mean, with Mama and Papa in the village...'

Lady Broxted gave her an odd little look. She put down her cup carefully.

'My dear, your uncle arranged it all with the Ainslowes last night. *I* had nothing to do with it. I said it was asking for trouble to go to the Court when your parents are living so close, but he thinks there is no reason why anyone should make the connection. And, of course, it does mean that we may be able to arrange for you to visit them while we are there. Discreetly, of course. But you would like that, would you not?'

'Oh, yes, very much.' Carlotta twisted her hands together. 'But what if someone at the Court should recognise me?'

Lady Broxted shook her head, smiling. 'Now how could that be? As you have said yourself, we took you away from Malberry before the Ainslowes moved in to the Court. Silly child, I think you are worrying unnecessarily.'

'But when Papa was working, I sometimes went up to the house with him...'

Lady Broxted sat up at that. 'Mercy me! Who saw you there?'

'The—the workmen, of course, and...and Kemble, Mr Ainslowe's clerk of works.'

Carlotta waited anxiously while her aunt frowned over this, tapping her fingers together.

'But there were no household staff there?'

'No, ma'am.'

'The workmen will have been paid off by now. And the clerk of works, you say? Well, it is very unlikely that he will remember you, for you are a very different creature now. And if you visited your father once or twice while he was working, I dare say this—this Kemble scarcely noticed you.'

'It—it was more than once or twice, aunt.' Carlotta screwed up her courage. 'I—um—I painted two of the ceiling frescoes.'

'You did what?'

Lady Broxted fell back against her pillows, her colour fluctuating alarmingly. Carlotta jumped off the bed.

'Shall I call your maid, ma'am?'

'No, no, I shall be better in a moment. You may fetch my smelling salts from the table over there…ugh! Thank you. That is better.'

Carlotta watched anxiously as her aunt lay back on her pillows, eyes closed. Eventually, she sat up again, a look of long suffering etched upon her features.

'I think you should tell me the whole.'

'Papa had broken his leg—'

'Yes, yes, I know that, for he was laid up when we called upon you.'

'Well, the house was so nearly finished, there were two small ceiling frescoes to be painted and no one else to do it, so…I painted them.'

'Good heavens. And…and this was on a ceiling, you say?'

'Yes, ma'am.'

'Which entailed….climbing a ladder?'

Carlotta nodded.

'And the workmen saw you?' Lady Broxted's colour began to rise again.

'It was not so very bad. You see, I was wearing breeches, and—'

Lady Broxted shrieked and put her hands over her face. 'Breeches! Oh, heavens, we are undone!'

'No, no. Dear Aunt, you said yourself that the workmen will be gone.' Carlotta sought to reassure her. 'And Mr

Kemble will not connect fashionable Miss Rivington with her curls and ringlets with little Carlotta Durini, even if our paths should cross, which is highly unlikely.' She paused. 'However, I think it might be best to cry off—could you not say that I am unwell, and we could retire to the country for the summer?'

Carlotta waited hopefully, but her aunt shook her head.

'No, your uncle would never hear of it. He was so pleased with himself for arranging the whole.'

'But why, ma'am? I know he is good friends with Mr Ainslowe, but surely it would not cause such great offence if we did not go—'

'It is not quite so simple, Carlotta.' Lady Broxted twisted the edge of the sheet between her fingers. 'Mr Ainslowe has invited a large number of guests to Malberry.'

'Then our absence will be less noticeable.'

'He has invited Lord Fairbridge and Mr Woollatt to join the party, and they have accepted.'

Carlotta smiled. 'Oh? I am sure they will all have a very pleasant time.'

'You do not understand! Broxted expects one of them to make you an offer!' The silence that greeted this statement was profound, broken only by the steady tick of the pretty little carriage clock on the mantelpiece. Lady Broxted's restless fingers smoothed over the covers. 'Your uncle is very anxious for you to make a good match, Carlotta. He is confident that you can do so. Lady Fairbridge has hinted that she looks favourably upon you as a bride for her son, and Mr Woollatt's standing up with you for a second time last night was most encouraging. When your uncle learned who was going to be at Malberry, he thought it could not be better; we have always said that if you should receive an offer, then your suitor must be told of your true circumstances. What better place to explain everything, with your parents so conveniently situated? And now you tell me that you were running all over the house, dressed as a…'

'I am very sorry, Aunt.' Carlotta sighed miserably.

'Well, we must make the best of it.' Lady Broxted threw back the bedcovers. 'Ring for my maid, my love. I will go and see Broxted and explain the whole.'

'Will he be very angry with me, do you think?'

'Perhaps, but we must see what is to be done. If he thinks we can still carry it off, then so be it.'

'Aunt!'

Lady Broxted regarded her, a question in her eyes. Carlotta knew it was time to tell Lady Broxted of her meetings with Lord Darvell, but even her brave spirit quailed at the thought of confessing so much. Perhaps he would not betray her. Perhaps she could persuade him not to betray her.

'Well, my dear?'

Carlotta's courage failed her, she shook her head. 'Nothing, Aunt.'

Later that day Carlotta was summoned to Lord Broxted's study. She went in cautiously, and found her aunt and uncle waiting for her. Lord Broxted's frown eased a little when he saw how anxious she looked and he gestured to her to sit down.

'Your aunt has told me of your conversation this morning,' he said in his ponderous way. 'I admit that I had some concerns when Ainslowe first issued the invitation, but we have already agreed that although one cannot like the circumstances of your parents' marriage—' Carlotta opened her mouth to protest, but he put up his hand to silence her. 'Pray let me continue. Your mother's running off to marry an Italian artist cannot be viewed as anything other than regrettable, but there it is: if the truth should out then we will deal with it. Besides, as your aunt has told you, if a suitable gentleman should make you an offer of marriage, then he must be told. Your announcement that you were—ah—more actively employed at Malberry Court than we first realised has been a shock, I confess, but the advantages of our visit far outweigh the slight risk of your being recognised.'

'Oh. I have no wish to embarrass you, Uncle. Would it not be better to go somewhere else this summer—Brighton, perhaps?' asked Carlotta, hopefully.

A look of distaste flickered over his face. 'I have never been one of the Prince's set and would prefer that you were not brought to their attention. No, we shall go to Malberry. Your aunt mentioned that the clerk of works had seen you at the Court. I know from Ainslowe himself that he has sent the man off to oversee the building of his hunting lodge in Leicestershire. It is therefore highly unlikely that he will return during our visit. It is my hope that by the end of our stay at Malberry Court, it will be unnecessary for us to worry further over your origins.'

'You mean, sir, that I should accept an offer of marriage if I receive one.'

'But of course you should!' Lady Broxted looked at her in surprise. 'After all, that is the reason we took you under our wing, is it not?'

'Yes,' said Carlotta, stifling a sigh. 'I suppose it is.'

'I do not wish to pain you, Carlotta, but you have very little choice,' her uncle pointed out. 'What does the future hold for you, if you do not marry? Perhaps you have some idea of making your living as an artist, but you must know how precarious that would be, and you must not be thinking that I should feel obliged to give you a pension,' he said, his face hardening. 'I am afraid I could not bring myself to condone your choice of a lifestyle that could only bring more disgrace upon our family.'

'So you consider Mama *disgraced* herself when she married an artist,' said Carlotta, angry colour warming her cheeks.

'No, of course he does not,' put in Lady Broxted quickly. 'I am sure—'

The earl raised his hand. 'Please, madam, I think it is time my niece realised her situation. When we offered you a home, Carlotta, it was in an effort to reinstate a branch of the family. It has never been my intention to allow you to follow in your mother's footsteps.'

Carlotta choked down the angry retort that rose to her lips. She had always known the whole point of bringing her to town was to find her a suitable husband—her aunt had never made a secret of the fact. How could she now say it was not what she wanted?

Chapter Eight

At the assembly the following evening, Mr and Mrs Price and their daughter could talk of nothing but the forthcoming visit to Malberry. They were discussing the subject when Carlotta and her aunt came up to them, and immediately drew Lady Broxted into the conversation.

'We were just saying how much we are looking forward to seeing Malberry Court,' said Mr Price in his blunt, jovial way.

'Yes, we have heard much of the refurbishment,' said Lady Broxted.

'Well, here is one gentleman who can tell us if it is worth all the fuss!' Mr Price looked past Carlotta and beckoned. 'Lord Darvell, well met, sir. We are discussing Malberry—you were there when the work was being carried out, I understand. Tell us, is it as fine as everyone says?'

Luke paused. He did not look at Carlotta, but he was very aware of her standing so close, those expressive eyes shuttered, her countenance impassive.

'Better,' he replied. 'My brother has spared no expense, the most fashionable architect was employed, and the finest artist available…'

From the corner of his eye he saw Carlotta jump and turn away. Damnation. He had intended to ignore her, but now, standing so close, he could not help himself; he would do anything to get behind the mask of indifference.

'Aye, so I heard. An Italian.' Mr Price gave a hearty laugh. 'I hope there's nothing on the walls that will shock the ladies!'

'Oh, I would not think that likely, in the house at any rate,' murmured Luke. 'What do you say, Miss Rivington?'

Carlotta wanted to glare at him, but she was aware of her aunt's nervous looks; it would not do to raise suspicions. She shrugged. 'As I have never been a guest at Malberry, I could not say. I am sure Mr Ainslowe has commissioned everything in the very best taste.'

She turned away, but his voice followed her.

'Miss Rivington is something of an artist herself. She is very good.'

'My niece?' Lady Broxted gave a nervous little laugh. 'Wh-whatever gives you that idea, my lord?'

Unable to escape, Carlotta turned back to confront her tormentor. She raged inwardly when she saw the devilish amusement dancing in his eyes.

'She told me so herself.'

'Oh, do you draw, Miss Rivington?' Mrs Price pounced on this news.

'I prefer to *paint*, ma'am,' Carlotta replied stiffly.

'Perhaps you will take Julia's likeness. I am sure she would sit for you, my dear.'

'Miss Price will need a little patience, ma'am,' said Luke. 'Miss Rivington has promised that *I* shall be her first subject.'

An agitated murmur came from Lady Broxted. Carlotta's cheeks flamed.

'We were funning, sir. I am no portrait painter.'

'No? I thought it was in the blood.' He laughed. 'You see how she colours up, Mrs Price? Miss Rivington displays a hasty temperament. Quite *Latin*, do you not agree?'

Mrs Price chuckled and tapped his arm with her fan. 'What nonsense, my lord. You know very well it is your teasing that has overset her. Pray leave the child alone or you will make her afraid of you.'

'Thank you, ma'am, but there is no danger of that,' retorted Carlotta. 'As well be afraid of a bag of wind!'

'My dear!' exclaimed Lady Broxted, mortified at her niece's lack of manners.

Biting her lip, Carlotta excused herself and walked away. To disguise her agitation she began to tug at her gloves, which had slipped down below the elbow.

'Take care, Carlotta, you are dangerously close to flouncing, you know.'

Luke had followed her. She almost screamed with vexation.

'Pray leave me, sir. I do not care for your teasing.'

'Well, that is unfortunate for you, my dear, because I have not done with this game. When you are angry you are quite…delicious.'

He reached out and drew one finger along the bare skin of her arm between the edge of her glove and the tiny puff sleeve. Carlotta shivered as his touch awakened the memory of being in his arms, of his kiss. It had been such a sweet moment and over far too quickly. She reminded herself how little that kiss had meant to him. She jerked away.

'I will not play your game, sir!'

He bared his teeth. 'Oh, I do not think you have any choice.'

Her eyes narrowed, but even as a sharp retort rose to her lips he bowed and lounged away, laughing.

Lady Broxted came up, frowning anxiously. 'My dear, what did Lord Darvell mean? You have not really promised to paint him, have you?'

'No, Aunt, I have promised him nothing,' retorted Carlotta.

'I am so glad.' Lady Broxted gave a huge sigh of relief. 'It would not do at all, my dear, and your uncle would be most displeased. I have noticed that Lord Darvell has been paying you more attention recently; he is very engaging, to be sure, but you know that his fortune is almost non-existent. Pray do not be losing your heart to him, especially now. Your uncle has hopes for something much better for you.'

'Lose my heart?' Carlotta gave a brittle laugh. 'What an absurd idea, dear ma'am. Lord Darvell is an entertaining flirt, but when he is gone I never give him a moment's thought.'

In an effort to prove the truth of her words, Carlotta threw herself into the dancing with an excess of energy. However, when she joined Miss Price a little later, the subject of Malberry Court was raised once again.

'I am so glad you are going to be there with me,' Julia said in her shy way. 'I feel I know you so well now.' She blushed a little. 'Viscount Fairbridge has been invited, too. Did you know?'

'Yes, I had heard,' replied Carlotta. She added with a twinkle, 'Perhaps he will propose to you while we are there—would you like that?'

Julia's blush deepened to crimson. 'I should like that very much.'

'So should I.' Carlotta smiled, not at all overset at the thought of losing one of her suitors. She only hoped her aunt and Lady Fairbridge would not be too disappointed.

'I have never received an offer of marriage,' murmured Julia. 'Have you, Carlotta? Has a young man ever proposed to you?'

'No, but—'

'But?'

Julia was watching her and Carlotta shook her head.

'Nothing. No one has ever proposed to me.'

But he was going to do so. The words ripped through her. She had been convinced Luke was going to propose…

* * *

He had escorted her home from Malberry Court after the storm. It had stopped raining and the clouds were breaking up, allowing a fitful moonlight to cast its blue-grey light over the park.

'It must be close to midnight,' he said. 'Wait here while I collect my horse, and I shall walk you to your door.'

She waited obediently, listening to his footsteps as he strode away into the gloom. She was not afraid of the dark and knew she was quite capable of making her way home alone, but she did not want to say goodbye to Luke. Luke—just thinking of his name spread a warm glow inside her, even though she knew she could not call him by that name, not yet.

When he returned, she stepped down on to the drive to join him.

'The ground is very wet,' he said. 'Shall I throw you up onto the saddle?'

'Thank you, but no. I would much rather walk with you.'

'Then give me your hand. I do not want to lose you.'

They walked in silence, the only sound their footsteps on the gravel and the drip, drip of water from the trees.

'Will you be leaving Malberry soon, sir?'

'Yes. I must go to my own house, it is in Worcestershire—Darvell Manor. I have business there. I have already delayed here too long.'

'Oh…' She hesitated. 'Your brother's affairs have taken more time than you expected?'

Glancing up, she saw his teeth gleaming in the dim light.

'No, sweet torment, I remained here for pleasure only.' She heard him sigh. 'I sought to pass the time here with a little idle dalliance, but—' Angrily she tried to pull her hand away. His hold tightened. 'Wait until I have finished, Carlotta. *But*, I found myself enchanted.'

'You cannot blame me for that,' she said stiffly. 'I never sought to entrap you.'

'No. That was my downfall.'

'Oh.'

He stopped and pulled her round into his arms. 'This is madness, my dear, our worlds are so different. I have been wild, reckless even; you are such an innocent you could not begin to understand. And yet why should we not be happy?'

He appeared to be talking to himself. Carlotta waited patiently, content to be in his arms. With a short laugh he turned and they began to walk again, but Luke kept one arm possessively around her waist.

'What are your father's plans for you, Carlotta?'

'Why, none, sir.'

'Is there no young man in Italy pining for you?'

She laughed at that. 'Of course not. We left Rome two years ago.'

'Perhaps your father wants you to marry another artist, to carry on the family business.'

'If he does, I know nothing of it.'

Puzzled by his questions, she walked on in silence. They followed the drive to the gates and turned to walk along the road towards the village. It was a much longer route than going through the woods, but she was glad of that—it gave her more time with Luke.

'Is your father well enough to receive visitors, Carlotta?'

'Why, yes, sir.'

The dark shapes of the village houses appeared through the gloom, and Carlotta could see the outline of her parents' cottage, standing square and proud in its own little garden. A candle burned in one of the windows.

'Mama has set a light for me,' she said.

'Will she be anxious for you?'

'Of course, but she knows I would not venture out until the storm had passed.'

'Then you had best go in.'

'Will you not come with me?' she asked, greatly daring. 'I am sure Mama would want to thank you for escorting me home.'

'No, no, it is very late, and I am not dressed for such an important occasion. I shall call upon you tomorrow.'

'Important, sir?'

He took her face in his hands and kissed her gently. 'Say nothing of our meetings; it would be best if I explained everything tomorrow. I would have no censure fall upon you, my dear. Any blame must be mine, all mine.' He kissed her again. 'Until tomorrow, my sweet life…'

He stepped away from her, took the horse's bridle and set off at a smart pace along the road. Carlotta watched him until the bend in the road hid him from her sight. A little bubble of happiness was growing within her. *Tomorrow*, she thought, her hand upon the latch, *tomorrow my whole life will change*.

Her life had changed, but not in the way she had hoped. She had not seen Luke again—until she had come to London. She realised Julia was still speaking, and gave herself a little mental shake. 'My apologies, Julia, what did you say?'

'I wondered why Mr Woollatt was not here tonight.'

'I believe he has gone out of town for a few days.' Carlotta smiled inwardly as she recalled her relief when she had heard the news.

'Mama says she thinks he will make *you* an offer, Carlotta,' remarked Julia. 'Would it not be splendid if we were both to find husbands at Malberry?'

'Yes,' agreed Carlotta in a hollow voice. 'Splendid.'

'Miss Rivington, do tell me that my luck is in at last, and that you are not engaged for the next dance?'

She turned to find Sir Gilbert Mattingwood at her elbow. Shaking off her sombre reflections, she bestowed a sunny smile upon him. 'I am not engaged, sir.'

He held out his arm and took her to join in a lively country dance. As they skipped and danced through the set she found herself thinking of the rumours she had heard of his impoverished state. It was a pity, she thought, for he was an engaging companion and might make a pleasant husband. He was certainly more entertaining that Mr Woollatt. Carlotta gave herself a mental shake. She was becoming positively obsessed with the subject of marriage. As the music ended Sir Gilbert took her arm.

'Let us go and find some refreshment.'

They strolled into the next room where a table was set out with several punch bowls. Lord and Lady Broxted were standing nearby with Mr and Mrs Ainslowe, and it was only natural that when Sir Gilbert had served Carlotta with a cup of punch they should join the group.

'So hot!' exclaimed Lady Broxted, fanning herself vigorously. 'I do not know how you young people have the energy to dance. I shall be very glad to go down to Malberry next week, for it is always so much cooler in the country.'

'Aye, so it is, ma'am,' agreed James Ainslowe. He turned to Sir Gilbert. 'I was telling Lord Broxted about that picture I won from you. I have sent it on down to Malberry Court.'

Carlotta sipped at her punch, wondering that Sir Gilbert should not be embarrassed at this allusion to his gambling debts. However, he did not appear to be in the least discomposed, and merely bowed.

'The canvas is so large I have always thought it more suited to a country house.'

'A Tiepolo, is it not?' interpolated Lord Broxted.

'Aye,' Mr Ainslowe nodded. '*Maeceanas Presenting the Arts to Augustus*, or some such thing. Is that correct, Mattingwood?'

'Yes, something in that line. I was never greatly interested in art.'

'Well, it does not matter, for I shall ask Signor Durini to have a look at it while I am there.'

Carlotta stiffened. Lady Broxted looked anxiously at her husband and plied her fan energetically.

'Your pardon, Ainslowe,' said Sir Gilbert. 'I did not catch that name?'

'Giovanni Durini, the artist I have working at the house.'

'I hope you are not suggesting my painting is not genuine,' cried Sir Gilbert, feigning outrage.

'Don't be such a fool, Gil.' James grinned. 'But since Durini is at hand I shall ask him what he thinks of it.'

'Is not the work on the house complete now, Ainslowe?' Lord Broxted's tone was so studiously casual that Carlotta had to suppress a nervous giggle.

'Oh, the house itself is finished,' replied James. 'Durini has been painting the temples in the gardens this summer. His work is magnificent; I cannot wait to show it off to you all.'

Carlotta swelled with pride at this, but her aunt's anxious face sobered her. Sir Gilbert touched her hand.

'Another cup of punch, Miss Rivington?'

'Yes, yes, if you please, sir.'

'And when do you set off for Malberry, Mrs Ainslowe?' asked Lady Broxted, anxious to move the conversation away from art.

'Friday next, to make everything ready for you all to join us the following week. I would have liked to go down sooner, but we are engaged to Lady Ottwood for her entertainment on the Thursday.'

Lady Broxted nodded. 'Yes, we, too, are going. I am told

we are to dine out of doors and there are fireworks planned for the evening.'

'Fireworks,' exclaimed Adele. 'How exciting. What a pity Luke will not be there. He says there is business he must attend to. But it does not matter—we will arrange something of our own at Malberry, will we not, my love?'

Mr Ainslowe patted her arm. 'I shall see what I can do.' He turned towards Sir Gilbert, who was returning with another cup of punch for Carlotta. 'You are coming to Ottwood, are you not, Gil?'

'Alas, no. I must go out of town for a few days.'

Adele looked up quickly. 'Oh, but it will not prevent you joining us at Malberry?'

Sir Gilbert bowed. 'Oh, no, ma'am.' He turned to smile at Carlotta. 'I am very much looking forward to that.'

The following day Mr Woollatt called at Broxted House. The ladies were in the morning room when he was announced; Carlotta gave him a faint smile, but her aunt flew from her chair and greeted him with uncommon warmth.

'My dear sir, you are very welcome. When did you arrive back in town?'

'Last night, madam.'

'Fie on you, sir, and it is now nearly dinner time! Why did you not call this morning? You must know how welcome you are here.'

Carlotta blinked and listened in surprise as her aunt pressed Mr Woollatt to join them for dinner.

'I would like that very much, ma'am, but my dress…'

Since Mr Woollatt was wearing a black tailcoat and knee breeches, Carlotta could not help wondering if he was half expecting the invitation. Lady Broxted was quick to reassure him.

'Pho, we stand upon no ceremony here, sir. Now if you were

one of these young bucks who think it acceptable to go round sporting a spotted handkerchief instead of a necktie, an untidy coat and top boots bearing only one spur, I should not be so forbearing, but you, sir, are always dressed with neatness and propriety!'

'If I am not inconveniencing you…'

'No, indeed, Mr Woollatt. Pray sit down, sir. You will excuse me for a moment while I order another place to be laid.'

She hurried away, and Carlotta was left alone with Mr Woollatt.

'I understand the town has been very hot of late, Miss Rivington. I trust you have not suffered while I have been away?'

'No, I have been very well, sir, thank you.' She wondered if he wanted her to say how much she had missed him. She could not lie, so she kept silent. He sat back in his chair, folding his hands across his chest.

'I am very much looking forward to going to Malberry Court next week. A country-house party is the very thing to raise the spirits. Your uncle tells me you will be travelling down early next week—it is my intention to be waiting for you there.'

The smile that accompanied these words made Carlotta look away, something very like panic welling up inside her. She was thankful that her aunt returned at that moment, and she was not obliged to reply. Mr Woollatt immediately turned his attention to his hostess.

'You are not to be thinking I came here merely to beg a dinner,' he said, chuckling at his own humour. 'I have come to issue an invitation for you and Miss Rivington to join me at the theatre tomorrow night. I have secured a box at the English Opera House in Wellington Street.'

'The theatre? How splendid—is it not, Carlotta?'

'But, Aunt, I thought we were promised to Mrs Winterton.'

'A card party! What is that when there is such a treat in store for us?' Lady Broxted dismissed the hapless Mrs Winterton with one white hand. 'You need not fret, my love. It was never fixed, after all. We will be delighted to join you, Mr Woollatt.'

'Excellent.' he rubbed his hands together. 'They are performing a farce and one of Mr Sheridan's comedies. I thought Miss Rivington might prefer that to more serious fare, and I shall be able to show you both the new gas lighting.' Carlotta thought she had misheard him, but she saw that her aunt was looking equally blank. 'Not only do they have the new lanterns at the entrance, but they are using gas to light the stage, too,' explained Mr Woollatt.

'How exciting,' murmured Lady Broxted. 'We are very much in your debt, sir. You will be able to wear your new silk gown, Carlotta.'

Mr Woollatt beamed. 'A new gown? I am sure you will look delightful, Miss Rivington, and as for being in my debt, well, ma'am, the sight of Miss Rivington in her new gown shall be my reward!'

The English Opera House gleamed in the evening sunlight, its new white stone pillars not yet blackened with the soot from the thousands of coal fires that warmed the metropolis each winter. Mr Woollatt escorted his charges to the theatre in his own carriage, informing them as he did so that the building had been designed by Mr Beazley to incorporate all the most modern comforts, as well as the celebrated gas lighting.

'You cannot appreciate this innovation while it is daylight,' he said, 'but you will see it when we leave the theatre tonight, and, of course, the stage will be illuminated. Our enjoyment should be greatly enhanced, eh, Miss Rivington?'

They took their seats in the box and Mr Woollatt hovered about the ladies, making sure that Carlotta had a good view of the stage, offering to put her shawl about her shoulders if she should feel a chill and bringing his own chair close beside her.

Carlotta turned with a look of entreaty to her aunt, who was sitting a little apart, but she merely nodded approvingly.

'Well, this is very cosy,' remarked Mr Woollatt as the play began. 'You told me you enjoy the theatre, Miss Rivington. I come to the plays regularly when I am in town. I hope this may be the first of many little outings we will make together.'

Carlotta smiled, but could think of nothing to say and after a few moments Mr Woollatt turned his attention to the stage. Carlotta wished she could go home.

When the farce ended several visitors arrived in the box, most of them friends of Mr Woollatt, but some came to pay their respects to Lady Broxted, including James Ainslowe and his wife. After Mr Woollatt's rather ponderous conversation, Carlotta was glad to see them, but her smile slipped a little when she saw Lord Darvell following them into the box. Mr Woollatt has risen from his seat when the visitors had arrived and he was now obliged to stand against the back wall to make room for them all. He directed their attention to the new gas lanterns on the stage, but no one seemed to hear him. The little box buzzed with conversation, Mr Woollatt presented his acquaintances to Carlotta and Mr and Mrs Ainslowe engaged Lady Broxted in a lively discussion. When Mr Woollatt's friends departed, he took a step back towards his chair, but Lord Darvell was there before him and slipped into the seat beside Carlotta, his knee almost touching her own. She tensed, prepared to spring away from him should he dare to touch her.

'Did you enjoy the farce, Miss Rivington?'

'Very much, my lord.'

She turned away, supposedly looking in the audience for her acquaintance, but was very much aware of him, sitting so close to her. Every nerve in her body seemed to be on edge.

'Mr Foote's comedies are always of a superior nature,' opined Mr Woollatt.

They ignored him.

'And what do you think of the scenery?' asked Luke.

Carlotta was immediately on her guard. She risked a glance at his face and fancied that the devil was in his eyes.

'I did not notice. I was enjoying the play.'

'I thought it was a little crude.'

'I believe they have several renowned artists here,' stated Mr Woollatt, on the defensive.

Luke kept his gaze fixed upon Carlotta. 'But I have seen better artwork, have not you, Miss Rivington?'

She did not answer, merely unfurled her fan and waved it languorously before her. He turned a little more on his chair until his knee was in contact with her thigh. It was the lightest touch, but it burned through the thin muslin of her skirts, making her tremble. It was all she could do not to move away. It was all she could do not to press against him. Carlotta swallowed hard. She dare not look at him as he continued.

'I thought the street in Rome looked a little contrived, too— what thought you, ma'am?'

'Oh, come now,' said Mr Woollatt. 'You cannot expect Miss Rivington to know such a thing. She has never been to Italy.' He paused. 'That is, *have* you visited Italy, Miss Rivington?'

She began to wave her fan much more vigorously. 'I was there with my parents,' she muttered. 'A long time ago.'

'Well…' Mr Woollatt puffed out his cheeks. 'How on earth did you know that, sir?'

'I—I expect my aunt and uncle mentioned it,' put in Carlotta quickly, aware of the wicked gleam in Luke's eyes. He was going to denounce her, she knew it. She put up her chin. She would not crumble beneath his mocking glance. Whatever he did to her, she would not give him that satisfaction.

'Yes,' he said at last. 'I expect they did.'

'Luke—' Adele put her hand on his shoulder '—we must be getting back to our own box, the play will begin very soon.'

Lord Darvell rose. 'A pity,' he murmured, 'When we were all getting along so well.' He turned to Mr Woollatt. 'Your servant, sir. Perhaps we may continue our conversation at a later date.'

Mr Woollatt watched him leave, his bottom lip jutting. 'Audacious young dog! He presumes to know you very well, Miss Rivington.'

Carlotta wondered if she should confess the truth—surely nothing could be so bad as the game of cat and mouse Luke was playing with her? She glanced at her aunt; she must be told the truth before anyone else, and a box at the theatre was not the place for that. So she must put off her confession to another day. She summoned a bright smile for Mr Woollatt.

'Lord Darvell is, as you say, sir, an audacious gentleman.'

Luke accompanied James and Adele back to their seats on the opposite side of the theatre, his senses full of Carlotta, her dark beauty, the perfume of the violets in her corsage, the warmth of her thigh when his knee had touched it—only a couple of thin layers of material had separated them. It was a wicked thought.

'Well, what do you think, is it a match?' Adele walked between the two men, looking up at each of them in turn.

'Woollatt seems very much at home there,' opined James.

'She won't have him,' said Luke shortly.

'Oh, I don't know.' James rubbed his nose. 'Woollatt is as rich as Dives and Lady Broxted is giving him every encouragement. Broxted won't want to let a fortune slip away from the family.'

'Well, we shall know soon enough,' said Adele, taking her seat. 'They will all be at Malberry and we shall have plenty of time to observe them. Now, let us be quiet and enjoy Mr Sheridan's play.'

Luke sat down, but he paid very little attention to the actors. Instead his eyes kept straying to the box opposite, where Daniel Woollatt seemed to be for ever hovering over Carlotta, leaning towards her to make some comment, whispering in her ear. And she was smiling at him, damn her! Luke's reason told him that she was merely being polite, but every smile, every gesture towards Woollatt, flayed his spirits. It did not matter that he knew her to be a shallow, heartless creature; it galled him to see her giving her attention to anyone else. Now Woollatt was pointing out something on the stage to her, their heads so close together they were almost touching. Heaven and earth, how much longer did he have to endure this?

At last it was over. As the audience applauded, he watched Woollatt tenderly placing Carlotta's wrap around her. Surely his hands lingered far too long on her shoulders? What was her aunt thinking of, to let the man maul her in such a way? Smothering an oath, Luke turned away to follow his brother out of the box. As they made their way out into the street, he muttered his excuses, wanting nothing more than to be alone. Adele turned to give him her hand.

'Good night, then, Luke.' She looked up at the front of the building and said with a laugh in her voice, 'Oh, look, these must be the new lanterns Mr Woollatt described to us. What thought you of the new gas lighting for the stage, Luke? Do you agree with Mr Woollatt that it is a splendid innovation?'

He scowled. 'No, I do not. I thought the smell of the gas quite nauseating!'

Chapter Nine

As the date for leaving town drew closer, Carlotta grew ever more anxious. She knew Darvell would be going to Malberry and she could not be sure how he would behave towards her. With less than a week until their departure, she decided she could bear the uncertainty no longer. They were all engaged to spend the day at Lady Ottwood's house on the edge of the town, but Carlotta cried off, pleading a migraine and begging that she should be allowed to rest at home for the day. With some difficulty she persuaded her aunt and uncle to go without her and, as soon as the carriage had rolled away, she dashed off a note to Lord Darvell. She did not know if he would come. As she moved restlessly about the house she remembered only too well how he had promised to come to her once before.

No morning had ever dawned so bright as that last day at Malberry. Carlotta woke early, a warm glow of expectation filling her even before she remembered why. 'Until tomorrow, my sweet life.' Recalling the look in Luke's eyes as he had taken his leave of her sent Carlotta's spirits soaring. She threw herself into the morning's activities, insisting on cleaning and tidying the little parlour before she set off to the market with Jack, their manservant, to collect their provisions. She was anxious to get back, but even so the choosing of a freshly plucked chicken could not be rushed and it was past noon before her shopping was complete and she returned to the house. Jack's arms were full with baskets and parcels so Carlotta went before him to the back door to let them in. She had scarcely put down her basket when Mrs Durini put her head around the kitchen door.

'Good, you are back. Make haste and come in, Carlotta, we have visitors!'

Carlotta's heart leapt. Pausing only to take off her bonnet, she hurried to the parlour.

'Here I am, Mama…'

She trailed off, her eyes widening as she found herself being regarded by a total stranger.

With her mind in confusion, Carlotta was introduced to her uncle and aunt, Lord and Lady Broxted. She listened to explanations of renewing family connections, reinstating her in society, giving her the opportunity to make a good marriage, but all she could think of was that it was past two o'clock. Surely Luke should be here by now.

'I do not like to rush you, Carlotta, but your aunt and I must return to London tonight.' Lord Broxted turned to his sister and gave a tight little smile. 'It has taken my people a long time to track you down, Margaret. We only received word of your direction yesterday and my dear Celia was anxious that we should visit you immediately.'

'We are off to the country at the end of the week, and we would like to take our niece with us,' Lady Broxted explained with a smile at Carlotta. 'I realise that this must be something of a shock for you all, and if you would rather take your time to discuss it, then of course you must do so, but we should not then be in a position to have her join us until the end of the year…'

Carlotta gave a little curtsy. 'And I am very grateful to you, my lady—Aunt—but it is all so sudden.' *Please, Luke, hurry. I need you.*

She uttered up her silent prayer. Everyone was smiling at her, convinced she must be delighted with the prospect of being taken off to live with the Earl and Countess of Broxted.

'You will be free to return home whenever you wish,' continued Lady Broxted. 'But I intend to spoil you so much that you will want to stay with us for ever!'

Carlotta looked at the smiling faces. A net, a fine mesh of love and good intentions, was closing around her. She rose.

'I—um—if you will excuse me for a few moments, I must go and see…'

'Carla, where on earth—?'

But Carlotta did not wait to hear her mother's words. She picked up her wrap and ran out of the house.

It was only a short distance to the inn and she ran all the way. Before she reached the tap-room door the landlord came out. He stopped when he saw her, blinked, then gave her a smile.

'Well, Miss Carla, what is it now? Surely your father cannot have finished all that fine wine I found for him?'

'No, no, it is not that, Mr Hitchen. I…' Carlotta hesitated, blushing '…I was wondering if your guest is within doors; the—um—the gentleman who has been staying with you.' She twisted her hands together, hope and anxiety mixing within her as she waited for his answer.

'Ah, you'd be meaning Major Ainslowe.'

'Yes,' she said eagerly, 'yes, that's right.'

'Well, he's gone, a good half hour since.'

'Gone!'

'Aye, that he has, Miss Carla. Now what was it he said?' Hitchen jingled the coins in his pocket. 'Let me think. He said he was tired o' country ways, and country people. I think he had grown bored, miss. Said he wanted excitement. You know how these rich gentlemen can be. Miss Carla, are you quite well?'

The landlord's kindly concern brought her head up.

'What? Oh, oh, yes, thank you, Mr Hitchen.'

She forced herself to turn away and with an effort began to retrace her steps. The bubble of happiness inside her heart had burst, shattering into tiny pieces. So he had gone. He had only been amusing himself after all. But she had known that all along, had she not?

By the time she reached her father's door she had mastered the urge to cry. Instead her chin lifted a little. She went inside and found her parents sitting with Lord and Lady Broxted in uncomfortable silence. Her mother started up as she came in.

'Carla, my love, whatever possessed you to run off in that way? Such rag-manners when your aunt and uncle have come so far to see you. '

'I needed to—I had to…' Carlotta took a long, steadying breath and looked directly at the earl. 'My lord, if you still want me to come away with you tonight, then I am very willing.'

A full twelve months had gone by since then and once again she was waiting for Luke. But Berkeley Square was a long way from Malberry and perhaps, after today, she would be free of him. It was shortly after noon when he was announced.

'Please show Lord Darvell into the book room.'

Carlotta waited for a few moments, steadied herself with a few deep breaths, then went to join him. She found him standing before the empty fireplace, one arm resting along the mantelpiece. He was dressed for driving in an olive green frock coat, buckskins and top boots with a pair of York tan driving gloves clasped in one hand. She thought idly how well the country style suited him and noted how the summer sun had lightened his brown hair to a honey-gold. As she entered the room, he turned and bent a frowning gaze upon her, but although he looked serious, she was relieved that there was no sign of the savage anger she had seen in his face in their recent meetings.

'Will you sit down, my lord?'

'What is it you want, madam? I came here in my curricle, and I do not like to keep my horses standing any longer than necessary.'

His harsh tone made her heart sink; it was not a promising start. She moved to a chair and sat down. She must not allow his incivility to upset her.

'Thank you, sir, for coming here so promptly.'

He shrugged. 'You summoned me.'

'I *asked* you here,' she corrected him, holding her temper under a tight rein, 'because I want to—to call a truce.' The sardonic lift of his eyebrow brought a flush to her cheek. 'It will be difficult to avoid each other at Malberry, my lord, and—um—I have no wish to cause embarrassment to your brother or any of his guests.'

His lip curled. 'I see no embarrassment, except for you, Miss Rivington.'

'Pray do not be so foolish,' she retorted. 'Think for a moment how difficult it would be for your brother, as host, if you exposed me.'

He moved closer, towering over her. 'Very well then, tell me why you want this…truce?'

She looked down at her hands clasped in her lap. He was watching her intently and his scrutiny disturbed her.

'I have told you I want no unpleasantness—'

'You have told me nothing that would warrant you writing to me, demanding to see me.'

The brittle curb on her temper snapped. Her fingers curled tightly in her lap. 'Very well—if you want the truth, you shall have it. My uncle expects me to receive an offer of marriage while we are at Malberry.'

* * *

So there it was.

Luke caught his breath, winded, as if he had received a blow to the stomach. He kept his hands at his sides, but could not prevent them balling into fists. 'Oh? Who could be the lucky man, I wonder? Woollatt?' He gave a savage laugh. 'I take your silence for confirmation, Miss Rivington. So, you have brought your rich suitor up to scratch.'

She winced visibly at his sneering tone and paused a moment before continuing. 'Of course, if he is serious in his regard for me, then I must tell him the truth, but *I* would like to be the judge of when it is the right time, not you. I would therefore be…grateful if you would give me your word to say nothing that might j-jeopardise the situation.'

She kept her head lowered. He could not see her eyes, but her scarlet cheeks betrayed her. In the silence that followed her words, Luke could hear only the steady tick, tick of the long case clock as she waited for his answer.

'No.'

Her head shot up. 'What did you say?'

'I said no. I will make you no such promises.'

She stared at him. He turned away from those haunting brown eyes, knowing that if he met her troubled look his own defences would crumble and he might admit that he would do nothing to cause her more pain. Then he would be lost. He summoned up his anger. He was justified to feel it; by heaven, she had almost brought him to his knees! He had been on the verge of offering her more than he had offered any woman before. Thank heaven he had discovered her true nature before committing himself.

'What have I ever done to make you hate me so?' She spoke so quietly he could hardly hear her. 'I admit I was angry with you when we met again in town, but that was understandable after you had left me so cruelly last summer.'

'I *left* you, as you put it, so that you could be launched into society. And I must say you seem to have taken to it admirably.'

'I had precious little choice in the matter, since you had already quit Malberry.'

'Aye, and thank God I made good my escape.'

She jumped up, white-faced, only her eyes burning with anger as she glared at him. 'What does that mean?'

'Heaven knows what I might have done, had I stayed.'

'You had no intention of staying,' she flung at him. 'Admit it; I was a mere distraction, something to pass the time while you were buried in the country.'

'And you would know about distractions, would you not? You have enjoyed enough of them yourself!'

Her lip curled. 'You have made several hasty judgements about me, sir, but I have done *nothing* to be ashamed of.'

'No? I saw you with my own eyes, flirting with Woollatt in Vauxhall Gardens.'

'Yes, when you were parading that…that *doxy* on your arm! Can you blame me for wanting to punish you?'

He gave a harsh laugh. 'Punish me? What in hell's name have I ever done to you?'

'You abandoned me!'

Carlotta had not meant to say that. The words were wrenched from her, a despairing cry torn from her heart, where she had carried her unhappiness in secret for so many months. Angry at her own weakness, she dashed her hand across her eyes.

'How foolish of me to try to reason with you,' she said bitterly. 'I would be obliged now if you would leave me.'

'Have no fear, madam, I am going!'

He was turning towards the door when it opened and an anxious-looking footman came in.

'A letter for you, miss. Come express it has, from Malberry.'

Carlotta was still reeling from her outburst and looked at him blankly for a moment until the implications of the words penetrated her mind.

'Malberry?' She almost snatched the letter and quickly broke the seal, her fingers shaking. Luke had not left the room. He was standing by the door, tugging on his gloves, but she ignored him as she read the short note. The words seemed to jump on the page.

'It—it is my father. He is hurt, badly hurt…attacked. Mama wants me to come at once…'

Her throat dried. She looked across at Luke. Thoughts tumbled through her head but she could not make sense of them. He was watching her, his face grim.

'Fetch your wrap,' he said quietly. 'I will drive you.'

'Thank you.'

There was no surprise, no hesitation, only the knowledge that she had needed him and he had not failed her.

Pausing only to fetch her cloak and bonnet and to scribble a hasty note for her aunt, Carlotta climbed into the curricle. She did not speak as Luke threaded his way through the busy streets, her brain too shocked to think coherently, but as they left the town behind she unfolded the letter and read it again.

'I do not understand—who would want to hurt Papa? *Why* would someone do this? I cannot think—'

'Hush.' His hand closed over hers. 'Do not torture yourself with conjecture.'

'You are right. I must wait until we reach Malberry; Mama will explain.'

He squeezed her fingers. 'Try not to worry.'

A stretch of open road allowed Luke to push his team on, thundering towards a turnpike.

'Billy, sound the yard of tin,' he ordered briskly. 'We have no time to lose here.'

They were through in seconds.

'We are making good time,' remarked Luke. He glanced at the stiff little figure beside him. 'It won't be long now.'

She did not reply, merely stared straight ahead, her hands clenched together in her lap. Luke found the silence between them uncomfortable. Unbearable.

'I *did* come,' he said shortly. 'That day in Malberry. I did come to your house, but…the earl was there before me.'

Luke shifted uncomfortably in his seat. He remembered how nervous he had been, wishing he had brought his valet with him and something finer to wear than his brown country frock coat—not the ideal dress for a gentleman about to make a proposal of marriage.

'I was outside the window when Broxted said he wanted to take you to town. It was your birthright, Carlotta. I could not deny you your chance.'

Broxted's words echoed again through his head with painful clarity. *Carlotta should come back with us now and take her rightful place in society. We would treat her as our own, give her every luxury—I will even settle upon her the portion that should have been yours, dear sister. Carlotta will have the opportunity to make a good marriage—nay, an excellent match— as befits the granddaughter of an earl.*

'So you went away again.' Carlotta's quiet statement sliced into his heart.

'Yes. I'm…sorry.'

He cursed himself for the inadequacy of his words. Should he tell her how much it had cost him to ride away that day? How he had thrown himself into the improvements at Darvell Manor in his efforts to forget her? He glanced at her again. No. She was unmoved by his apology. It was too late.

Chapter Ten

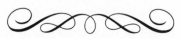

They swept into Malberry High Street less than three hours after leaving Berkeley Square.

'I'd wager there ain't a cove living who could beat that,' remarked Billy as the curricle pulled up.

Carlotta barely heard him. As soon as the curricle stopped she began to climb down; by the time Lord Darvell had given his instructions to his groom, she was at the door, pushing past the maid and running up the stairs.

'Mama, Mama!'

Mrs Durini appeared on the landing and Carlotta threw herself into her arms.

'How is Papa? What happened? Where is he?'

'Carlotta! Gently, gently, my love.' Her mother hugged her fiercely. 'How glad I am that you are here, and so quickly!'

'Of course. Your note—'

'Oh dear, did I frighten you? I should have waited to write to you, but I was in such a panic, and for a few hours the doctor thought—but that was last night. Today your papa is much better and Dr Johnson is confident he will make a good recovery.'

'May I see him?'

'He is resting now, but you may come in.'

Nodding, she led Carlotta into the bedroom where her father

was lying in the middle of the large bed. The sheets were pulled up to his chin, but one side of his face was misshapen and heavily bruised, the purple-and-red blotches an alarming contrast to the white bed linen.

Carlotta put her fist into her mouth to stifle a cry of anguish and sank down beside her father.

'He is sleeping,' said her mother softly. 'The doctor has given him a draught and says he must rest as much as he can.'

Carlotta reached out her hand to touch his swollen cheek. 'Who could have done this?'

She felt her mother's hand on her shoulder.

'Come downstairs, love. Bessie shall sit with him while I tell you what I know.'

Carlotta followed her down the stairs, clinging to the rail as her knees threatened to give way. They went into the little parlour, where Luke was waiting for them.

'I hope you will forgive the intrusion, Mrs Durini,' he said. 'The door was open…'

'This is Lord Darvell, Mama. He brought me here.'

Her mother moved forward, hands outstretched in welcome. 'Then you have my heartfelt gratitude, my lord,' she said. 'I dared not hope Carlotta could be here so soon.'

He bowed. 'I was with Miss Rivington when your letter arrived. It was the least I could do. May I enquire how your husband goes on?'

'He is recovering, sir. He suffered a serious beating around his head and shoulders, but we are hopeful that there will be no lasting damage.'

'Mama,' said Carlotta, 'will you tell me what happened?'

Mrs Durini hesitated, and Luke said quickly, 'Pray allow me to stay, ma'am. I may be able to help.'

With a nod Mrs Durini sank onto the sofa, drawing Carlotta down beside her.

'Giovanni was working late at the Court last night and he was set upon as he returned… Footpads. They were lying in wait for him as he crossed the stile. If it had not been for Jack he might have been—' She broke off to wipe her eyes with one corner of her apron. 'Jack—our m-manservant, my lord—was throwing rubbish on the midden when he heard Giovanni cry out. Jack went to find him and—and the attacker ran off.'

'Attacker. There was only one?' asked Luke, frowning.

'Jack saw only one.'

'And did he get a clear look at him?'

'N-no. It was too dark.'

'What is it, my lord?' said Carlotta quickly. 'What do you suspect?'

'How many people use that path and the stile?' he countered.

'The servants from the Court, when they come to the village,' said Mrs Durini.

'How often would that be, once or twice each day?'

'Possibly. It will be more when the master and his guests arrive.'

Carlotta fixed him with an anxious gaze. 'Lu—Lord Darvell?'

He hesitated. 'It seems an odd place for footpads to lie in wait.'

As his words sank in, Carlotta felt the chill running down her spine. 'You think they were waiting for Papa?'

Her mother gave a smothered gasp. 'No, it cannot be! Giovanni has no enemies.'

'You are sure of that?' he asked.

'Of course I am sure. He is very well liked here in Malberry.'

'Be that as it may, if you will permit me, I shall set my groom to make enquiries in the village—perhaps a stranger has been seen here. Can you think of anyone who might harbour a grudge?'

'My father is an honest man,' replied Carlotta, holding her head up. 'He pays his debts and has never cheated anyone.'

He regarded her steadily. 'I believe you, but until we get to the bottom of this matter, it would be as well for you to take extra care.'

'We shall do so, my lord.' Carlotta nodded at him. 'Thank you.'

'Yes, thank you, my lord, and thank you again for bringing my daughter to me so quickly. But I have offered you no refreshment, let me—'

Luke held up his hand. 'No, I will not trouble you, ma'am.' He rose. 'My groom is waiting for me at the George—I am going on to the Court, but I shall call again tomorrow, if I may.'

His words dispelled the anxiety that had been growing within Carlotta.

'You are not going back to Town?'

'No.' His look and the little smile that accompanied it warmed her. 'I shall stay at the Court now until James arrives.'

'And you will be very welcome to call here at any time, my lord,' put in Mrs Durini.

'Thank you, ma'am. Miss Rivington, it now occurs to me— we came here in such a hurry, would you like me to send Billy back to town tonight for your clothes…?'

'Thank you, sir, but I would not have you put to such trouble; I have sufficient gowns here.' Carlotta gave a little smile. 'They may not be fashionable, but they are perfectly adequate.'

Her mother nodded. 'Indeed they are, my love, for you will not be venturing out of doors while you are here.' She glanced towards the ceiling, as if anxious to get back to her husband. 'Well, my lord, we must not keep you longer. Until tomorrow, then. Carlotta, since Bessie is still upstairs, perhaps you will show his lordship out?'

Carlotta picked up his hat and handed it to him, then led the way back into the little passage. At the door she turned to him, suddenly shy. 'My lord, I—'

He put one finger against her lips. 'I will call again in the morning.' He looked at her, his hazel eyes warm with concern. 'Unless you would like me to stay…?'

The idea made Carlotta's insides tie themselves in knots. She would like nothing more than to have him stay with her for ever, but that was not what he meant. She summoned a smile. 'Thank you, sir, but we shall manage. We will check that all the doors and windows are locked, and Jack shall sleep with a thick staff beside him.'

'Make sure he does,' he said, giving her a faint smile. 'Goodnight, *cara*.'

Carlotta returned to the sitting room to find her mama looking out of the window, watching Lord Darvell's retreating form.

'Well,' she said, 'what a very kind gentleman he is, to be sure. And is he related to Mr Ainslowe, who owns the Court?'

'His brother, Mama.' She flushed at the speculative gleam in her mother's eyes.

'Ah. And is he the rich suitor your aunt has mentioned in her letters?'

Carlotta's blush deepened. 'Lord Darvell has no fortune; Uncle Broxted considers him a wastrel.'

'Well, that is a pity, for he seems a most pleasant gentleman, and uncommon kind to bring you all this way.' She sighed. 'But there, it would do no good for you to throw yourself away on a handsome face, my dear. Your prospects are so much better now.'

It was strange, after the luxuries of Broxted House, to be waking up again in the tiny bedroom of her parents' cottage. It took Carlotta several moments to collect her thoughts and separate dreams from reality. Despite knowing that her father lay injured in the next room, she felt none of the anxiety and distress that had filled her days in London. Lying very still, listening to the birdsong outside her window, Carlotta thought about the calm sense of well-being that enveloped her. The answer came to her in the form of a memory, a pair of hazel eyes smiling warmly at her. She was no longer at odds with Luke. Something had changed yesterday when she had received the letter from Malberry. Instinctively, in her need she had turned to Luke for help and he had answered her mute appeal without hesitation. And he had called her *cara*—dear one. Her heart singing, Carlotta slipped out of bed and scrambled into her clothes. Luke had promised to call again this morning!

As soon as she was dressed Carlotta went to see her father. It was clear that her mother had kept an all-night vigil at his bedside and Carlotta immediately took her place and sent her off to rest. There was little to do, for her father was sleeping quietly, but she knew her mother would not be easy unless someone was keeping watch. An hour dragged by; sitting in the quiet bedroom, Carlotta thought back to the journey to Malberry, riding beside Luke in his curricle. She had been so anxious for her father that she had given little thought to Luke's explanation that he had come to the cottage, but had turned away again when he heard her uncle's plans for her.

She closed her eyes. If only he had seen her, talked to her. She shook her head. Too late for that now. Suddenly, in the airy stillness of the little room, she thought of how Luke must have felt on that day—not the confident, strong young buck that she knew, but a nervous young man, uncertain of his welcome, knowing that, despite his title, his financial position would fall a long way short of the ideal match Lord Broxted planned for his niece.

'Oh, Luke,' she whispered, 'your fortune or lack of it did not matter to me—it has never mattered!'

She sat up with a start as her mother came into the room, carrying a large basket.

'Look, Carlotta, is this not generous?' she said, smiling broadly. 'Lord Darvell brought it himself; the fruit is from the hothouses up at the Court. He said his brother's visitors would not miss a few peaches and grapes, and when I protested he pointed out that the fruit is so ripe it needs to be eaten! What could I do, but accept it gratefully?'

'Lord Darvell has been here?'

'Yes. I was resting on the daybed in the sitting room when Bessie announced him, and you can imagine how flustered I was to be found out. I have not the slightest doubt that my cap was askew! But he was very kind, and said he only wished to leave the fruit basket and would not disturb us. He is going to call again tomorrow, to see how we go on.'

Carlotta fought down her disappointment. There was no reason why he should ask to see her—in fact, she was not at all sure that he would want to do so.

Carlotta was carrying her father's breakfast tray down the stairs when Luke arrived the following day. She heard his voice as Bessie admitted him and she hurried on to the kitchen with her dirty dishes. She hesitated only for a moment to consider running back up to her room to check her appearance in the mirror. That would waste too much precious time, so she contented herself with removing her apron and shaking out the skirts of her old dimity gown before hastening to the parlour. At the door she stopped, her hand hovering over the handle—perhaps he would not want to see her. If that was the case, she needed to know, and the sooner the better.

Taking a deep breath, she opened the door and went in.

Luke was standing by the window. His tall, broad-shouldered frame seemed to fill the little room. With his back to the light she could not see his face and Carlotta was suddenly too nervous to speak. Her mother was addressing her, and she made an effort to attend.

'So your father has finished his breakfast?'

'Yes, Mama. I left him with Jack, who has promised to shave him.'

Mrs Durini smiled and turned back to her guest. 'I think that answers your question, my lord. My husband is feeling much more the thing this morning.' She rose. 'If you will excuse me, I had best go to him; he may even now be thinking of getting out of his bed.' She added with a slightly distracted air, 'I have instructed Bessie to bring in refreshments for our visitor, Carlotta. Pray look after him.' She was gone upon the words.

Carlotta cleared her throat. 'My mother is very anxious for Papa...'

'You do not need to explain.' As he moved away from the window she was relieved to see he was not frowning. 'She has left the door open; there can be no impropriety.'

Carlotta nodded, thankful for his efforts to put her at her ease. Bessie came in, carefully carrying a tray bearing glasses and two decanters. They watched in silence as the maid put her burden down upon a side table, bobbed a curtsy and scurried out again. Carlotta looked at the tray in dismay.

'Oh dear, I expected her to bring in some small beer for you; I have no idea what is in these...'

'I am being treated as an honoured guest,' he remarked, a smile lifting the corner of his mouth. 'Allow me.' He walked over to the table. 'One is quite clearly brandy. The other...' he lifted the stopper from the decanter and sniffed it '...sherry, I think. By your leave, Miss Rivington, I shall help myself to a little brandy. May I pour you a glass of something?'

'N-no, thank you.' Already nervous, Carlotta knew it would be unwise to accept, especially when she had never tried either of those beverages. She watched him fill his glass and take a seat opposite her.

'You had no unwelcome visitors?' he asked.

'No, my lord. I explained everything to Jack and he insisted upon bringing Mack, his dog, into the house, but we have not been disturbed.'

'And have you spoken to your father about the attack?'

She nodded. 'He was well enough to talk about it yesterday. He remembers very little, except being set upon as he climbed over the stile.' She sighed. 'We can none of us think of a reason for such an attack. It must have been footpads.'

'Perhaps.'

'You sound doubtful—what do you know?'

'Nothing, but robberies usually take place upon known highways, not little-used paths.'

She shuddered. 'I hate to think that someone wishes to harm Papa.'

'Perhaps I am wrong; I do not wish to make you anxious. All I ask is that you take care.'

The concern in his voice touched her. She tried to put on a brave face.

'Well, Papa will be confined to the house for a few weeks at least, and Jack will not leave his side.' Carlotta hesitated. It was important that he realise how grateful she was for his help. She cleared her throat. 'While we are alone, sir, please let me thank you for bringing me from London—'

'It is not necessary.'

'I think it is, especially—especially when I think of what I said to you.' Her voice failed. She took a deep breath to regain control. 'I was very much at fault.'

'We were both at fault,' he responded quietly.

She clasped her hands tightly together. 'Then, is it—do you think we might be…friends?'

Luke regarded her sombrely. As the silence lengthened Carlotta's heart sank. Perhaps too many insults had been traded. Perhaps she had given him too great a disgust of her. Nervous, hurried words began to tumble from her lips.

'I am aware that there have been misunderstandings and I regret that, very much. But—but if you could only bring yourself to forget everything that has passed between us, I...I would very m-much value your friendship.'

Her fingers were digging into her palms as she fought down the urge to weep. She could do no more. Her apology was heartfelt, but perhaps it was not enough.

'My memory is yours to command, ma'am.' He spoke lightly, and there was a strange look in his eyes, but his words gave her hope.

'Oh, yes, please, my lord! If we could begin again, from today, perhaps we could be true friends.'

'If that is what you wish, consider it so, Miss Rivington.'

Carlotta sighed and closed her eyes, feeling that a great weight had lifted from her shoulders.

'Thank you, you are very good.'

A rustle of skirts and hasty step announced Mrs Durini's return. She came bustling into the room, tutting.

'Well, what a good thing I went up. Giovanni had persuaded Jack to bring his clothes and was preparing to come downstairs! If ever I saw the like—I told him he must not even think of getting out of bed until the doctor has seen him again.'

'And when will that be, ma'am?' asked Luke.

'Tomorrow, although how we will persuade him to remain in bed until then I do not know.'

'We shall hide his clothes, Mama. Then he will be obliged to keep to his room.'

'Yes, we can do that.' Mrs Durini sank down on the sofa.

'Doctor Johnson has told me that he must rest, but he is not an easy patient. Thank goodness I shall have you to help me, Carla, at least for a few days.'

'Oh, but I shall not quit you now, Mama. Not until Papa is better.'

'But of course you must go,' exclaimed Mrs Durini, regarding her in some surprise. She put one hand to her head. 'But of course, you do not know—oh, I shall go distracted, I vow! Your aunt has written; she sent it express and it arrived while you were with Papa this morning. They are coming down to Malberry as planned and will collect you on their way.'

'No!' Carlotta shook her head vehemently. 'I cannot leave— she does not know how matters stand here!'

'Well, naturally she knows that if Giovanni was seriously ill there would be no question of you leaving us, and she says as much in her note. But that is not the case, my love. And she has explained to me about—I mean—she has explained how important it is for you to join her at Malberry.'

Carlotta flushed scarlet at the knowing look her mother gave her.

'No—I—that is—'

'Your mother is right,' said Luke quietly. 'If your father continues his recovery, there is no reason why you should not join the house party at the Court. You may rely upon my discretion.'

'That is very good of you, my lord.' Mrs Durini fidgeted uncomfortably. 'I do not know what my daughter has said to you about the arrangement with Lord and Lady Broxted…'

'Nothing to the detriment of her parents, ma'am, I assure you. However, I am aware it is not generally known that you are living at Malberry.' A noise from upstairs made him look up. 'I am keeping you from your patient. I must go.'

Mrs Durini rose and held out her hand to him. 'I am very grateful for your kindness to us, my lord. Remember, you are welcome to call here at any time.'

'Thank you, ma'am. You are most kind.'

Luke kicked viciously at the thistles in his path as he walked back to Malberry Court. So she wanted to forget everything. Hah! If only that were possible. What he would give to banish her from his mind, to forget how sweet she had tasted, how soft and yielding she had felt in his arms, but that night at Malberry was burned into his memory. He would never forget it, even if she could. But he had agreed that they should start again as friends. Friends! His mouth twisted into a bitter smile. She wanted to keep him as a friend while she accepted an offer from Daniel Woollatt—as though he could stand by while she became another man's wife. Luke stopped. That was just what he must do: if Woollatt was her choice, then so be it. After all, what had he to offer her except an impoverished title and an estate that would take years to turn a profit? No, he could not ask that of her. She wanted him as a friend—needed him as a friend. Aye, that was some small comfort. That is what he would be, although every moment he was near her, knowing she could never be his, would twist the knife a little deeper into his soul.

When Lord Broxted's travelling coach swept through the gates of Malberry Court a few days later, Carlotta was once again dressed as befitted a member of the earl's family. Lady Broxted had insisted she put on her cream flounced gown, holly-green spencer and matching silk bonnet before setting out for the Court and now she nodded in approbation, declaring that her niece was once more fit to be seen.

'So now we shall see these famous frescoes we have heard

so much about,' remarked Lady Broxted, leaning forward to gaze out of the window at the approaching house.

'My dear, I think the least said about the paintings the better,' returned the earl repressively.

Apart from an airy wave of her hand, Lady Broxted ignored him. 'You must show me the ones you worked upon, my love. What a pity it is that we cannot tell anyone about your painting, because you are a clever little puss, when all's said and done.'

Carlotta repressed a smile. 'Thank you, Aunt. I painted the two smaller roundels on the ceiling of the portico, here at the main entrance.'

The carriage pulled up at the foot of the shallow steps and a liveried footman hurried forward to open the door.

'You will do nothing to draw attention to these paintings, madam,' muttered the earl as he handed his wife out of the carriage.

'No, of course not, but I must see them.'

As they ascended the steps she glanced up at the ceiling behind the soaring pillars that supported the portico.

'Oh, my heavens!' Lady Broxted began to ply her fan furiously. 'My dear child! The nymphs—'

'They are maenads, Aunt,' said Carlotta. 'It is Dionysius surrounded by dancing maenads.'

'Never mind what they are called.' Lady Broxted lifted her fan to cover her mouth while she whispered to Carlotta, 'They are *naked*!'

'No, no, they have a diaphanous veil that covers them, a little,' Carlotta replied soothingly. 'But *my* efforts are the smaller roundels: the grapes and the lyre. I did not paint the maenads.'

'No, but you were very close to them!' Lady Broxted lowered her eyes and hurried into the house. 'Heaven and earth, Carlotta, I hope we are never found out!'

Suppressing her giggles with difficulty, Carlotta followed her aunt inside.

* * *

The hall was very crowded and Carlotta's first, alarming thought was that everyone had come to greet them, but a quick glance around showed her that they were all in riding dress. James Ainslowe separated himself from the crowd and came forward, grinning broadly.

'Welcome, my lord, Lady Broxted...Miss Rivington. We did not know what time to expect you and have this minute sent word to the stables. We could put off our ride for an hour, if you would like to join us...'

Lord Broxted put up his hand. 'No, no, Ainslowe, you must carry on.'

'Of course they do not want to come riding with us,' exclaimed Adele, stepping forward to greet the new arrivals. 'They will want to rest and refresh themselves after their long journey, is that not so?'

Her smiling question encompassed them all, and Carlotta was tempted to say that her journey had been no more than a mile, and that she would dearly love to go riding. She was obliged to press her lips together to prevent any such impulsive utterance. Carlotta glanced at the assembled group; she knew them all: Mr and Mrs Price and Julia, Lord Fairbridge, Sir Gilbert Mattingwood, Lord Darvell—Carlotta gave Luke a shy smile, hoping he would come over to her, but even as her eyes found his, Mr Woollatt was pushing past him and bustling forward, his face wreathed in smiles.

'Miss Rivington, the day is suddenly all the brighter now that you are here. I am sure our host will understand if I cry off from our ride now.'

Luke raised his brows. 'Oh, why should you want to do that, sir, if, as you say, the day is suddenly so much brighter?'

A bubble of laughter rose in Carlotta's throat and she was obliged to turn it into a cough. Mr Woollatt was in no way put out.

'I was speaking metaphorically, my lord. If you will allow me, Ainslowe, I shall not ride with you. Instead I shall go upstairs and change. Then I shall be on hand to entertain our new guests until you have all returned from your ride. There, now, what have you to say to that?'

In the face of his smiling self-satisfaction, Carlotta could find nothing to say and it was left to her aunt to speak up.

'An excellent idea, Mr Woollatt. How kind of you to think of our comfort.'

'Well, then, if that is settled, we had best get on,' declared Mr Ainslowe, shrugging.

'And I must find my man to help me change,' muttered Mr Woollatt. 'Never seems to answer my bell, whereas *your* man always seems to be on hand, Mattingwood. I'm always tripping over the fellow!'

Sir Gilbert, who had been casting an admiring glance at Carlotta, laughed at him. 'Reed is very conscientious and likes to be close by in case I need him.'

'Well, there is no need for him to be hovering in the corridors,' put in James. 'There is a bell-pull in every bedchamber so you can ring for him from your room. Perhaps you should explain that to him, Mattingwood.'

'Thank you,' replied Sir Gilbert. 'I will.'

A flurry of activity followed and for a few moments noisy chaos reigned in the hall. The riding party made its way outside, narrowly avoiding the puffing footmen who were carrying in the corded trunks bearing the Broxted coat of arms. Mr Woollatt exchanged a final few words with Lady Broxted before disappearing up the stairs while Lord Broxted was assured by his host that the housekeeper would be down soon to show them to their rooms.

* * *

'Carlotta, my dear, are you ready?'

Lady Broxted peeped into the little bedchamber and Carlotta turned from her mirror.

'I am, ma'am. I just need my fan…'

'How quick you are,' declared her aunt, coming into the room. 'You will see that I am not yet changed. Jarvis has only now unpacked the gown I wish to wear. But if you are dressed there is no need for you to wait for me; you may go on down to the library and I shall join you shortly.' She handed Carlotta her fan and propelled her towards the door.

'Oh, but I would much prefer to sit here and read until you are ready, Aunt,' said Carlotta, resisting.

'No, you must go on. By all means take your book down with you, love. I am sure the light will be much better there and after all, the library is the proper place for book-reading.'

Smiling, Carlotta made her way downstairs. She was honest enough to admit that she was happy to have the opportunity to explore the house while most of the guests were absent. She was curious to see how the rooms looked now they were furnished. She could not linger in the hall, liveried servants were on duty there, but the new bell system, installed while her father had been working at the house, meant that it was no longer necessary to have footmen waiting in every room. She forced herself to hesitate as she reached the foot of the stairs, as if unsure of her way; after all, it was meant to be her first visit to Malberry Court.

She passed through the small ante-room where doors led to both the library and the drawing room, then went into the library, closing the door carefully behind her. The lofty ceiling was painted in shades of blue, from deepest indigo to near-white, the intricate pattern matched exactly by the huge Axminster carpet that covered the floor. She remembered her father's apprentice had carried out most of the painting in this room, for there were none of the impressive murals that were her father's trademark, any wall space not covered by book-shelves being left bare to display Mr Ainslowe's art collection. This mainly comprised family portraits and conversation pieces, but on one wall there was a single large canvas showing a more classical scene. It must be the Tiepolo, she thought. She was moving towards the picture to study it more closely when she heard the door open.

'My dear Miss Rivington.' Mr Woollatt quickly crossed the room and picked up her hand, pressing a kiss upon her fingers in an old-fashioned gesture that she found slightly unnerving. 'How fortunate that I have found you alone.'

'Is it, sir?' Carlotta withdrew her hand and moved away. 'I am waiting for Lady Broxted to join me.' She prayed her aunt would come in *very* soon.

'Of course, of course. In the meantime, we must entertain each other, eh?' He gave a series of little grunts, and Carlotta realised with a jolt that it was laughter. He began to pace up and down, his hands clasped behind him. 'Yes, Miss Rivington, I am delighted to have this opportunity to speak to you alone. You must know what is on my mind.'

Carlotta swallowed nervously. 'No, sir.'

He beamed at her. 'Ah, such innocence. Charming. Utterly charming. Then let me speak plainly, my dear. For some time now I have been contemplating a change to my situation. As you know, I am what is known in modern parlance as a *warm man*.'

'W-warm, sir?'

'Yes, full of juice—although I would more modestly call it a comfortable fortune. It is only right that at my time of life I should be looking to set up an establishment.' He cleared his throat. 'To, ah, provide myself with an heir.'

With sudden, frightening clarity Carlotta knew she did not want him to continue. Where was her aunt? 'Sir, I—'

'I have been in town for more Seasons than I care to remember and, if you will forgive my arrogance, I think I can say that I could have my pick of the eligible young ladies paraded at Almack's. But none, my dear Miss Rivington, has ever made such an impression upon me as you have done.'

'Mr Woollatt—' Carlotta put out her hand to silence him, but he merely caught it in his own.

'Your kindness, your gentle ministrations to me that night at Vauxhall Gardens, convinces me that I have made the right decision.'

Carlotta hung her head, her cheeks burning as she remembered that night, and Luke's damning accusations.

'No need to colour up, my dear, although such maidenly modesty does you credit. Lady Broxted was quite right when she told me you were totally unspoiled.'

Carlotta had a sudden, vivid recollection of the scene in the hallway when they arrived earlier that day. She remembered her aunt talking earnestly to Mr Woollatt and in that moment she realised this tête-à-tête had been arranged. Lady Broxted had told Mr Woollatt that he would find her alone. Panic welled up within her as he began to pull her towards him.

'Miss Rivington, let me say—'

'Beggin' your pardon, sir.'

Mr Woollatt dropped Carlotta's hand and jumped back at the words, uttered in a rough, country burr. Carlotta looked around to see the gardener coming into the room carrying a large vase of flowers. He placed the vase carefully upon the table, then proceeded to separate the stems in a methodical, unhurried fashion. Carlotta glanced at Mr Woollatt. His face was flushed with indignation and he glared at the gardener, who ignored him and continued to arrange the blooms to his satisfaction. Offering up a little prayer of thanks, Carlotta muttered her excuses and fled.

Once she had reached the safety of her bedchamber, Carlotta allowed herself to recall the events in the library and even to smile a little at the scene. There was no doubting that Mr Woollatt was most aggrieved to have his rehearsed proposal of marriage interrupted. However, she felt no desire to smile when she thought of her aunt and uncle. They would be very angry with her when they heard that she had run away, and rightly so—their purpose in coming to Malberry Court had been to secure for her a suitable husband, and everyone was agreed that Mr Woollatt was eminently suitable.

Carlotta stayed in her room until the dinner hour, then, steeling herself to face her aunt's displeasure, made her way downstairs. This time the doors to the ante-room and the drawing room were thrown wide and the sound of voices told Carlotta that the guests were gathering in readiness for the dinner hour. As she entered the drawing room, Lady Broxted beckoned to Carlotta.

'What in heaven's name has occurred?' she hissed, pulling Carlotta towards her. 'Mr Woollatt is quite put out—did you refuse him?'

'No, Aunt, we were disturbed,' Carlotta explained in a whisper. 'I—I panicked, and ran away.'

'Silly child, what on earth is there to frighten you? Don't tell me Mr Woollatt was anything other than a gentleman.'

Carlotta flushed. 'No, of course not, Aunt.'

'Well, let us hope all is not lost,' murmured Lady Broxted. She patted Carlotta's hand. 'There, there, child. I suppose it is only natural that you should be a little nervous. We must see what we can do to help you. Come now, do not look so down-hearted—your pretty smile will help to win the day.'

Carlotta tried to oblige. She raised her head, forcing her lips into a smile, only to find herself staring straight into the eyes of Lord Darvell. Lady Broxted's fan rapped across her knuckles.

'For goodness' sake child, do you wish to drive away your suitor? Keep your smiles for Mr Woollatt, if you please! You must be careful to give him no reason to think you a flirt, my love. Behave yourself during dinner and afterwards. We must do what we can to win back Mr Woollatt's regard for you.'

Carlotta bit her lip; she was quite certain that she did not want Mr Woollatt's regard.

Chapter Eleven

To Lady Broxted's intense disappointment and Carlotta's relief, Mr Woollatt was seated at the far end of the dining table. Carlotta happily accepted Adele's invitation to sit near her, but she was disconcerted to find Luke slipping onto the chair beside her. Her aunt had warned her not to smile at other gentlemen, but it was so difficult not to respond when Luke was looking at her with that warm glint in his eyes. She sought nervously for something to say.

'Did—did you enjoy your ride today, my lord?'

'Very much,' he replied soberly. 'The countryside around Malberry provides some fine views and the park is ideal to gallop the fidgets out of horse and rider.'

Carlotta stifled a sigh. 'I wish I could have come with you. I dearly love to ride.'

'I thought Lord Broxted had provided you with a mount in town.'

'Yes, he hired a hack for me; she was the prettiest little thing, but very slow. There was no spirit in her—I doubt if she had ever galloped in her life.'

'Then we must ask Adele to find you a more lively ride while you are here.'

She thanked him warmly, and as the meal progressed she

found herself chatting away quite happily. He described for her his life in the army, and was entertaining her with some of the more light-hearted moments when she caught her aunt's eye. There was no mistaking the warning.

'Ah,' murmured Luke, intercepting the exchange of glances, 'I am being too familiar.'

'No, oh, no,' exclaimed Carlotta. 'It is just that…'

She trailed off unhappily, but Luke merely nodded.

'I understand,' he said gently. 'If you are seen to be on friendly terms with me, it might frighten away other suitors.'

A spurt of anger flashed through Carlotta, burning her cheeks. 'Surely there can be no harm in our talking at dinner. I can hardly ignore you—that would be uncivil.'

He grinned. 'It would indeed. But perhaps we should restrict ourselves to the commonplace. Let me recommend the turbot, Miss Rivington.'

Carlotta lifted her napkin to hide her smile—Luke could never be commonplace!

After dinner Lady Broxted kept Carlotta by her side while she did her best to charm Mr Woollatt back into a good humour. It appeared to work, and when Carlotta retired for the night, he pressed a kiss upon her hand and squeezed it, his smile indicating that he had forgiven her.

'Well, I have done my best; it is up to you to win back your suitor now.'

Carlotta was sitting up in bed, sipping at her hot chocolate when her aunt came in the following morning.

'I have seen you in the saddle, Carlotta, I know you ride well, so I rely upon you to impress Mr Woollatt.'

'Oh,' said Carlotta, brightening. 'Are we riding today?'

'Your uncle and I do not go, but Mrs Ainslowe assures me

that she will look after you, and Mrs Price says she will be riding, too, with Julia.'

'Oh, famous!' Carlotta scrambled out of bed. 'I knew nothing of this—when was it arranged?'

'It was decided last night, after you had gone off to bed. Knowing how much you like to ride, I had no hesitation in putting your name forward. Mrs Ainslowe says she can find you a suitable mount.'

'Thank you, Aunt Broxted!' Carlotta flew across the room and hugged her ruthlessly.

'Well, well, that is enough now. You may show your gratitude by charming Mr Woollatt.'

An hour later Carlotta was trotting out of the stable yard on a pretty little grey mare, trying to convey her thanks to her hostess. 'She is beautiful, and so lively. I cannot wait to try out her paces. May we gallop once we are in the park?'

'By all means,' replied Adele. 'She is called Flame and I am pleased you like her. She used to be my own favourite before I married, but James made me a present of Zephyr and I must ride her to please him.' She laughed and leaned forward to pat the glossy black neck of her mount.

'I am honoured that you have loaned Flame to me,' said Carlotta.

'Luke told me that you liked a spirited animal and Miss Price is a more nervous horsewoman. She prefers a *quieter* mount.'

Carlotta looked across at Julia. She was riding a heavy bay hack whose dull eye and rolling gait seemed to indicate that he would not move any faster than a walk. Carlotta knew she would have disliked riding such a slug, but Julia looked happy enough, especially with Viscount Fairbridge riding beside her.

'Your horse looks very fresh, Miss Rivington,' commented Mr Woollatt, trotting up beside them.

'She is, sir. She is longing for a gallop.'

He gave her an indulgent smile. 'Do not fret, for I shall ride alongside you, and catch your bridle if she looks to be getting away from you.'

Carlotta looked at her hostess, saw her eyes were brimful of merriment and was forced to bite back her own laughter. After all, she had promised not to upset Mr Woollatt. Before she could say anything more, Mr Price's voice gave her thoughts another turn.

'My man tells me there's talk of footpads in the village, Ainslowe. Attacked your painter, I understand.'

James nodded. 'Damned scoundrels. Might have killed him, too, if his servant had not been at hand.'

'Mercy me!' declared Mrs Price, coming up at that moment.

'No need to worry, ma'am.' Her host smiled. 'I set my men to scour the area as soon as I heard of it, but there is no sign of the scoundrels. I'd say they are long gone, now.'

'Gypsies, perhaps,' said Sir Gilbert, trotting up.

'Possibly. Unusual, though. No one has reported any strangers in the area.'

'And how is your artist now?' asked Mr Price.

'A sore head, but thankfully nothing more serious. I told him to rest for a while, but I have no doubt he will be back at work in a week or two.'

'Surely there is nothing more to do at the Court,' said Sir Gilbert with a little laugh.

'Oh, not in the house itself, but there are still a few temples to be painted yet. I do not see him leaving me before the New Year.'

'My husband is determined to have every surface decorated,' called Adele from the other side of the group.

James raised his hat to her. 'In your honour, my dear, in your honour!'

Adele chuckled. 'James is determined to have everything of

the finest,' she said to Carlotta. 'But I must not complain. He has bought me the prettiest little carriage to ride around the estate.'

'Dear me. Not a high-perch phaeton, I hope?' exclaimed Mr Woollatt. 'Most dangerous. There have been any number of accidents in town, you know, some of them fatal.'

'No, no, sir, mine is a gig, and perfectly safe. You must let me take you up in it, Miss Rivington.'

'I should like that very much, ma'am.'

'And you are not afraid I shall overturn you?' asked Adele, giving her a mischievous, sideways glance.

Carlotta chuckled. 'I will take my chances.'

Mr Woollatt shook his head at her. 'You are altogether too careless of your own safety, Miss Rivington.'

Carlotta quelled a little spurt of irritation and schooled her features into a smile. 'I am very honoured, sir, that *you* should be so careful of it,' she said sweetly.

Mr Woollatt blinked, then he puffed out his chest, looking very pleased with himself.

They had reached the open parkland by this time, and Carlotta's mount began to prance.

'Are you ready to gallop the fidgets out of that nag of yours?'

Luke's voice close behind her made her look round. Her eyes strayed over his horse, a raw-boned black hunter that sidled and danced, eager to be off.

'I doubt I can keep up with that rangy brute.'

He gave her a slow smile and deep within her she felt the responding tug of attraction, setting her nerves tingling.

'Try,' he murmured.

The provocation was too great, and as the hunter leapt forward Carlotta kicked her little mare on in hot pursuit, ignoring Mr Woollatt's protests.

The mare was fresh and agile, but could not match the

hunter's pace. Carlotta pulled her to one side to avoid the mud kicked up by the hunter's huge hooves. She bent low over the horse's neck and gave herself up to the chase, revelling in the wind in her face, the smooth rhythm of the mare as she flew over the ground. The scent of new-mown grass and leather and horses combined into a heady mix that set her senses buzzing as she crossed the open ground, urging her mare on to keep up with Luke. All too soon they were approaching the trees that bordered the park and the hunter's pace slowed. A quick glance showed Carlotta that the rest of the party were some distance behind them, spread out across the park. Luke rode on until he was in the shadow of the trees before he pulled up to wait for her. Carlotta cantered up, laughing with sheer exhilaration. Luke was grinning.

'Well done. Where did you learn to ride like that?'

'Mama taught me, in Italy. She is an excellent horsewoman; we also used to ride bareback there, sometimes.'

'Astride?'

'Of course.'

'Miss Rivington, I am shocked!'

She put her head on one side as she looked at him. 'Are you, truly?'

'No, of course not. You have mud on your face.'

'Oh dear, have I? That is because Flame was close behind you for most of the way.' She hunted for her handkerchief.

'Bring your mare closer; I will wipe it off for you.'

'Quickly, then, before any of the others come up.' She held out her handkerchief and turned her face up towards him, smiling, but her smile faltered when he caught her fingers. The shock of his touch set her heart beating so heavily she felt sure he would hear it. 'Perhaps we should not—' She made to draw back, but his grip on her hand tightened.

'We are friends, are we not?' he said lightly.

Meeting his eyes, Carlotta saw there was nothing alarming about his smile and she relaxed a little, allowing him to take her chin with the fingers of one hand while the other gently drew the wisp of silk across her cheek. Carlotta trembled. He was so close, she could see the tiny laughter lines at the corners of his mouth, the flecks of gold in his hazel eyes. She wanted to throw her arms around his neck and beg him to kiss her, but it would not do. She had enjoyed one brief, heady flirtation with the Wicked Baron; she would not risk such pain again. She closed her eyes, afraid that he would read her thoughts.

'There, it is done.' Carlotta opened her eyes to find him smiling at her so warmly that her bones turned to water. 'Just in time. The others are coming up now.' Luke caught at Flame's bridle. 'While we are alone, I want to tell you I called upon your parents this morning.'

'You have seen my father? How is he?'

'Much better. He sends you his love.' A smile lifted the corners of his mouth. 'He hopes you are behaving yourself.'

She stifled a sigh. 'I am *trying* to do so. Thank you for bringing me news of Papa; it is very good of you to go to so much trouble for me.'

She could not read his look and was about to ask what he was thinking when she heard the thud of hooves, and a re-proachful voice behind her.

'My dear Miss Rivington, was that wise, to set off at *such* a pace on an animal you do not know?'

The magical moment was gone. Luke looked up.

'You must blame me, Woollatt,' he called cheerfully. 'I could tell at a glance that Miss Rivington is at home to a peg on horseback and thought she would like to gallop the fidgets out of the mare.'

'Then I call you thoughtless, my lord, to risk the young lady in such a way.'

'No, I am the thoughtless one,' put in Carlotta quickly. 'I was very eager to try out Flame's paces, and she was raring to go. You can see that she is perfectly docile now—I could have stopped her at any time, you know.'

Having promised to behave herself, she knew it behoved her now to make her peace with Mr Woollatt. She cast a swift, apologetic glance at Luke; much as she would have liked to spend the whole morning in his company she knew her duty. She turned her horse and trotted off beside Mr Woollatt.

For Carlotta, nothing else that day could match the enjoyment of her gallop across the park and those few stolen moments alone with Luke. Even the impromptu dance that evening could not compare, for although she stood up with Luke for two country dances, Mr Woollatt hovered around her and remained in close attendance for the whole of the evening.

When Lady Broxted carried her off to bed that evening, she had nothing but praise for her niece.

'I confess I was a little anxious that Mr Woollatt might be offended, after your treatment of him yesterday, but you have made up for it today, my love, and no mistake. He was full of praise for you tonight! I have great hopes that he will declare himself tomorrow.'

'Do you think so, Aunt?'

'Without a doubt, my love. And now that you have had time to grow accustomed, you will not be tempted to run away again, now will you?'

'No, Aunt. But…should I not tell him about—about Papa before he makes me an offer?' asked Carlotta, clutching at a final straw.

They had stopped at the door of Carlotta's chamber.

'No, no, my love, your uncle will discuss everything with Mr Woollatt afterwards. There is no need for you to worry about that.' Lady Broxted patted her cheek, saying fondly, 'That's a good girl. Just think how happy your dear mama will be when we tell her of the splendid match you have made! Now, hurry off to bed, child—I want you looking your best in the morning!'

Carlotta obeyed her aunt and made haste to get into bed, but sleep eluded her. She lay between the covers, tossing restlessly while the house gradually sank into silence and at last she drifted into an uneasy sleep.

She woke again as it was growing light and lay quietly, listening. She knew it must be very early, for the house was silent, sleeping still, but Carlotta was wide awake. She slipped out of bed and went to the window. There was only the faintest line of gold on the eastern horizon, the rest of the sky ranging from flushed pink to deep blue, and the land below was still tinged with grey.

Her room was in the west wing of the house, overlooking the walled garden with its statues that gleamed in the ghostly morning light. Carlotta fumbled with the catch and quietly pushed up the sash window. The air was pleasantly cool, and she leaned her elbows on the sill, breathing deeply while she considered her situation. It could not be so very bad to be married to Mr Woollatt. He was undoubtedly kind, and so rich that she need never want for anything. Perhaps they would have a house such as Malberry Court, and a stable full of horses. She smiled to herself; she would have to ride them very quietly.

Carlotta wondered why she was so anxious; she knew that many married couples lived very comfortably together: Mr and Mrs Ainslowe certainly appeared extremely happy, and she had never known her aunt and uncle to disagree in all the time she had lived with them. There was no reason why she should not be as happy in her marriage. She thought of Julia and Lord Fairbridge; she had watched them dancing together and had seen the glowing looks they had shared. Her heart clenched. If only she could look that way upon Mr Woollatt. But she knew there was only one man who evoked such emotion from her. She gave herself a little shake. She must not think of him. It was not at all helpful.

A movement below caught her attention. She peered down into the gardens. A shadowy figure was gliding close to the wall towards the house. One of the servants, she thought, returning from meeting his lover in the village. The thought deepened Carlotta's depression. With a sigh she went back to her bed, hoping for an hour's sleep before the maid brought her hot chocolate.

The restless night made Carlotta very tired the following morning and she sent her maid away, only to be woken some time later when the servant came back to announce that she had missed breakfast and that her aunt wished her to make her way directly to the library. She knew immediately the reason for the summons. Suddenly her sprig muslin with its tiny puff sleeves seemed far too flimsy to combat the chill that came over her. Carlotta knew this was merely nerves and resisted the temptation to wrap herself in her paisley shawl before running downstairs.

She opened the door to the little ante-room and found Lord Broxted waiting for her. He beckoned her to come forward, and as she did so her aunt came out of the library.

'Ah, there you are, my love.' She shut the door carefully. 'And in your new gown, too. Very pretty. Mr Woollatt is waiting for you.'

The knot in Carlotta's stomach twisted even tighter. 'Aunt—I—that is—'

Her uncle reached out for her hand. 'Go into the library, my dear,' he said gently. 'You know what you have to do.'

Carlotta looked from his smiling face to her aunt, who was

nodding encouragement. Squaring her shoulders, she crossed the small ante-room, but at the library door she turned back. 'Aunt, I do not think I can do this.'

'Nonsense, my love. What is there to do? Mr Woollatt is not an ogre.'

'I know that, but—'

Lord Broxted put up his hand. 'Carlotta, this is no time to be difficult. Mr Woollatt's intentions have been clear for some weeks; if you are averse to his suit, then you should have made that plain to us before now.'

'No, no, it is not that…'

Carlotta twisted her hands together until Lady Broxted came up and caught them in her own gentle clasp.

'I understand, my dear; you are afraid, and that is very natural, but your fears are unfounded. Do you think your uncle has not made enquiry? Mr Woollatt is known to be a good man; he will make you an excellent husband.'

'And he has hinted that he is prepared to be very generous over the settlements,' put in Lord Broxted. 'The match will be very advantageous to your parents.'

'I am sure Mr Woollatt is everything you say, but—' She broke off as hasty footsteps approached from the hall.

'Oh, excuse me.' Luke's long stride brought him into the ante-room before he realised it was occupied. 'I left my riding gloves in here earlier.' He looked from Carlotta to Lady Broxted. 'I beg your pardon. I hope I am not interrupting anything?'

'Please, my lord, just go,' said Carlotta, dismayed.

'It is a delicate matter, my lord, but I think you may be able to help us.' Lady Broxted moved swiftly to close the door behind him. 'You have proved yourself a true friend to my little niece, and your advice now would be welcomed.'

'No,' whispered Carlotta, but so quietly that no one heard her.

'Aye, perhaps she will listen to you, sir,' muttered Lord Broxted testily. Luke raised his brows. 'Mr Woollatt is beyond that door,' explained the earl, pointing towards the library. 'My niece has only to go in and accept his offer of marriage and she will have every luxury showered upon her. She is a very fortunate young lady. Yet she hesitates. I pray you, Darvell, add your voice to ours, urge her to take the small step that will secure her comfort and happiness—and that of her family.'

Carlotta's cheeks flamed. She dare not look up as she waited for Luke to speak.

'Miss Rivington must do as she thinks fit,' he said at last. 'Woollatt is a good man; I believe his reputation to be unblemished.'

'There, my love, what did I tell you?' Lady Broxted beamed. 'It is a match any mother would want for her daughter. Go in now, Carlotta. You have kept the poor man waiting long enough.'

The world seemed to be tilting. Carlotta put her hand against the doorpost to steady herself. She closed her eyes. Had this been planned, that Luke should come in and add his persuasion? If that was so, then truly he could not love her. The crushing pain in her chest made it difficult to breathe. Carlotta forced her eyes open, forced herself to look across the little room to where Luke was standing. His face showed nothing but polite indifference. He gave her a little bow, saying coldly, 'I wish you every happiness, ma'am.'

She watched him turn away. He began to play with the little Dresden ornaments on the side table. She looked at his back, ramrod straight, the broad shoulders unyielding beneath the fine wool of his riding coat. The sight offered her no comfort; she read rejection in every stiff line of his body.

'My love, Mr Woollatt is waiting for you.'

Lady Broxted's words recalled Carlotta's wandering senses. She put up her chin, turned and walked into the library.

Luke moved the little porcelain shepherdess closer to her mate; he heard the door close and the soft sigh of relief uttered by Lady Broxted. Carlotta was about to make a most advantageous match and he had not stood in her way. He should feel happy for her. She would command every luxury, every comfort. But there had been no comfort in the look she had given him, only anxiety and fear and…

'Damnation, I cannot allow this—' He swung round, only to find Lord Broxted blocking his way.

'One moment, Darvell. You are not indifferent to my niece, I think. Consider, if you please, before you commit an act that you may both regret. What can you offer her, compared to Daniel Woollatt? Granted, you have a title, but no fortune, and a reputation that is not to be envied.'

Angrily Luke shook off the earl's restraining hand. 'Perhaps we should let Carlotta choose!'

'I think she has already chosen.'

The words hit him like icy water. His hands balled into fists and for a moment unreasoning anger threatened to overwhelm him. He wanted to knock Broxted to the ground, but one did not brawl with fellow guests. Besides, what would it achieve? It would merely add to his reputation as the wild, wicked baron.

Lord Broxted patted his shoulder. 'Let be, Darvell,' he said gently. 'It is best this way. She will be happy. Woollatt can give her everything.'

Unlike you. The words were unspoken, but Luke felt them in the air; they wrapped themselves around his heart, heavy as lead.

'I pray you are right, Broxted.' With a nod, he scooped his gloves from the table, turned on his heel and walked out.

* * *

Luke strode from the house, a red mist of anger, frustration and bitter disappointment clouding his thoughts. Billy was waiting for him in the stable yard.

'Mr Ainslowe has gone on ahead, my lord. Says he will wait for you in the park,' he announced formally as Luke swung himself into the saddle. 'Would you like me to accompany you, sir?'

'Of course not. I have no need of a damned nursemaid!'

Billy jumped back as Luke swung the big hunter around and trotted out of the yard. Somewhere deep inside him, reason told Luke that he would have to apologise to his groom, but that would come later. For now he just wanted to ride away and forget. So she would marry Woollatt and have everything her shallow heart desired. She had called him friend, but she had no need of him now.

A gallop across the park helped him to regain control over his temper, but did nothing to improve his mood—he found it impossible to raise a smile when he caught up with the main riding party.

'Luke! Thought you had decided not to join us.' James looked at him closely. 'Are you well, brother? You look unusually grim. Is aught amiss?'

'I am well enough—that is—urgent business calls me away.' *Why not?* he thought. *What is there to keep me here?* 'I only came here to tell you.'

'What, you are going now, *riding* to town? Luke, wait—'

But he was already cantering away, ignoring his brother's bewildered shout. He was determined to quit Malberry immediately. He would send word back to Billy and to his man—damnation, he could manage very well for one night without them and the thought of returning to the house, knowing that *she* was within its walls and unattainable, was not to be borne.

* * *

Soon he was trotting out of the gates, lost in his own black thoughts until he became aware of an unusual amount of activity on the edge of the village. Outside the Durinis' house, in fact. But he must have made a mistake; it did not *look* like the Durinis' cottage. Then he realised what was different: one half of the house was a blackened ruin.

Chapter Twelve

This cannot be real. I am dreaming. The thought echoed again and again in Carlotta's head. It was as if she was outside herself, watching Mr Woollatt as he paced up and down the Axminster carpet, outlining his circumstances and pointing out to her the advantages of becoming his wife. She felt too detached. Surely it was not her voice that was speaking, expressing her obligation, saying how happy she would be to accept his kind offer. It seemed no sooner had these words been uttered than Mr Woollatt was kissing her hand, declaring himself to be the happiest of men. Then the doors opened and her aunt and uncle came in, Lady Broxted laughing and crying all at the same time and soon Carlotta was crying, too.

'Oh, my dear, I am so happy for you.' Lady Broxted hugged her. 'And you have a ring already!'

Carlotta raised her left hand and looked at the large diamond that winked and glittered as she moved her fingers. It felt very heavy, like a manacle, shackling her to her fate.

'Yes…' Mr Woollatt came over, looking very smug. 'I know how much these little trinkets mean to you ladies, so I took the precaution of bringing it with me.'

'And it fits perfectly.' Lady Broxted beamed at him. 'How clever of you, sir.'

* * *

It was not to be expected that the engagement should be kept secret. Lady Broxted was eager to dash off to the breakfast room to tell the other houseguests and she would have dragged the happy couple with her, had not Mr Woollatt held up his hand.

'I shall come in briefly to accept their felicitations, of course, but then you must excuse me, ma'am. My mother must be informed of this felicitous event. There is no time to lose, for I would rather tell her myself immediately than risk word reaching her in a roundabout way. Naturally, I discussed my intentions with her before coming to Malberry, but she will want to know if my hopes have been realised. Lord Broxted, I shall bring my lawyer back with me to agree the settlement. After that we can send an announcement to the newspapers, make it all official.' He raised Carlotta's hands to his lips, one after the other. 'I am grieved to have to leave you so soon, my dear, but I shall not be gone above a couple of days. I shall be counting the hours until our next meeting.'

Carlotta murmured her reply and watched him walk away. All the time she felt nothing. Nothing.

Carlotta had hoped that once Mr Woollatt had departed she would be allowed some peace, but it was not to be; Lady Broxted kept her beside her for the rest of the day while the guests came in turn to congratulate her. Mrs Price called her a sly little puss and made Julia blush by telling her that she would have to hurry up and find a husband if she was not to become an old maid. Sir Gilbert looked thoughtfully at the diamond and wished her every happiness, while Mr and Mrs Ainslowe beamed at her, declaring they felt personally responsible for her good fortune. Only Luke was missing from the happy crowd and it was not until they were all gathered in the drawing room before dinner that she learned he had left the Court.

'Urgent business in town,' explained James.

'Staving off his creditors, more like,' grinned Mr Price, winking at his host.

James's smile hardened slightly. 'No, no, it has not come to that yet,' he said gently.

Mrs Price gave a little laugh, although there was more than a hint of wistfulness about her as she said, 'I doubt we are exciting enough for the Wicked Baron.'

'I assure you, my brother-in-law is more than happy with the company here,' said Adele. 'Only a matter of grave importance would take him away.'

'It is a great pity that Mr Woollatt has left us, too,' continued Mrs Price. 'What shall we do with so few gentlemen? Methinks Lord Fairbridge and Sir Gilbert will have to work twice as hard to keep us all amused.'

The viscount flushed at this, but Sir Gilbert merely laughed.

'Oh, I am sure we shall contrive to amuse ourselves,' replied Adele smoothly. 'Now, shall we go in to dinner?'

'If I had known Darvell was going to town, I would have given him a draft on my bank,' said Sir Gilbert as everyone rose to make their way to the dining room. 'I had a little luck with the cards recently, Ainslowe, and I would buy that Tiepolo back from you. I thought this might be a good time for it, because I could have Reed take it back to town for me.'

'My, my, Sir Gilbert, how would you manage without your valet?' cried Mr Price, winking at his wife.

'Very well, sir, I assure you. I am not such a frippery fellow that I cannot dress myself for a couple of days. But I would like to get the painting back to town.'

'Oh, you would, eh?' retorted James. 'Well, I hate to disappoint you, Gil, but it ain't for sale.'

Sir Gilbert laughed. 'Surely, Ainslowe, you would not deny me my own again.'

'Unfortunately for you, Sir Gilbert, I have taken quite a fancy to it,' laughed Adele as she walked by on Lord Broxted's arm. 'I have to agree with James that it looks very well in the library—you will not get it back now, I think!'

Carlotta was thankful that her betrothal was no longer the main topic of interest and settled down to her meal, although she was so tired that every mouthful was an effort; she was relieved when Mrs Ainslowe shepherded the ladies back to the drawing room, leaving the gentlemen to their brandy. The ladies disposed themselves gracefully on chairs and sofas, Lady Broxted explaining to Mrs Price that Mr Woollatt had gone north to apprise his mother of the happy change to his circumstances.

'I think he would have been better advised to wait a little, until he could take Miss Rivington with him,' opined Mrs Price, 'When—*if* my Julia receives an offer while we are at Malberry, I should not want to separate the happy couple so soon.'

'True, but there is also a case to be made for allowing them both to come to terms with their new situation,' replied Lady Broxted.

'Yes, poor Carlotta is looking quite worn out with all the excitement,' observed Adele.

Carlota seized her chance.

'Indeed, I am a little tired, Mrs Ainslowe. I think if you will excuse me now I would like to retire.'

'Of course we will excuse you.' Adele patted her hands, smiling at her. 'We must put the bloom back into your cheeks before your fiancé returns, must we not?'

Carlotta forced herself to smile at this, and with a little curtsy she moved towards the door.

'Poor love, would you like me to come with you?'

'No, thank you, Aunt, there is no need to disturb yourself. I shall be quite well if I can only lie down.'

Carlotta slipped out of the room and leaned against the

closed door. She let out a long sigh of relief. Lack of sleep was beginning to catch up with her and her bones ached with the effort she was making to smile at everyone. The company was keeping country hours at Malberry Court and the daylight had not yet faded. However, a gloom was settling over the north-facing hall, making the glow of candles coming from a side room all the more noticeable. It was Mr Ainslowe's study. The door stood ajar, allowing the light to spill out on to the tiled floor of the hall. She heard voices and glanced in through the half-open door. With a gasp she stopped, staring. Luke was talking earnestly with his brother, but, as if aware of her presence, he looked up and saw her. There was no escape, so Carlotta moved forward, blurting out the words that were in her head. 'I thought you had gone!'

James opened the door wider. 'Come in, Miss Rivington.'

She walked into the study, keeping her eyes upon Luke. He looked very grim, but then he had looked no different when she had seen him in the ante-room that morning.

'I thought you had left for town,' she said again. She looked at his muddy boots and dirty coat. 'Have you been riding all day?'

'No, not exactly,' he said. 'I have this minute come back from the village. There was an attack last night, on your parents' house. A fire—but do not be alarmed,' he added quickly, 'they are unhurt.'

Carlotta glanced anxiously at James.

'You need not worry, Miss Rivington, Luke has told me your history. As yet no one knows that he has returned. The rest of the gentlemen are still at their brandy. They are not aware why I was called away from the dining room.'

She hardly heard him, but turned back to Luke.

'What of the maid, and Jack?'

'Both safe.'

'Thank heaven. What happened?'

'Someone piled wood and bracken against the back door and set fire to it, but the dog's barking woke the servants in time to put the flames out before anyone was hurt. Half the house is damaged, but it is not irreparable.' A faint smile tugged at his mouth. 'That is why I am so filthy, I have been helping your father to salvage what he could from the wreckage and move it into the undamaged part of the house. There is room for the servants to sleep there, but I have taken your parents to the George.'

Carlotta put her hand to her throat as she looked at the two men. 'But who would do this? I mean—coming so soon after the attack upon Papa…'

James hesitated.

Luke said quietly, 'I think we should tell Miss Rivington the truth, brother.'

The silence was unnerving. Carlotta forced herself to speak. 'Thank you. Yes, if you please. Do you know who—who would do this?'

'No,' said James gravely, 'but there was something. Whoever started the fire left a message painted on the wall of the house.'

'A message?'

'Two words,' said Luke, watching her. *'Leave now.'*

'I—don't understand.'

'Someone wants your parents to quit Malberry.'

'B-but why?'

'That is what I have been asking Signor Durini.' Luke regarded her sombrely. 'Perhaps you can help us?'

She shook her head, frowning. 'I have no idea why anyone—it is preposterous. Papa has no enemies.'

'It would appear that he does,' Luke corrected her gently.

'But who could it be?' she challenged him. 'Why would someone want him to leave here?'

James looked uncomfortable. He glanced at his brother, then said diffidently, 'Forgive me, Miss Rivington, but it would be less embarrassing for Lord Broxted if your parents were not living quite so close.'

She stared at him. 'You cannot think my uncle capable of this!'

'Since he brought you to town, he has been careful to keep your parentage a secret,' Luke reminded her.

'Yes, but only because he is afraid any eligible suitors will be discouraged.'

'Any man who truly cares for you will not care a button that your mother married an artist,' muttered Luke.

'Yes, that is what my uncle thinks,' she said eagerly. 'He has always said that once a man shows a true regard for me he will explain everything. He would have told Mr Woollatt if he had not been in such haste to get away this morning.' She fixed her eyes upon James, pleading silently with him to understand.

'Broxted is very conscious of his own importance,' murmured Luke, 'but I do not think him capable of this.'

Carlotta gave an emphatic shake of her head. 'No, of course not.'

'But if that is not the reason for the attacks, what is?' asked James.

'Until we find that out, we must do something to protect the Durinis.' Luke looked at his brother. 'Well, James?'

'I shall move them to my Leicestershire estate. The gatehouse there is empty. Then we will spread the word that they have fled we know not where.' He turned back to Carlotta. 'You may rest easy, Miss Rivington. I shall look after your parents.'

'Thank you, sir. You are very good. How soon will they leave?'

'As soon as they can be packed and ready. Tomorrow, I hope.'

'I must go and see them—'

'No! It is too dangerous.'

Luke's vehemence startled her. She began to protest until James said gently, 'It would be best if you did not visit them,

Miss Rivington. Few people here know your background—to own it now might put you in danger, too.'

'But I could visit them after dark. They would not be asleep. Mama never retires before midnight, and sometimes Papa works through the night—'

'And do you truly believe it would relieve their worries to think of you wandering abroad at night? No, be guided by me, it is best that you do not see them.' James raised his head, listening. 'I hear voices. The gentlemen are on their way to the drawing room, and I think we should join them—that is, you and I should join them, Miss Rivington, Luke must go upstairs and change. He is not fit to be seen.' He held out his arm to her.

'I—I was about to retire,' she confessed.

'If that is what you wish. However, we could tell everyone that you overheard the news and are too disturbed to sleep, if you go now, you may be obliged to hear the story several times over in the morning.'

'Very well, sir, you have persuaded me. And it is the truth that I could not rest now.' She laid her fingers on his sleeve. 'Will you tell them everything that has occurred?'

'Only that someone tried to set fire to my artist's house. The rest shall be our secret. You may wish to confide in your aunt and uncle, of course, and with your permission I should like to tell Adele that you are Signor Durini's daughter, but you may be assured it will go no further.'

'Yes, of course.'

He patted her hand. 'Very good. Now, shall we go in?'

Carlotta lay on her bed and counted the chimes from the clock tower on the stables. Eleven o'clock. It was time. She dragged her cloak around her and went to the door. The landing was deserted, but she knew that some of the guests might still be downstairs. She strained to listen for footsteps, but all she could hear was the thudding of her own heart. It was only a few yards from her bedchamber to the backstairs, but it would not do to be discovered creeping out of the house so late at night. Nothing stirred. Carefully she closed her bedroom door and flew across the landing to the backstairs. Her soft kid boots made no noise on the wooden treads, but she was fearful that a creaking stair might betray her. By the time she reached the door leading out into the garden, her nerves were stretched to breaking point and when a dark figure detached itself from the bushes beside her she almost fainted. She turned to flee, but even as she drew breath to scream a pair of strong arms wrapped about her and a hand was clamped over her mouth.

'I have been waiting for you.'

Carlotta stopped struggling. The hand was removed from her face and she swung around.

'Luke,' she hissed. 'What are you doing here?'

He looked down at her, his face in deep shadow.

'I told you, I was waiting for you. I knew you would go to see your parents, with or without consent. I saw it in your face when James forbade you to go.'

'He did not forbid it, he merely advised.'

'And your uncle? I assume he knows the truth now about the attack.'

'Yes, I explained it all to him and to my aunt when we retired. They were deeply shocked.'

'And did they condone this night-time escapade?' He waited. 'Well?'

'I did not tell them,' she replied in a small voice.

'I thought as much.'

'How did you know I would be here?

He reached up and cupped her chin with his hand. Gently he ran his thumb across her bottom lip. Despite her anxiety, the familiar flame of desire stirred at his touch.

'I have seen that obstinate look before—it was a simple matter to ascertain the nearest way out of the house from your chamber.'

'I suppose you will insist that I return.'

She heard him laugh softly. He pulled her hand on to his arm.

'No, but I insist you let me accompany you.'

Relief flooded through her. '*Thank* you!'

'Save your thanks until we are safely indoors once again,' he muttered. 'And pull your hood up to cover your face. That's better. We will take the longer path, through the trees to the far side of the lake. I would not expect anyone to be looking out of the window at this time of night, but we will take no risks.'

After the attacks upon her father, Carlotta had not been looking forward to walking through the dark grounds of Malberry Court, but with Luke beside her she was no longer afraid. They left the shelter of the walled garden and followed the path around the perimeter of the park. They walked in silence with only the occasional screech of a fox or hooting owl to disturb the peace.

When they reached the stile, Carlotta glanced around her anxiously, knowing that this was where her father had been attacked. The trees and lush undergrowth made the area particularly dark, and she was glad to have Luke's comforting presence as they made their way past her parents' house, one side of it blackened and damaged. The gaping black holes where the windows had been made her shudder, and she was pleased that Luke hurried her on towards the George, where lights still blazed from the taproom despite the lateness of the hour. He led her under the arch, but at the doorway he stopped, pushing her behind him.

'Wait here. I will make sure there is no one on the stairs… Good, it's clear. Come along.'

Carlotta could hear voices and laughter coming from the taproom. The smell of stale cabbage and onions permeated the dark corridor. Taking her hand, Luke led her up the narrow staircase and along a dimly lit passage, stopping at the end to knock on a solid door. A bolt scraped back, the door opened, and Carlotta fell into her father's arms.

Carlotta sat between her mother and father, looking from one to the other to assure herself that they were safe while they explained what had happened.

'It is not so very bad.' Her father shrugged. 'We lost some clothes, a few pots and pans—'

'A few pots and pans!' cried Mrs Durini, 'My whole kitchen was destroyed.'

Signor Durini threw up his hands. 'Hah, of what importance is a kitchen?'

'Of great importance, if you want to eat,' returned his wife, drily. 'Not only that, the flames reached the room above it, where most of my gowns were stored.'

'I shall buy you more gowns, *cara*. But if it had reached my *pittura*, or the *miniatura*, now *that* would have been serious. As it is, Signor Ainslowe has said he will send his carriage tomorrow morning to take us to another, safer house, and we can continue to work there. Signor Ainslowe says the final two temples can be completed some other time, he has enough for now.' He squeezed Carlotta's hand. 'So you must not worry about us, Carla. In fact, I think we should celebrate our good fortune! I shall fetch a bottle of wine, if our landlord is not abed!'

'I'll go with you,' said Luke.

'Papa is remarkably calm about all this,' said Carlotta as the two men left the room.

'Your father is an artist. He lives for his painting. Besides,

Lord Darvell and his brother have promised to help us, and they are good men, I think. Although I cannot condone his lordship bringing you here tonight, and so late.'

'It was my idea, Mama.'

'Well, you should not have come, my love. It is not safe.'

Carlotta put up her chin. 'I had to come; I could not let you go away without seeing for myself that you were unharmed. Please do not be angry with me.'

'Of course not, my love.' Mrs Durini smiled fondly at her. 'And you have something to tell us, too, have you not?' She lifted Carlotta's hand, turning it so that the ring on her finger glinted in the candlelight.

Carlotta's cheeks grew warm. 'Yes, Mama. I—I am betrothed.'

'Oh, my dear, that is wonderful! To…?'

'M-Mr Woollatt.'

Mrs Durini blinked. 'Mr Woollatt? The man your aunt mentioned in her letters, the rich suitor?'

'Yes, Mama. The *very* rich suitor.'

'Then why are you with…?'

'Lord Darvell is m-my friend,' Carlotta replied, flushing.

Mrs Durini frowned. She took Carlotta by the shoulders and pulled her round to face her. 'My love, listen to me. A young lady cannot have male friends, especially when she is betrothed. People will talk.'

'Let them; I do not care what they say!'

'Of course you do not, but your fiancé might well care.'

'Please do not worry, Mama. Luke only came with me to protect me; no one knows we are here, and we shall be careful to make sure we are not seen as we go back through the park.'

Her mother did not look very reassured. 'We will have no more than one glass of wine together, *cara*, then you must go home as quickly as possible. Do not tarry. Promise me.'

'Of course, Mama, but there is no danger, Luke is with me.'

She pulled Carlotta into her arms and hugged her tightly. 'Oh, my sweet child,' she murmured, 'there is every danger!'

'Well, are you happy now you have seen your parents?'

Carlotta and Luke were walking back through the park, their path through the trees dappled with moonlight.

'Yes, I am.'

'Then what is worrying you, Carlotta?'

She looked up quickly, but Luke's face was in shadow.

'Is it so obvious?'

'It is to me.'

She sighed. 'Mama says…I must… She says you cannot be my friend.'

'She is right. That is why I was going to leave Malberry today.'

'Then why did you return?'

'Because I could not leave knowing you might be in danger.'

A bubble of happiness began to grow inside her; she reached out for him. 'So you *do* care.'

'Yes.'

He squeezed her hand, and the fragile little bubble burst as Carlotta felt Mr Woollatt's ring pressing into her fingers.

The gibbous moon was high above them, sailing through the clouds, serene and untroubled. Luke had a sudden impulse to throw back his head and howl, letting out his despair and frustration.

'It is too late. I would to heaven I had declared myself.' He was not aware that he had spoken aloud until he heard Carlotta's heavy sigh.

'My uncle would not have countenanced it, he—he deplores your loose ways. Besides, Mr Woollatt is far richer than you, is he not?'

Luke hesitated. Should he tell her how much he loved her? What good would it do now? If she broke off the engagement to Woollatt, she would be labelled a jilt and lose her place in society—her rightful place and one that she had known for such a short time. He could not do that to her—and if he did, would she not come to hate him for it? He forced himself to speak lightly.

'Yes, Woollatt is a much better man than I am, in all ways.'

The little hand in his trembled. He stopped. Something about the stance of the slender figure beside him stabbed at his heart. Her hood had fallen back, but she stood with her face averted. He took her shoulders and pulled her into a patch of moonlight. Still she would not look at him and he cupped her chin with his hand, tilting her face up. As she raised her eyes to look at him, he saw that they were glistening with tears.

'Ah, love, don't cry.' The words were wrenched from him. He folded her in his arms, felt the stiff little body resist for a moment before collapsing against him, sobbing piteously.

He held her, crooning softly and caressing her hair, hating her pain, but at the same time revelling in the closeness, the feel of her leaning against him, dependent upon him for comfort. Desire stirred; her nearness was arousing him, but he tried to ignore it. He rested his cheek on her hair, breathing in the fresh, flowery scent. If only this could go on for ever, if they did not have to face the morning. If only…

He realised she had stopped crying and was standing passively within his arms, her head resting against his chest. He loosened his hold and reached into his pocket.

'Here,' he said, holding up a handkerchief. 'I would rather you wiped your eyes on this than my shirt front.'

A watery chuckle greeted his words. 'Thank you.' She raised her head, smiling slightly, but as she reached for the handkerchief he pulled his hand away.

'No, let me do it.' She stood quietly, her face uplifted, while he wiped her cheeks. 'There, that's better.' He kissed the tip of her nose. She stood mutely looking up at him, her eyes huge and dark in her pale face, her lips full and lush. Irresistible. Gently, he slid his lips over hers. Just one kiss, he told himself, just one moment of happiness before he gave her up for ever.

Carlotta closed her eyes as his mouth found hers. It was supremely comforting, having Luke so close to her. Her hands slid up around his neck. Just once, she told herself, just one last, treasured moment to remember in the bleak years that stretched ahead of her. It was her last conscious thought. Luke's mouth became harder, more demanding and she gave herself up to the pleasurable sensations he was arousing within her. She pressed herself against his hard, aroused body and felt her insides liquefy. An urgent and irrepressible need consumed her. Luke pushed aside her cloak, his hands sliding over her shoulders, then he was cupping her breast, his thumb circling, teasing until she was pushing hard against him, her thighs aching, her body tingling with an anticipation she did not understand. His mouth trailed lightly across her neck, his breath tickling her skin, his touch sending little darts of heat through her body. She drove her fingers through his hair and gave a little moan of pleasure.

Desire surged through Luke, fuelled by elation as Carlotta leaned against him, her body inviting his caresses. He pushed her back gently, trapping her against a tree. His tongue flickered over the silky smooth skin of her shoulder, nibbled gently at her collarbone before his mouth moved on to explore the soft swell of her breasts. He pushed aside the thin muslin and took one hard erect nipple in his mouth, his tongue circling slowly while Carlotta arched against him, her responses driving all other thoughts from his mind. Her hands tangled in his hair, then, as the fingers of her left hand slid down to caress his cheek, he felt the hard, unyielding metal of the ring upon her finger.

It was a little touch, but it was enough. It reminded him that

Carlotta was to be another man's wife. Slowly Luke raised his head, listening to his own ragged breathing. He would not do this. He would not take what did not belong to him. Carlotta was looking up at him, her eyes large and luminous with desire. He could take her now; he knew she was willing, but he remembered the vow he had made to himself twelve months ago, that he would not ruin her. His own private devil whispered that no one need ever know, she would not be the first bride to go to her husband without her virginity, but it would not do. *She* would know, and she was too honest, too innocent to live with that secret—it would ruin any chance she had of happiness with her husband.

'Luke, what is it?'

He kissed her, one final, light touch of the lips. 'No more, sweetheart. I am promised to protect you, and I must get you back to the Court before I dishonour you completely.'

She was watching him, the signs of doubt on her face. 'Do you not…want me?'

He heard the uncertainty in her voice. It tore at his heart. 'Want you! Heaven and earth, love, you'll never know how much!' He cupped her face with one hand, saying gently, 'I will not take another man's bride, Carlotta. It would bring us all pain. Believe me, I know, I have seen it happen too many times.' He moved away from her, away from temptation. 'I will not lie to you—I have had my share of mistresses, but it has always been a game understood by both parties. We enjoyed each other, then moved on, with no regrets, no broken hearts—until now. I will not risk yours.'

Carlotta was confused. Her heightened senses were aware of the balmy stillness of the night and the moon sailing overhead, so calm and serene. Yet here, within the shadow of the trees, there was an atmosphere of suppressed passion. She felt as if she had been rudely awakened from a lovely dream, where she and Luke loved each other, and nothing else mattered. Now he talked of risks, and broken hearts. She gave a shaky laugh. 'It is too late for that, I think.'

'But not too late for you to be happy.'

She put a hand to her head, trying to think clearly. 'I—I do not understand.' She heard him sigh.

'No, you are too innocent, but believe me, it is for the best. You must marry Woollatt with a clear conscience. You deserve that. *He* deserves it.'

A line from a poem darted into her head and she murmured the words,

'"I could not love thee, dear, so much, loved I not honour more."'

He looked at her. 'What was that?'

She gave him a sad little smile.

'You are a good man, Luke Ainslowe.' She held out her hand. 'Will you take me back to the Court, now?'

Hand in hand they walked through the park; as Luke opened the gate into the walled garden, Carlotta looked up at him.

'You will not go?' she said. 'Even though my parents are moved to safety, you will stay?'

'I am promised to help James track down the attackers.'

'Then I won't lose you just yet.'

He followed her into the garden. 'It would be less painful if we did not see each other.'

'But we must grow accustomed,' she reasoned. 'We move in the same circles, we cannot avoid seeing each other.'

'I will not be in town so often in the future. I have spent much of the past year on my estates, trying to bring them back into shape. I have made some progress, but there is a great deal yet to do.'

She sighed. He had withdrawn from her, as he must. They

were moving silently along in the shadow of the garden wall towards the side door of the house, creeping along like a couple of robbers, or lovers. With a gasp Carlotta stopped and reached out to grab Luke's sleeve.

'I have just remembered something. Last night, I did not sleep very well and was looking out of my window—it was just before dawn, the sun had not risen, but it was growing light—I saw someone here, in the garden. A cloaked figure keeping to the shadow of the wall. It could be nothing. At the time I thought it was a servant, coming back from a tryst with his maid—'

'You are sure it was a man?'

'Yes, I think so…that is—yes, it was a man; it moved like a man.'

Luke frowned. 'The figure was coming towards this door? This wing is used only for guests and their personal servants.'

'Do you think someone from here set fire to my parents' house?' She shivered, suddenly fearful.

'That is what we must discover,' murmured Luke. He pulled her into his arms for a brief moment. 'You must try not to worry, *cara*.'

'I am not at all afraid when you are with me,' she murmured into his coat. Gently he disentangled himself from her arms.

'You must go back to your room,' he said softly. 'Let us see if the side door is unlocked, as we left it.'

Chapter Thirteen

'Carlotta, my dear, are you ill? You are looking very pale.'

No wonder, thought Carlotta, entering the breakfast room, *I spent half the night wandering the park with Luke, and the other half lying awake, thinking about him. Damn the man! Oh, Luke…*

'I slept ill last night, Aunt.' She smiled at the guests gathered around the table, as if to apologise for not looking her best for them. Luke, she noted, was not present.

'Too much excitement, perhaps, Miss Rivington?' Sir Gilbert waved away the footman and held the chair for her himself. Carlotta would have preferred to sit beside her aunt rather than across the table, where she must face her close scrutiny, but she could not bring herself to refuse Sir Gilbert's courtesy.

'I know what it is,' declared Mr Price. 'She is missing her swain. Am I not right, Miss Rivington?'

'Perhaps.'

'I am afraid I cannot divert you with any outdoor pursuits,' announced Adele. 'The inclement weather has put an end to hopes of that.'

Everyone present glanced towards the windows and the steady rain pouring down.

'I only hope we will not have to cancel our shooting party,' remarked Mr Price, addressing himself again to his breakfast.

'Lord, no.' Sir Gilbert laughed. 'That is two days hence; the weather will have changed by then.'

'But it will be excessively muddy,' pointed out Mrs Ainslowe.

'Then it is a good thing we shall not be dining with you.' Her husband laughed.

'The gentlemen have decided that when they have finished shooting they will retire to the bathhouse,' explained Mrs Ainslowe, observing Lady Broxted's puzzled look. 'We shall be left to enjoy a quiet dinner here at the Court, where we may gossip and chatter to our hearts' content.'

'It means we shall not be bringing our dirt back to the house.' James grinned. 'There is nothing that annoys the ladies more than to have our muddy footprints all over the floors.'

Lord Broxted turned to his wife. 'Ainslowe mentioned it to me yesterday, and I had meant to tell you, my dear—I hope you do not object?'

'Not in the least. I am sure you will all enjoy getting excessively dirty, and we shall spend a very pleasant day without you, I have no doubt.'

'I just wish it was fine today.' Adele sighed. 'I did so wish to take Carlotta for a ride in the gig.'

'Perhaps it is for the best that you do not go,' put in Lady Broxted. 'Mr Woollatt is very anxious for Carlotta's safety.'

'Then we must hope tomorrow is dry, so that we can drive out before he returns,' retorted Carlotta. Her aunt's look of surprise made her flush and she added more gently, 'I am sure it is perfectly safe, ma'am, and I would not have him worry over me.'

'Of course he will worry!' Mrs Price put down her piece of toast and shook her head at Carlotta. 'Lord, what a strange notion! It is a very good sign that Mr Woollatt is concerned for you, my dear, it shows he means to take very good care of you when you are married!'

Carlotta pinned on a smile, but inside she was already feeling constricted by that invisible mesh of solicitude.

The rain was succeeded by a drizzling mist that kept the house party indoors. Adele invited everyone to the library to play charades, an idea eagerly taken up by most of the younger guests and improved upon by Sir Gilbert, who suggested that the ballroom would offer more scope for their theatricals. Lady Broxted and Mrs Price decided to adjourn to the morning room and Carlotta chose to remain close to her aunt, determined to avoid all male company. The older ladies settled down to while away the afternoon with their books and desultory conversation, and Carlotta carried her embroidery frame to a chair by one of the far windows where she was not overlooked. She kept her head bent over her work, and, if the memory of Luke's embraces sometimes made her set a stitch awry, at least there was no one to observe it.

However, she was heartily bored with her occupation by the afternoon and was relieved when Adele came in and announced she was going out.

'The weather is clearing and I am going to take a walk before dinner. Who will join me?'

'Dear me—walking, so late in the day?' said Lady Broxted, glancing at the pretty ormolu clock on the side table.

Adele laughed. 'There is an hour or more before we need to even think of changing for dinner, that is time and enough to take the air.'

'I stand in awe of your energy, Mrs Ainslowe,' said Mrs Price, waving her fan. 'I vow I am quite fatigued, and was about to suggest to Lady Broxted that we should retire now to rest until the dinner hour.'

'An excellent idea, ma'am,' agreed Lady Broxted. 'I fear you will have to excuse us from your little outing, Mrs Ainslowe.'

Carlotta wondered how they could possibly be tired when they had done nothing but sit down since breakfast. Something of her thoughts must have shown in her face, for Adele was looking at her with a very decided twinkle in her eyes.

'Then Julia and I will be going for a walk on our own, unless I can persuade Miss Rivington to join us?'

'Just the two of you, ma'am? No gentlemen?'

'Alas, no. They have decided they would prefer to play billiards. So you see, it will be a very small little party. Will you come?'

Reassured that there would be no danger of meeting Luke, Carlotta gladly put aside her embroidery and accepted the invitation.

'How fresh the air is!' declared Adele as they set off into the park. 'I declare I am quite *stifled*, being confined to the house all day. We are all wearing very sensible half-boots, I see. I thought we might take the path around the lake, it is newly completed and should not be too muddy, despite the rain. Are we agreed? Good. Onward, then!'

Adele's brisk walking pace suited her young companions very well. A stiff breeze had blown away the low cloud and after the recent rain the colours of the park seemed enhanced in the sparkling sunlight. Carlotta was very glad to be out of doors. The exercise soothed her ragged nerves and she walked along in silence, happy to allow her mind to wander freely. Adele was drawing Julia out, gently encouraging her to talk, but Carlotta paid little heed to them or to their direction until the meandering path brought them in sight of a large square building, its fluted columns and stone portico reminiscent of a Greek temple. When she had seen it last it had been little more than a neglected shell, but now the windows had been glazed and the solid oak doors repaired.

'Ah, the bathhouse,' said Adele. 'There are some very fine murals in here, I understand. Shall we go in and look?'

Julia stopped. 'Oh, but…is this not the gentlemen's bath-house?'

'Well, certainly the gentlemen use it, but they will not be here today,' replied Adele. 'Come.' She squeezed Carlotta's arm. 'I am sure *you* would like to look inside.'

'Indeed I should,' agreed Carlotta. It was one of the last buildings to be decorated by her father, and she was eager to see it, eager for some link with her parents. With a jolt she realised how much she was missing them.

Adele led the way up the shallow steps to the double doors situated beyond the pillars.

'Perhaps it is locked,' said Julia, not unhopefully.

Adele reached into her reticule and pulled out a large key. 'I came prepared!'

The doors opened smoothly and they stepped inside. They found themselves in a square, vaulted room with windows set up high in the walls. There was a rectangular plunge bath in the centre of the floor with a flight of shallow stone steps leading down into it. Adele stooped to put her hand into the water, sending little waves rippling across the surface.

'I am told it is deep enough for swimming. It is very cold, of course, but the gentlemen do not seem to mind that.' She giggled. 'The high windows mean that they cannot be spied upon.'

'I—I am sure we should not be here,' stuttered Julia, staring wide-eyed at the walls.

Carlotta looked around her; a series of murals depicted classical scenes, men and women bathing in a river. She had been brought up in an artist's studio and was quite at home with the near-naked figures, but Julia was clearly shocked. Adele merely laughed.

'Of course, we should not be here, but you are not children;

I do not believe you will be irrevocably harmed by what you see. Besides, we need not tell anyone.'

Julia gave a nervous giggle. 'No, I suppose not.'

'Come along, then; let us go into the warm room.'

They moved on past the plunge pool and through the doors beyond. Carlotta was surprised to find herself now in a very different space. There was a large fireplace set into one wall and a number of padded couches placed around the room. The windows here were also high and the walls beneath them were covered with scenes of what Carlotta suspected might be an orgy. She smiled to herself; Papa was very liberal, but he would never have allowed her in *here* while he was working!

'The gentlemen come in here to relax,' explained Adele. 'There is a little room at the side where water can be heated for the hip baths. Then, when the gentlemen have finished their day's shooting, they can bathe and refresh themselves in the plunge pool before taking an informal dinner here, before the fire.'

'It sounds very…decadent,' observed Carlotta, her lip quivering.

'Yes, but amusing,' replied Adele.

The three ladies looked at one another and giggled.

'P-perhaps we should hold a dinner of our own here one day,' suggested Adele.

Julia put her hand to her flaming cheeks. 'Oh, no, I could not…!'

Carlotta took her arm. 'You need not be anxious, Julia. I do not think it would be allowed.'

'Certainly not for *unmarried* ladies,' agreed Adele, twinkling.

Carlotta returned from the walk with her spirits much improved and looking forward to her dinner. At the back of her mind there were nagging doubts about her engagement to Mr Woollatt, but he was not expected to return for a few more days and in her present buoyant mood she found herself reluctant to think too much about the future.

As the ladies hurried up the stairs to change they found James waiting for them on the landing.

'Ah, there you are. Did you enjoy your walk?'

'Very much, my love,' replied Adele. 'And we are now ready for our dinner!'

James grinned. 'Then you had best go and change, but perhaps Miss Rivington would spare me a moment? I have a message for her.'

Carlotta looked at him in surprise, but Adele patted her arm.

'From Daniel Woollatt, I don't doubt. Very well, James, but do not keep her too long!'

'Is that it?' asked Carlotta, 'Do you have a message for me from Mr Woollatt?'

James beckoned to Carlotta to follow him to one of the deep window embrasures that overlooked the south lawn. He waited until the other ladies were out of sight, then he pulled a note from his pocket and handed it to Carlotta.

'Better than that—it is from your father. My coachman returned from Leicestershire this afternoon and he has brought a note for you from Signor Durini.'

Eagerly she unfolded the paper and scanned it. 'Thank you, Mr Ainslowe. I had asked Papa to let me know that they were safe.'

'Well, now you can rest easy.' He smiled down at her. 'And when Woollatt returns we shall see the smile back in your eyes, I hope. Oh don't colour up, my dear; Adele noticed that you had lost a little of your sparkle, but that's to be expected, with your fiancé gone away.'

Carlotta blushed, confused, and strove for something to say. 'May I write a letter to my parents, sir?'

'Of course—give it to me when it is finished and I will see

it safely delivered.' With a final reassuring smile James stepped quickly out of the embrasure. 'What the—!'

Carlotta heard his exclamation. As she moved forward she saw he had come to a halt at the head of the stairs.

'Reed! What the devil are you doing there?'

Sir Gilbert's manservant was almost at the top of the grand staircase, but at these words he stopped and made a low bow.

'My apologies, sir. My master sent me to the library and I thought, this being the shortest route and with all the guests in their rooms, dressing for dinner—'

'Well, quite clearly they ain't all in their rooms,' retorted James coldly. 'Please use the service stairs in future.'

'Yes, sir.'

Watching from the window, Carlotta observed the smirk on the man's ferret-like features as he bowed again.

'One moment, Reed!'

'Yes, sir?'

'Where's your book?'

'Sir?'

'If Sir Gilbert sent you to the library, it must have been for a book.'

'I was *returning* a book for him, sir,' Reed said quietly. Then, with another bow, he continued on his stately way.

'Insolent dog,' muttered James.

'I understand that all valets think themselves superior,' murmured Carlotta.

'Aye, they do, but most of 'em make a better pretence at sub-servience than that creature. In fact, most of 'em keep out of sight. Ah, well, Mattingwood tells me the man has been with him for many years and long-serving attendants are the very devil, Miss Rivington. Now, I had best let you get on, or we shall both of us be late for our dinner!'

* * *

Luke wished the interminable day would come to an end. He had spent his time avoiding Carlotta, as much for his sake as hers. It was bad enough that he couldn't get the thought of her out of his mind; when he walked through the hall the perfume from the flowers on the console tables made his step falter and for a moment he was back beneath the trees, burying his face in her hair and breathing in her sweet, flowery fragrance. Just going out of the front door and looking up at the frescoes reminded him of Carlotta. Now, at dinner, he had to steel himself to face her. He had deliberately come down late to the drawing room, but not late enough, for James was laughingly informing the assembly that his wife had kept the young ladies out of doors for far too long, and they were even now at their dressing tables.

Luke positioned himself in a far corner and watched the door, waiting for a first glimpse of that beloved, heart-shaped face. When Carlotta did come in, he thought how well she looked, the effects of the walk still discernible in her glowing countenance. He had hoped to avoid her, but it was as if some magic thread drew her gaze to his. She looked away immediately, as anxious as he was to avoid detection, but that one fleeting glance set his pulses racing, made the blood course faster through his body.

With an effort he turned his back to her and joined Sir Gilbert and Mr Price for a lively debate on horses, but he was aware of her presence and found himself straining his ears to hear the soft words she was exchanging with Adele. Luke soon realised that he was not the only gentleman showing an interest in Carlotta. He noticed how often Sir Gilbert's eyes wandered over to the little group, and when the ladies engaged upon an argument regarding *The Mysteries of Udolpho* and Carlotta was about to run to the library to fetch Mrs Radcliffe's novel, Sir

Gilbert swiftly stepped in, offering to go in her stead. Damn the man, he had not shown such great interest in Carlotta before she became engaged to Woollatt. Was he trying to set up as her flirt even before she was married? Scowling, Luke tried to give his attention to Mr Price, but from the corner of his eye he watched as his brother joined the little group.

'So, my love,' said James, 'did you and your young friends enjoy your stroll through the park?'

'Very much. We completed a full circuit around the lake. The new path makes it a most pleasant walk with beautiful views across the park. We passed the bathhouse.' Adele threw a mischievous glance towards Julia, who blushed vividly. 'We were *most* impressed.'

The devil, thought Luke. They have been inside. He imagined Carlotta looking at the bathing scenes. Had they also visited the inner sanctum? He glanced across at Carlotta and immediately looked away again, biting his lip. Of course they had. Her sparkling eyes and the telltale flush on her cheek gave her away. He wondered if she, too, was imagining how delightful it would be to swim together in that cold pool—could she swim? If not, he would teach her. Afterwards they would lie naked in front of the roaring fire in the warm room. He turned away suddenly. It could never be, of course—she was Woollatt's fiancée. But still the thought was far too arousing.

'We are very tempted to join you in the bathhouse when you have done with your shooting,' murmured Adele.

Luke swung back in time to see the look of horror on Miss Price's face. James wagged a playful finger.

'We have entertained you with dancing and rides and I know not what every day thus far, madam wife. You will now allow us to enjoy ourselves in peace! Besides, have we not promised that we shall join you here for supper?'

'Your wife is teasing you, Mr Ainslowe,' put in Mrs Price.

'We have plans for our own entertainment that day, I assure you. More to the point, is anything arranged for tomorrow? If it remains dry, I would very much like to take the lakeside walk—Mrs Ainslowe's description has given me a desire to try it.'

'Yes, I, too, would like to see it,' added Lady Broxted.

'Let us all go,' suggested Sir Gilbert, returning from the library.

'Yes, James may escort you,' declared Adele. 'And since we have already seen it, I shall take Julia and Carlotta out in the gig.'

'Th-thank you, but Lord Fairbridge has already promised to take me out for an airing in his curricle,' stammered Julia.

James laughed. 'Miss Price has seen your driving, my dear, and is in dread of being overturned! And you, Miss Rivington—will you risk life and limb?'

'I understand it was you who taught Mrs Ainslowe to drive,' replied Carlotta in the same bantering tone. 'Have you no faith in your pupil?'

'Bravo, Carlotta! James knows I am a very good driver, else he would not have given me my own carriage.' Adele nodded at Carlotta. 'I thought we could drive up through the woods to the south of the house; there is a fine view from top of the hill. We will set out directly after breakfast, if you would like it.'

'I should,' said Carlotta. 'I should like it very much.'

A bright, sunny day greeted Carlotta when she awoke the following morning, but despite the promise of driving out with her hostess, there was a tiny shadow over her anticipation. Mr Woollatt might well return that day. With a sigh Carlotta slipped out of bed. The diamond ring was resting on her dressing table, a physical token of the promise she had made. She forced herself to slip it onto her finger. She should be happy; she was betrothed to a good man with a handsome fortune. If she had not met Luke—she cut off the thought. She *had* met him, nothing could change that, and nothing could change the fact that she was engaged to Daniel Woollatt. There was no going back. Therefore she must make the best of it. Perhaps if she and Luke were not in the same house, if they did not see each other every day, then it would be easier to bear. She could forget him—well, perhaps not quite forget him, but at least this crippling, aching longing might ease a little. Carlotta decided that she must persuade her aunt to take her away from Malberry. Away from Luke. The thought made her eyes prickle with hot tears, but she brushed them away, resolutely turning her thoughts to the more pleasant prospect of driving out with Mrs Ainslowe.

Adele drove the gig from the stables at a smart pace, sending up a shower of gravel as she swung sharply around the corner to bring the equipage to a halt at the front steps.

'There,' cried James, waiting on the steps beside Carlotta, 'do not say I did not warn you! My wife is a demon when she is handling the ribbons.'

Carlotta heard the affection and pride in his voice and said nothing as he helped her up into the gig and tucked the rug around her.

'Have I kept you waiting?' said Adele. 'I beg your pardon— Perkins was nowhere to be seen and Little Jones, the stable boy, was struggling to yoke poor Brigadier all on his own. But we are here now, you see.'

'Will you return to take luncheon, my love?' asked James.

'Oh, I am sure we shall be back by then.' Adele arranged the reins between her fingers. 'When do you set off for your walk around the lake?'

'As soon as we are all ready,' said James. 'But I doubt we shall make such good time as you did yesterday.'

'No. We set a very smart pace, did we not, Carlotta?'

'Well, go a little more slowly today,' he said, stepping back. 'Be careful, my love.'

Adele smiled at him. 'Am I not always? Stand aside, sir!'

With a flourish of her whip she set the team in motion. Carlotta turned to wave to Mr Ainslowe, her smile slipping a little when she spotted Luke staring out of the study window.

'Tell me, Carlotta,' said Adele. 'If you and my brother-in-law are so in love, why did you accept an offer from Mr Woollatt?'

Carlotta jumped. 'H-how did you know? We have been so careful…'

'That is what made me suspicious. You both prowl around each other, being far too rigidly correct. Oh, have no fear, I doubt if anyone else has noticed, even darling James.' Adele paused while she guided the horse out of the gates and turned away from the village to drive up the hill. 'Perhaps it is being so in love oneself that makes one especially aware—or perhaps it is being with child.'

'You are—oh, Adele, that is wonderful news!'

'Yes, isn't it?' she laughed. 'That is why James is so concerned that I should be careful. He would have me lie abed all day if he could, but I am not such a poor creature.'

'But you will drive steadily, will you not?'

'Pho.' Adele laughed at her. 'I will not overturn you, I promise. But you have not told me why you are marrying Daniel Woollatt.'

Carlotta had twisted slightly in her seat with her right hand resting along the back rail, but as the gig swayed alarmingly on the uneven road she hooked her arm around the rail and held on tightly.

'Well?'

'It is a very good match.' This sounded lame even to Carlotta, and she added, 'He is extremely rich.'

'But you love Luke.'

'Yes.'

'And what does he say about this?'

Carlotta felt the hot tears burning her eyes. She swallowed the lump in her throat and tried to speak lightly. 'H-he agrees it is a good idea.'

'The devil he does!' exclaimed Adele in a most unlady-like manner.

'He told me so,' said Carlotta miserably. 'When...when he knew Mr Woollatt was going to make me an offer.'

'Then he is a fool, and I shall tell him so to his head!'

'Oh, no, pray, Adele, you must say nothing of this. We are agreed that it is too late, and we must forget each other.' She sniffed. 'L-Luke will soon find himself someone else.'

'Unfortunately, my dear, I am afraid that is more than likely,' said Adele. 'Luke has something of a reputation.'

'I know.' Carlotta gulped back a sob.

'You could cry off from your engagement.'

Carlotta shook her head. 'I have thought of that, but it would not do. I would be labelled a jilt; my aunt and uncle would be mortified and Mama and Papa would be very disappointed in me. There would be gossip; everyone would learn about m-my parents and I should not be welcome in polite society.

'But I could bear all that, I really could, if only... You see, if Luke married me, everyone would blame *him*, too. We w-would be outcasts. That would not trouble me very much, because I have not lived in society very long, but I could not ask Luke to give up everything he has known. It would make him unhappy, and he would end up hating me for it.'

Carlotta gazed ahead, considering her future and unappre-ciative of the bright sunshine or beautiful woodland that sur-rounded them.

'I must say it is a pretty coil,' confessed Adele after a moment. 'I was very fortunate, you see. I fell in love with James the first moment we met; although he was a younger son and not the most important of my suitors, Papa could see how much in love we were and eventually gave his consent.' She sighed, but after a moment she turned her head to give Carlotta a reassuring smile. 'You must not be cast down, my love. I am a firm believer that everything happens for the best. Something may yet turn up. And if it does not, and you do marry Mr Woollatt, well, just think how much pin money you will have to spend!'

Carlotta did not find much to comfort her in this thought, but she nodded and tried to enjoy the drive. They had emerged from the trees and were now travelling through open grazing land towards the summit of the hill. As the road levelled out, Adele gave an expert little flick of the whip and the horse picked up its pace.

'There are some outstanding views up here,' she said. 'They will make you forget—'

The sentence was never finished. The gig gave a sickening lurch. Carlotta's arm was still hooked around the back rail and instinctively her fingers clung on as the carriage dropped away from her. Her arm was almost wrenched from its socket; the gig tipped onto its side and Adele tumbled past her.

Chapter Fourteen

Carlotta scrabbled to find some ledge for her feet since the footwell of the gig was now tilted at a steep angle. She managed to push her toes against the side wall of the carriage and relieve some of the strain upon her arm, but her tentative foothold was shaken as the gig shuddered, then lurched again. She looked up to see that the horse was trapped in the tangle of harness and gig shafts and was frantically lunging forward, trying to pull free. She was not that far from the ground, and thought she might well be able to jump down if the gig would remain still. She was aware of voices, heavy footsteps running up. Turning her head, she saw one man drop his shepherd's crook and run to the horse's head, calming the frightened animal. Another was reaching up for her.

'It's all right, miss, I've got you!' Strong hands were around her, trying to lift her down.

'Wait, wait—my hand!'

The muscles of her right arm had seized up and would not obey her brain. With a great effort she managed to uncurl her fingers from the back rail and ease her arm free. She felt herself being lifted bodily from the carriage.

'Adele,' she panted. 'Where is Mrs Ainslowe?'

'Let's be sure you's taken no hurt first, miss,' her rescuer replied in a soft country drawl. 'Can 'ee stand on yer own? Good. Now then, let's look to yer friend.'

'Adele!'

Carlotta staggered a few steps and fell on her knees beside the still form stretched out on the grass verge. Adele had lost her bonnet and was lying on her back with one hand thrown above her head. To Carlotta's terrified gaze she looked extremely pale.

'She's stunned, miss. Took a nasty tumble, I'd say.' The man scratched his head. 'We needs to get 'er to a doctor. Are you from the Court?'

'Yes, yes, we are,' said Carlotta, taking off her spencer to make a pillow for Adele's head.

'Well, I'll run down and fetch some help. T'ain't far if I goes down through the trees. Abel will stay with 'ee.'

'Aye.' The man holding the horse's head nodded slowly. 'An' I'll try to get the poor 'oss out of this tangle.'

Carlotta turned a grateful gaze upon her rescuer. 'Yes, please, fetch help as quickly as you can!'

'Don't you worry, miss, I'll be back in two shakes of a lamb's tail.'

Carlotta watched him set off at a lumbering run down the hill and he was soon lost to sight amongst the trees. The man he had called Abel was talking soothingly to the horse, at the same time quietly grappling with the buckles and straps of the harness. Carlotta struggled to her feet and fetched the rug from the gig. It had fallen to the ground when they had crashed and was lying abandoned on the track. It was only a few steps, but Carlotta felt very unsteady and she was glad to sink down again beside Adele once she had covered her with the rug. Adele stirred.

'Carlotta?'

'Hush, now. Pray be still.' Carlotta put her hand on Adele's shoulder to prevent her from rising. 'We have sent for help.'

'What happened?'

'You lost a wheel, ma'am,' called Abel.

Only then did Carlotta notice that one of the gig's wheels was lying some distance away.

'Oh, good,' murmured Adele. 'James cannot blame me for overturning us.'

'Miss'll be relieved to hear you talkin', ma'am,' continued the shepherd. 'She was afraid you was a goner.'

Adele lifted one hand and Carlotta grasped it.

'No,' said Adele with a weak smile. 'I'm not gone yet.'

Even as Carlotta squeezed her fingers, Adele's eyes closed again as she sank into unconsciousness.

Carlotta had no idea how long she sat beside her friend at the roadside. She was aware that Abel had managed to move the horse from the shafts of the carriage. Once the animal was securely tethered, the man made no attempt to approach, but remained at a respectful distance, chewing on a straw. She was glad of the summer sunshine, but the hillside was quite exposed and without her spencer the fresh breeze felt chill on her bare arms. She was aware of how quiet it was; only the whisper of the wind in the distant trees and the exuberant trill of a skylark disturbed the stillness. Then she heard the faint but unmistakable sounds of a carriage approaching at speed and a few minutes later the silence was replaced by a bewildering amount of noise and bustle. Two carriages hurtled up the hill and came to a stand, the horses stamping and blowing. James Ainslowe ran to his wife, barking commands. Carlotta tried to rise, but her trembling limbs would not work. She staggered and fell against a comfortingly solid body. She was lifted off the ground by a pair of strong arms. Raising her eyes, she found herself looking up into Luke's anxious face. He smiled down at her.

'It's all right, you are safe, *cara*.'

She snuggled her cheek against his shoulder. 'I am now,' she sighed.

* * *

Carlotta was aware of an intense disappointment when she came to her senses and found herself lying on her own bed rather than in Luke's arms. Lady Broxted hovered about her and tried to insist that she should rest until the morning, but Carlotta would have none of it. Her right arm ached quite dreadfully from being wrenched when she had clung on to the overturning gig, but she had sustained no other injury and was determined to go down to dinner. This could be the last opportunity for her to speak to Luke before Mr Woollatt's return. Surely it could not be thought improper for her to thank him for his kindness?

As she entered the drawing room, Mrs Price immediately sprang to her feet.

'Ah, dear Miss Rivington! Is this wise—should you be out of your bed?'

'Why yes, I am very well now, I assure you. I was a little shaken, but nothing serious—nothing to compare with Mrs Ainslowe. I believe she is still laid up in her room.'

Mr Price sighed and shook his head. 'Indeed she is. When Ainslowe carried her into the house she was as white as her lace, and the poor man looked exceedingly grim. As he is not here, I can only suppose that he is still with his wife—what do you say, Darvell, am I right?'

'I believe my brother intends to join us for dinner and is even now in his room, dressing.'

Carlotta observed the anxiety in Luke's face. She wanted to go to him, but Julia was urging her to sit down beside her.

'You must have been very frightened, Miss Rivington.'

'There was no time for fear, the gig collapsed so suddenly.'

'We were on the far side of the lake when we heard the news,' said Mrs Price. 'You can imagine our surprise when Lord Darvell's groom came running up to tell us what had occurred.'

'Aye,' declared Mr Price. 'By all accounts, Sir Gilbert's man was ready to dash off immediately to the rescue, but Darvell's groom insisted on fetching his master and Mr Ainslowe.'

'And a good idea it was,' nodded Mr Price. 'The carriages were ready and waiting by the time we arrived back at the house, so there was little time lost and the four of us could set off to find you.'

Carlotta frowned, trying to hold a fleeting memory. 'Were there four of you? I remember only Mr Ainslowe, and Lord Darvell…'

'Bless you, my dear, how could you be expected to know what was going on?' said Mr Price. 'Lord Fairbridge and I came along to render what assistance we could. And I dare say Sir Gilbert would have joined us, too, if he had been there.'

'I had decided to take a ramble in the woods,' explained Sir Gilbert, coming forward. 'I was never more shocked than when I returned and Mrs Price told me of the accident—' He broke off as James came in. 'Ah, Ainslowe—we were just talking about the dreadful events this morning. How is Mrs Ainslowe?'

'Sleeping.' James looked tired and strained, but he came towards Carlotta and took her hand. 'I am glad to see you are up and about, Miss Rivington. Can I assume you were not hurt in the crash?'

'I bruised my arm a little, nothing more. I trust Mrs Ainslowe has suffered no *lasting* injury?'

She raised her eyes to his face as she spoke and he seemed to understand her, for he gave a tight little smile and returned the slight pressure of her fingers.

'The doctor is hopeful, but it is too soon to tell.'

The meal dragged on. Carlotta had found herself sitting at some distance from Lord Darvell and it was not until the gentlemen came into the drawing room after dinner that she found the opportunity of speaking to him. Mrs Price had persuaded

Julia and Lord Fairbridge to sing a duet; while the little group arranged themselves around the pianoforte, Carlotta moved across the room to stand beside Luke. She dared not look up at him and could only hope her voice would tremble less than her hands, which were clasped tightly together.

'I have not been able to thank you for your assistance this morning, my lord.'

'It was my pleasure, Miss Rivington.'

The cool note in his voice brought her head up and she saw the reason for it. Mr Price was standing very close to them.

He nodded at Luke, saying cheerfully, 'I beg your pardon, my lord, if I could just reach past you and take these candles to the pianoforte—my wife needs more light to read the music…'

Luke waited until he had moved away. 'I have never been more afraid,' he murmured. 'The shepherd said one of the ladies was unconscious, but I had no idea which of you was hurt until I came upon you.'

Carlotta put one hand up to her throat. His nearness unsettled her; she found it difficult to breath and her heart was beating such a tattoo that she was sure he must hear it. They were standing in shadow now, but even so Carlotta could see the glow of desire in his eyes, feel the longing emanating from him. It was like a magnet, a force beyond her control, pulling her in. She edged closer and put out her hand. His fingers closed over hers and she trembled. Her whole body tingled, her skin felt very tender, aware of the slightest touch. They were only inches apart; she need only take one little step and she could rest against him, put her cheek on his chest and listen to his heart.

Abruptly he released her hand and stepped away. 'You must not tempt me, *cara*,' he muttered. 'If you stand too close, I cannot think properly. When I carried you to the carriage this morning, you do not know how much I wanted to keep you with me for ever. I wanted to whip up the horses and drive off with you, to take you far away from here, from everything.'

He gave a ragged sigh and walked away. Carlotta watched him through curtain of hot tears.

'How I wish you had,' she whispered sadly.

A cold, grey dawn reminded Carlotta that the summer was coming to an end. She gazed out of her window at the blanket of low cloud shutting out the morning sun. The dull scene reflected her depression. Today she must persuade her aunt to take her away from Malberry, away from everything that could remind her of Luke. With a sigh she made her way downstairs and was about to cross the hall to the breakfast room when she saw Luke coming in through a side door. She dragged up a smile. 'You are up and about early, my lord.'

'Yes. I have been in the stables, looking at the gig.'

Something in his tone caught her attention. She stared at him, frowning slightly. He hesitated, then drew her away from the breakfast room. After a quick glance at the footmen standing motionless around the hall, he escorted her to his brother's study and carefully shut the door upon them.

'When I looked at the carriage yesterday, on the hill, I was surprised that the wheel had come away so cleanly. James commissioned that gig for Adele only months ago. It is of the very latest design—you will know by now that my brother likes to have everything of the best. The gig was brought back to the stables and I have been to check: the wheel is fixed with a pin and two nuts. If Perkins was in a rush, I can imagine that he might forget to put in the pin, or to secure one of the nuts, but he would never miss all three.' He paused. 'James's coachman—Perkins—insists he went over the gig thoroughly the previous day because Adele had warned him she might want to go out at a moment's notice. Now we know Perkins left the Jones boy to fetch the gig yesterday and the lad did not remove the axle caps to check the wheel nuts and pins were in place. After all, why should he, knowing his master had already done so?'

'What—what are you saying, Luke?'

'The grass where you took your tumble is kept very short by the sheep that graze it. The men who brought the gig back found the wheel nuts, but not the pin. I think someone removed it and loosened the nuts before replacing the axle cap. It was only a matter of time before the wheel would work itself free.'

Carlotta felt the blood draining to her feet. 'You—you think it was deliberate? Someone was trying to harm Adele?'

'No, Carlotta,' said Luke slowly. 'I think someone was trying to harm *you*.'

'Oh, heavens.' Carlotta sank down on to a chair. 'You think, then, that this is connected to the attacks upon my father?'

'I do—it is too great a coincidence.'

'But *why*? What have we done?'

He shook his head. 'That I do not know, but it would appear to be the work of someone within the Court. The doors to the stable yard are locked at night; no one from outside could gain entry. It could be the same person you saw returning to the house the other morning.'

'What should I do?' Instinctively she reached out her hands.

Luke took them in a comforting grasp. 'I am not sure. I must talk to James. I wish we were not obliged to go shooting, but if we call it off it might make your attacker suspicious; he may go to ground, and I do not want that. I want to find him.' He dropped to his knees in front of her. 'Promise me you will not leave the house today. I will tell Billy to remain here. If you need anything you may send for him, but you are to stay in the house, and with your aunt, wherever possible. Do you understand?'

Carlotta gazed at him. Her heart flipped over at the anxiety she saw in his eyes. Knowing he cared so much was a tiny crumb of comfort she would squirrel away for the future. For the time when she would not see him.

He spoke again. 'Promise me, *cara*. You must stay indoors and in company.'

'I promise.'

'Good.' He rose, pulling her to her feet and into his arms. He made no attempt to kiss her, but held her tightly for a moment. She felt his mouth on her hair.

'I will not let anything happen to you, sweetheart, but we must find out who is behind this. I cannot bear the thought of sending you away from Malberry with this riddle unsolved, with the threat still hanging over you.' He drew a deep breath and resolutely put her away from him. 'You must go now. Tell no one. I will talk to James and we will decide what to do.'

'Oh, but I need to know—'

He put a finger to her lips, a rueful smile lighting his eyes. 'Hush, little termagant. We will do nothing without consulting you, never fear.'

The low cloud persisted all day, but it did not rain, and the ladies amused themselves indoors with their books, their painting and their embroidery. Carlotta found it difficult to settle to anything and in desperation she asked if she might be allowed to sit with Mrs Ainslowe for a while. The suggestion was put to Adele's dresser, who graciously agreed to let Carlotta visit her mistress while she took a short rest in the afternoon. Carlotta duly presented herself at the door of the bedchamber and entered to find Adele awake, and smiling a welcome.

'Carlotta, my dear. So my gorgon has permitted you to come and sit with me, has she? You are honoured, for she has refused admittance to everyone else.'

A slight smile softened the dresser's severe countenance. 'Now, ma'am, you know the doctor said you was to have complete rest. And you, miss—' she turned her fierce eyes to Carlotta '—you are not to be overtaxing the mistress.'

'No, no, of course she will not,' said Adele. 'She will sit here and tell me all that is going on downstairs; I shall not move a finger.' She watched as her handmaiden left the room, and then beckoned Carlotta to come closer. 'Pull up that chair beside the bed, Carlotta, where I can see you. I have been so quiet today without James, but I told him he had to leave me, for his guests could not go shooting without their host, now could they?'

'I think he would have preferred to stay here with you, ma'am.'

'Perhaps, but there is nothing he can do for me. The doctor says I shall be well again presently, but for now I am to lie very still. Not an easy thing for me, my dear. You know how much I love to be out and about. But he says it is necessary, if I am to save the baby.' Adele paused, placing her hands on her stomach. With a sigh and a smile she looked up. 'So now, my love, tell me all that is going on downstairs. Has Viscount Fairbridge proposed to little Julia yet? Has Mr Woollatt returned?'

'No, and no, ma'am, but both events are imminent.'

They talked for some time and when the conversation began to flag, Adele waved towards the table at the side of the bed.

'I have Mrs Radcliffe's story here that I would dearly like to finish, but reading makes my head ache so. Would you read to me, Carlotta? Just for a little while.'

Carlotta readily agreed and they spent a pleasant hour immersed in *The Mysteries of Udolpho*. They had just started on the second volume when Adele's formidable maidservant returned and suggested her mistress should now rest. Carlotta rose immediately, giving Adele no opportunity to argue. With a promise to return again tomorrow, if Adele should still be in her bed, Carlotta went off to take the first, finished, volume of Mrs Radcliffe's tale back to the library.

The house was very quiet and Carlotta saw no one except the statue-like footmen in the hall as she made her way to the library. It was Mr Ainslowe's orders that all rooms should be kept in readiness for his guests, and candles were already burning, casting a warm glow over the library. It was a stark contrast to the gloomy dusk that was settling outside the long windows. Carlotta paused at the door. She had spent very little time in the library and was unfamiliar with the book-lined shelves. She walked slowly around the room, reading the titles engraved on the spines. Most were learned tomes, but at the far end of the room she found what she was looking for, volumes of popular novels tumbled together on a shelf. She smiled, recognising Adele's disregard for order. She slotted the book back in amongst its fellows and turned to make her way back to the door.

As she crossed the room, the low sun burst forth from the clouds and for a brief moment it shone in through the long windows and illuminated the large canvas that dominated the far wall. It was the painting James had won from Sir Gilbert. Carlotta remembered Papa talking often of the artist, Tiepolo. He had died before Papa was even born, but she thought her father would like to know that she had seen it. As quickly as it had come, the sun disappeared again, plunging the room into comparative darkness. Carlotta picked up a branched candle-stick and moved towards the wall to study the picture. It was a classical scene: Maecenas at the feet of the Roman Emperor. Carlotta held her candles aloft, staring at the painting. She frowned. There was something very familiar about the style, the vivid colours and flowing brushwork. Stepping closer, she peered at the richly patterned cloak that tumbled from Maecenas' shoulders and filled the centre foreground of the picture. She gasped. There, nestling amongst the patterned folds, was a tiny, delicate little snail.

Carlotta stepped back, her heart and mind racing. Her overriding thought was that she must tell Luke, and quickly. She ran back to the hall and ordered one of the footmen to fetch Lord Darvell's groom. She was in the morning room finishing off her brief note when Billy knocked on the door. She ran to him, folding the paper as she went.

'You must take this to your master at once—will you be able to find him? They may still be shooting.'

The groom glanced out of the window at the heavy clouds. 'The light is fading now, miss. I reckon they might have gone back to the bathhouse by now.'

'Very well. You must hurry, but do not attract attention to yourself.'

'Best if I run down, then,' he replied, putting the note in his pocket. 'But my lord did say I was to stay here and look out for you, miss.'

'I know, but this is very important—' She broke off, glancing out of the open door. 'What was that? Is there someone out there?'

Billy stepped out into the hall and looked around. 'There's no one there, miss, only the lackeys on the far side.'

'I should have told you to come in and close the door,' Carlotta scolded herself.

'Well, no harm done, miss,' Billy reassured her. 'All the guests have gone to their rooms to prepare for their dinner, and the servants know better than to dawdle here.'

'You are right; I am stupidly nervous tonight. Very well, you must be off now.'

'But the master said—'

She shook her head at him. 'I promise I shall go to my room directly, and remain at my aunt's side for the rest of the evening. I cannot possibly come to any harm. And it is important Lord Darvell receives my message as soon as possible.' She hesitated, biting her lip. 'He might be in danger.'

Billy nodded. 'Very well, miss, I'll go now, but you promise me that you will stay with Lady Broxted.'

'Yes, yes. Now *go!*'

The dinner hour dragged by. Carlotta had no appetite for the stuffed fish or the lamb's feet prepared so carefully by Mr Ainslowe's expensive French chef, although she did take a little veal ragout. Her nerves were at full stretch: she strained her ears for any sound of an arrival and her eyes flew to the door each time it opened, which happened frequently as the servants brought in each fresh dish. Carlotta tried to calculate how long it would take Billy to find his master. Surely once Luke had read her message he would understand and be on his guard. She was struggling to give her attention to her neighbour, who was advising her to try the blackberry sauce with the apple pie, when she felt something brush her arm. Her heart leapt to her throat as she looked down to see a small, folded paper in her lap. Trembling, she dropped her napkin over the note and looked around. Who could have put the note there? Several footmen were behind her, all intent on their duties. It must have been one of them, she reasoned. Perhaps Luke had slipped unnoticed into the house and bribed one of them to pass the note to her.

The agony of sitting with the note unopened was almost unbearable, but she dare not risk detection. At last she saw the signal to withdraw, and as the ladies filed out of the dining room she excused herself and found a quiet corner where she could scan the paper unobserved. She recognised her own writing immediately: it was the note she had given Billy, but now on the bottom was a short scrawl.

Come to the bathhouse at eleven o'clock. I will wait for you. Tell no one, and avoid the main path. You must not be seen. D.

With trembling hands Carlotta pushed the note into her reticule. Her heart pounded wildly. Luke had sent for her! He had promised nothing would be decided without consulting her—*that* must be the reason for a secret meeting. Eleven o'clock—it would be very dark, but she dare not take a lantern. She would have to trust to the moon to light her way to the bathhouse. A shiver tingled down her spine at the thought of it, then she straightened her shoulders. Luke needed her—she would not let him down.

Carlotta pulled her cloak around her shoulders. Outside the stable clock was chiming the half hour. Ten thirty. She turned to the maid appointed to wait on her.

'Remember, Mary, if anyone asks for me, you must tell them I am asleep and not to be disturbed.' She slipped a silver sixpence into the girl's hand. 'Do this for me and you shall have another upon my return.'

As she opened her bedroom door she could hear the faint murmur of voices from the drawing room, where the ladies were waiting for the gentlemen to join them for supper. No one had questioned her decision to retire early, pleading a headache, but they would want to know what she was doing now, so late and out of her room. Thankfully she met no one on the back stairs and was soon standing in the darkness outside the side door.

A chill breeze had sprung up and was dispersing the cloud, allowing a pale moon to peep through. Carlotta ran swiftly through the walled garden and out into the park where she hurried to gain the cover of the trees and began the long walk down to the bathhouse. The knowledge that Luke was waiting for her spurred her on and helped her to overcome any fear of walking through the park alone. It was difficult to see the old worn path and Carlotta was forced to go carefully to avoid tripping up. She put out her hand to guide her and the diamond in Mr Woollatt's ring flashed. Quickly she pulled back her hand and buried it in the folds of her cloak. She had not gone far when she heard voices, and the scuffing of boots on the main track. In the fitful moonlight she could see little more than black shapes, but she knew it was the shooting party, on its way to the house. She shrank back into the shadow of the trees as Mr Price's laugh boomed out across the night. She waited until they had passed, then, when there was no chance that they would see her, she pressed on, anxious to reach Luke.

The square shape of the bathhouse gleamed palely in the moonlight, the columns at the entrance were silver-grey against the black shadow of the porch. She thought she could make out a dim glow from the windows, but it could have been the reflected moonlight. As soon as she reached the clearing she ran across the short grass and up the steps. The door opened easily to her touch. She stepped inside.

The bathhouse felt warm after the chill of the autumn night air. Candles in two of the wall brackets were burning, giving a soft glow to the stonework. As she entered the sudden draught made the flames flicker wildly and Carlotta stopped as the figures on the walls seemed to move. Her nerves skittered in panic even as she told herself not to be foolish.

'Luke?' She whispered his name softly and the word echoed around the room. 'Luke?'

The door closed behind her. She swung around and found herself face to face with Sir Gilbert Mattingwood.

Chapter Fifteen

As the gentlemen walked back across the park Luke wanted to stride on ahead. He had enjoyed the day, but there had always been an underlying anxiety for Carlotta. He told himself she was perfectly safe in the house with so many people around her, and Billy would be keeping watch, too, but he was eager to get back, to see her for himself. It was irksome in the extreme to have to dawdle at this slow pace.

'Not a bad day's work,' said James. 'Of course, next month we shall be able to go after pheasant, but I hope you agree we had good sport today.'

'Aye, but I wish we had not sent the cart on ahead,' grumbled Mr Price. 'I had not realised it was such a walk, and uphill, too.'

Some of the gentlemen laughed at that.

'What, sir' Lord Fairbridge grinned 'would you want to sit in the cart with the duck, partridge and snipe?'

'Better that than walk another yard in these boots,' grumbled Mr Price. 'New, you see. Decided to try that new bootmaker in Davies Street. He's a damned charlatan, for they pinch my toes like the devil! The sooner I can take off the damned things the better.'

'Well, we are nearly there now,' said James. He touched

Luke's arm. 'I like to thank the servants at the end of each day's shooting,' he murmured. 'I order a bowl of punch to be prepared for them all, but as it is—Adele—'

'I know, you are anxious to see your wife as soon as may be,' replied Luke. 'Leave it to me, brother. I will see the servants for you.'

When the party reached the house, Luke made his way directly to the servants' hall to pass on his brother's thanks. He was a little surprised that Billy was not there. He looked into the kitchen as he passed on the way out to the stable block; that too was empty save for the cook and the kitchen maid carrying a large kettle to the fire. Outside the stable yard was in darkness with only a low light showing in the carriage house. Luke crossed quickly and found James's coachman there with the stable boy affectionately known as Little Jones.

'Oh, it's you, my lord.' Perkins lifted one finger to his head in brief salute. 'We was just finishin' up here, hanging up the cleaned tack ready for another day.'

'Have you seen my groom?'

'No, my lord.'

'I seen 'im,' piped up the stable boy. 'I was fetchin' our dinner from the kitchen and 'ee was there.'

'Are you sure?'

The lad nodded. 'One of the footmen came in and said Miss Rivington was wanting 'im.' The boy cast an anxious look at the coachman, who clapped a fatherly hand on his shoulder.

'Little Jones is pretty reliable, my lord'

Luke frowned. 'Very well—I will enquire in the house.' He turned to leave but at the door he stopped. 'Oh, The master has ordered rum punch to be served to you all. It is being prepared now, in the kitchen.'

'If it's all the same to you, my lord, I won't, not after last time.' Perkins shifted uncomfortably. 'The wheel on the mistress's gig… Master has said he will turn me off if I can't do my duty. I wouldn't blame 'im, neither.' He added fiercely, 'It's never happened to me before in all my years in service. That ashamed of meself, I am…'

'Ah. I see.' Luke turned to go.

'You said it might've been a bad bottle o' rum,' said Little Jones, helpfully. ''Acos Mr Reed told you 'ee had a bad 'ead, too.'

Luke swung round. 'What was that?' His gaze swept over Perkins, whose countenance showed a mixture of anger and embarrassment. 'Well?'

'I promised 'im I'd say nothing, me lord, Reed's that afeard of his master—'

'Are you saying you were drinking with Reed the night before Mrs Ainslowe's accident? You had best tell me,' he added as Perkins hesitated.

'Reed and me, we'd been chatting, you see. He seemed a friendly sort, not high and mighty like some o' your household staff, who holds up their noses at those of us as works outside.

'Well, we found we was both partial to a game o' cards now and then, so t'other night Mr Reed brings down a pack o' cards and a bottle o' rum after dinner, and we had a few games. Only…' Perkins shrugged, his ruddy face turning a deeper shade of red. 'Well, I misremember what 'appened, me lord. Put to bed in me boots, I was, and woke up with such a fearful 'eadache there was no getting up, so when the mistress ordered the gig, Little Jones here had to get it ready.'

'An' I did me best, sir, 'onest I did,' added the boy, staring anxiously at Luke.

'Can't blame the lad for not taking off the axle hubs and checking the wheels was secure,' said Perkins. 'I told master that, when he came back from fetching the mistress. The blame is mine, though I'd swear I checked both wheels the day before.'

'And it was Reed who brought the rum?'

'Aye, me lord, but when we was both bad on it, he asked me not to tell anyone that he'd been drinkin' with me, 'cos his master would turn him off. Right scared he was.' Perkins looked anxiously at Luke. 'I wouldn't want to get 'im into trouble, me lord…'

'No…' said Luke slowly. 'No, of course not.'

Luke ran back into the house and met his brother's stately butler in the servants' passage. 'Where is Sir Gilbert's man?' he asked him tersely.

'I believe he is gone back upstairs, my lord. He has just brought his master's boots downstairs for cleaning.'

'And Miss Rivington?'

'She retired early, my lord.'

Luke went on up to the hall, where he saw his brother coming down the stairs. James smiled.

'I have just left Adele. She is much better today and is even talking of coming downstairs tomorrow… Luke? Is something wrong?'

'Come into the study and we will talk.' He followed James into the room and closed the door carefully behind him. 'I have found our villain.'

'The devil you have! Who is it?'

'Mattingwood's man, Reed. Perkins says they were drinking together the night before the gig crashed. I believe he drugged Perkins by slipping something into the bottle of rum he brought with him, then he tampered with the wheel. Perkins was the only person who might possibly go over the gig again before sending it out, and he was too sick to get out of bed.'

'That would explain the crash,' said James, 'but there is

nothing to bear out your suspicion that the target was Miss Rivington.'

Luke shrugged. 'Two attacks on Durini, then the wheel comes off the carriage bearing his daughter—that is too much of a coincidence to my mind.'

'But what in heaven's name does the man have against the family?'

'Perhaps it is not just Reed, perhaps it is his master,' said Luke slowly.

'Gil?' James gave a little snort of laughter. 'How could he possibly be involved with an artist and his family? Why, he told me he has very little interest in art—' He broke off and fixed a sudden, intense look at Luke. 'The Tiepolo?'

Luke made for the door. 'Let's go and see.'

'But, Luke, can you tell if it is real?' said James they hurried to the library. 'Have you acquired some special knowledge of art in the past few years?'

'Not exactly, but there is one thing I know to look out for.' Luke strode into the library, picked up a branch of candles and carried it across the room. Holding the candles close to the painting, he began to study it closely.

'What are we looking for?'

'Something... Ah. There it is.' He pointed 'Look there, on the cloak.'

James peered closer. 'It's some kind of snail...'

'Yes. A *lumaca*. It's Durini's mark. I remember Carlotta telling me that he used to copy paintings for visitors doing the Grand Tour. She was adamant that they were not forgeries, because he signed each one.'

James stared. 'Do you mean Mattingwood gave me a worthless painting?'

Despite his anxiety, Luke smiled. 'Not worthless, James— Durini is a fine artist.'

'But Mattingwood tricked me over a debt of honour.' James gave a low whistle. 'He would be ruined if this got out.'

'That is why he has tried to stop Durini or his daughter seeing this painting.'

James was already heading for the door. 'Very well,' he said grimly. 'Let us find him!'

As they crossed to the stairs a figure emerged from the servants' door. 'My lord!'

Luke swung round. Billy was coming towards him. His clothes were dishevelled and he was gingerly feeling the back of his head with one hand.

'What the devil has happened to you?'

'Attacked, my lord. I was on my way to the bathhouse when someone clobbered me from behind. Pushed me down a culvert, too—must have thought I would be drowned, the drain being quite full after all the recent rains, but I came round to find myself caught by my belt on a tree root.'

'I told you to stay here and look after Miss Rivington.'

'That you did, my lord, and I was doing so, but Miss Rivington insisted I bring a note to you, urgent like.' He reached into his pocket, a look of consternation growing on his bruised face. 'Funny, I know I put it in here…'

'When did she give you the note?' asked Luke, a chilling suspicion growing within him.

'Just before dinner, sir. I was to find you and give you the note as soon as I could.'

'Damnation!' Luke raced up the stairs, James and Billy following. 'Tell me which is Carlotta's room,' he demanded as James caught up with him.

'Is she not in the drawing room with the ladies?'

'No, Wicks told me she retired early. Will you show me her room?'

James looked at him for a long moment, then silently led the way towards a door at the far end of the west wing. Luke knocked softly. After a few moments Carlotta's maid peeped around the door.

'I must speak to Miss Rivington.'

Perhaps it was Luke's brusque tone that caused the maid to look so frightened, but it roused his worst fears.

'She—she is asleep, my lord. I—'

Ignoring her feeble protests, he walked into the room. A few candles glowed about the room, but in the dim light it was clear that the bed had not been slept in. He turned back to the maid. 'Where is she?'

'I—I…'

'Come, girl, you must tell us what you know,' said James, following Luke into the room.

The maid shook her head, twisting her apron nervously in her hands. 'She didn't say, sir, only that she was going out and I was to tell anyone who asked that she was asleep.'

Luke stared at his brother, who nodded.

'We must talk to Reed.'

Seconds later Luke was banging on another bedroom door. Reed's ferret-like face appeared.

'Sir Gilbert is sleeping, my lord. I must ask you to—'

He got no further. Luke pushed past him, walked up to the bed and threw back the hangings. The bed was empty. He heard a scuffle behind him and found James and Billy struggling with the valet. They forced Reed onto a chair.

'The fellow tried to make a dash for it,' grunted James, holding him down.

'Because he knows you will want to thrash him for trying to kill your wife,' retorted Luke.

'No, no, it wasn't me,' squeaked Reed, alarmed by the ugly look on James's face.

'Oh, I think we can safely say it was you,' said Luke, dragging his arms roughly around the back of the chair.

'No, no, it was not my idea—I was o-ordered to do it.'

'Then you'd better tell me everything, if you want to save some of your hide,' growled James menacingly.

The valet licked his lips, looking fearfully at the three men standing over him.

'It—it was my master. He—he heard that Mrs Ainslowe had ordered the gig for the morning and he t-told me what he wanted me to do.'

'And the attack on Signor Durini in Malberry village?' asked Luke.

The valet shook his head. 'No, I swear, sir, that was not me—Sir Gilbert came on ahead of me.'

'What about the fire at the Durinis' cottage?' barked James.

Reed hesitated, as if deciding on what to say, and James took a step towards him.

'You came back through the walled garden just before dawn,' said Luke. 'Do not deny it—you were seen.'

'All right, it *was* me. But I was acting on orders. S-Sir Gilbert said he wanted Durini scared off. He didn't want him to come to the house again.'

'Because the Tiepolo is a copy,' growled James.

The valet nodded miserably. 'The master purchased it from the *signor* in Rome several years ago.'

'And he found out that Miss Rivington is Durini's daughter,' Luke persisted. 'Well, man, how did he do that?'

James put his hand to his head. 'It was that day on the stairs,' he muttered. 'When I gave Carlotta the note from her father— Reed was there. You overheard us.'

Reed swallowed hard. 'Aye. Sir Gilbert pays me well for any information I can bring him.'

'So where is Mattingwood now?' Luke demanded.

'He—he's still at the bathhouse.' Reed's ferret-like eyes darted to Luke's face. 'Waiting for Miss Rivington. She thinks she is going there to meet you.'

The chill that had been growing in Luke seemed to sharpen into ice.

'Billy,' he said quietly, 'go to the stables and saddle a horse for me, quick as you can.'

'Make that two,' called James as Billy ran out of the room.

Luke pulled loose the cord from the bed-curtains and began to tie Reed's hands to the chair back.

'I'll call a couple of my people to watch him until we return,' said James, going to the door.

'Thank you. And, James—fetch your pistols.'

Chapter Sixteen

'I—I was not expecting to see you here, Sir Gilbert.' Carlotta tried to sound innocent and bewildered. Could she convince him she was involved in a romantic intrigue? She thought not, since he showed no surprise at her presence. She began to talk rapidly. 'I thought everyone would be gone by now. Were you delayed?' She glanced at his stockings and buckled shoes. 'L-looking for your boots, perhaps? One can hardly walk back through the park without them, can one?'

'Reed has taken my boots back to Malberry Court. By now they will be lined up with all the others, waiting to be cleaned.' His growing smile made her shiver. 'Everyone will assume I am in my bed.'

'R-really?' She began to back away. 'I—um—I told my maid I was coming here to collect something. She will be anxious if I am not back soon—'

He laughed at her.

'You are the most delightful little liar, Miss Rivington. We both know you did no such thing. The note said "tell no one." You will have followed the instructions to the letter.'

Carlotta stared at him. 'How do you know what was in the note?'

'Because Reed took the original off Darvell's groom and brought it to me. *I* wrote the reply.'

Her heart dropped. There had been a faint, unacknowledged hope that Luke might rescue her, but now that hope died. She swallowed painfully. 'What is it you want with me?'

'Not your virtue, if that thought is making you clutch your cloak around you so tightly. Unfortunately, you know my secret.'

'Secret?'

'Come, come, Miss Rivington—or should I call you Miss Durini? Let us pretend no longer. You of all people should know that the Tiepolo is a copy.'

'Yes…but it is not so very bad; I dare say if you explained everything—'

'Explain it? I have *cheated*, my dear—cheated on a debt of honour. The *ton* would have no mercy, I should be shunned, no member of society would acknowledge me, and how long do you imagine it would be before my creditors started hounding me? I would be ruined.'

'But no one else need know of it,' she said quickly, 'I will say nothing—'

'I am afraid, my dear, I cannot take that chance. You must be disposed of.'

'You—you would not dare,' she whispered, still moving away from him.

'Oh, I would.'

'But it will do you no good. Sooner or later someone else will notice, too.'

'Before that happens I hope to have the picture back in my possession. I am sure I can persuade Ainslowe to sell it back to me.'

Carlotta shook her head. 'I doubt it; Mrs Ainslowe has already told you she has grown to like it.'

'That is, of course, a minor problem, but she is not yet recovered. I think if Mrs Ainslowe were to take a turn for the worse, her husband might be far too overset to care about a mere painting—in fact, he might be pleased to be rid of it, if it reminds him of his wife. Yes, that might work out very well. At the time I thought it a pity that she should be in the gig with you, but now I see it could be an advantage.'

'So the crash was your doing?'

'Yes. I was waiting in the woods, ready to administer the final blow, should either of you survive, but those damn fool shepherds were up on the hill and decided to come so gallantly to your rescue. But there is no one here this time to rescue you.'

Carlotta's lip curled. 'You are insane if you think you will get away with it.'

'But I *am* getting away with it. The attack on Durini has been blamed on gypsies, and as for the gig—Ainslowe's coachman was too drunk to do his job. If he were my man, I would have turned him off immediately for such gross ineptitude.'

An icy chill spread through Carlotta as she listened to Sir Gilbert. He was rambling on, and she began to think he was truly deranged. She forced herself to consider her situation. Mattingwood stood before the entrance, blocking her escape. She guessed there would be a smaller, servants' door beyond the warm room. If she could only reach the back room, then perhaps she could get out into the park. She turned on her heel and ran, heading for the inner door. She felt the tug as Mattingwood caught at her swirling cloak, but the ties were loosened and it slipped easily from her shoulders. The door was only feet away, if she could get through and slam it shut—it would give her precious seconds to find a way out.

'Got you!' A strong hand gripped her shoulder, yanking her backwards.

'Let me go! Help! Help me!'

'Scream all you like, there is no one to hear you.' He pinioned her arms at her sides and held her against his chest.

As she stared up at him, she saw the look in his eyes change. 'Hmm, shame to kill you before I have sampled your charms.' He leered down at her. His hold tightened and his head came down towards her. She turned her face away, squirming as she felt his lips on her skin. She tried to struggle, but he was too strong for her, pulling her closer until she could feel his body pressing against hers. Revulsion and fear shuddered through her. She stopped struggling, gathering her strength for one final, desperate push.

'That's right,' his voice was muffled as he nuzzled her neck. 'Relax and enjoy it, my dear.'

His arms slid around her, binding her to him. She turned her head against his; the smell of the oil on his blond hair made her feel sick, but she ignored it. She reached round and sank her teeth into his ear. He yelled with pain.

Savage satisfaction raged through her and she fought desperately to break away. She freed one hand and clawed at his cheek, her nails drawing blood before he pinioned her arms again and dragged her with him into the plunge pool.

The shock of the cold water paralysed Carlotta, but it took only a moment to realise that Sir Gilbert's vice-like grip on her had slackened. She kicked out and felt the stone steps beneath her feet. She struggled towards them, but before she could crawl out of the pool he had grabbed her again, pulling her back into the deeper water. She scrabbled wildly, her legs entangled by the clinging skirts of her gown. Sir Gilbert's weight was on her shoulders, pushing her down. She ducked away from him and came up to the surface, gasping. Then he lunged at her once more and forced her head under the water again.

Carlotta's lungs were bursting, burning with the effort to hold her breath. She knew it must end soon. The blood was pounding in her ears. She began to exhale, allowing the air to slip from her body. She could see the bubbles rising past her face. Soon she would have to breathe in and the cold, deadly water would fill her up. She would drown. She tried to hold back, but it was impossible; the last of the air escaped her and the empty, burning void of her lungs screamed for her to take a breath. *Give in*, said the tiny voice in her head. *Give in—a moment's pain and it will be all over*. She knew she was weakening as the blood and water pounded in her ears. It was too much effort to fight any longer.

Then, miraculously, the weight above her was gone. Strong hands were lifting her, dragging her out of the water. She lay face down on the cold stone, coughing and gasping. When at last she dared to open her eyes, she saw she was lying in a pool of water that was expanding outwards as more dribbled from her clothes and hair.

'Just in time, thank God.' Luke's voice was shaking, but his hands were firm and comforting on her shoulders as he helped her to sit up. Raising her eyes, she saw Sir Gilbert on his knees with James standing over him, a pistol in one hand. James met her eyes and gave her a little smile.

'Thank heavens we did not have to jump into the pool to rescue you.'

She shifted around to look at Luke. 'How—how did you know?'

'Billy came to find me—'

Sir Gilbert raised his head. 'Impossible. He's dead.'

'No, he is very much alive,' retorted Luke, nodding towards the door where Billy stood, legs slightly apart, looking belligerent. 'Reed thought he had disposed of him, but my man is not so easy to kill.'

Carlotta reached up to touch Luke's hand. 'I wrote a note. I thought you had sent for me...' Her voice trailed off and she began to shiver.

Luke helped her to her feet. 'There will be time for talking later. Take Mattingwood back to the house and secure him, James. Billy will help you.'

'You are not coming?'

Luke swung Carlotta up into his arms. 'No. I must get her warm, and quickly. I do not care if that villain catches a deadly chill, but I'll not risk Carlotta. Tell her maid to pack up some dry clothes for her mistress and send them down in the carriage.'

James nodded. 'Very well, brother.' He reached out to grab the back of Sir Gilbert's collar. 'Come along. It's Newgate for you, my man—and a fate far worse than being shunned by society, I think.'

He dragged Sir Gilbert to his feet while Luke carried Carlotta through the doors to the inner room. It was very dark, only moonlight from the high windows and a faint glow from the dying fire illuminating the furniture, but Luke did not hesitate. He walked swiftly across the room and gently laid Carlotta down on one of the couches.

'First, we need some light, then we must get you out of those wet clothes.'

Dazed, Carlotta watched as he pushed a taper into the embers and proceeded to light the candles. Soon a golden glow illuminated the disordered room. It was still littered with the remains of the gentlemen's dinner party. Dishes, bottles and glasses covered the side tables. Luke moved to one of the chests and pulled out a large bathsheet and a brightly patterned dressing gown. 'Here, take these. I will make up the fire; we shall soon have you dry again—and me.' He grinned as he dragged off his frockcoat and threw it over a chair. 'Just carrying you in here has soaked through my coat.'

Carlotta struggled with the buttons of her spencer while he crouched before the hearth, feeding the glowing embers with kindling and small logs.

'That's better.'

She glanced at the flames leaping upwards in the hearth. She had managed to remove her spencer, but was still struggling to unlace her sodden boots. She was shaking so much that her fingers would not work; they felt clumsy and terribly weak. Luke came across to sit beside her.

'Here, let me do that.' Gently he lifted her foot onto his knee, deftly loosened the laces and tossed the boot on to the floor. 'I have had years of practice at removing a lady's clothing,' he said lightly, lifting her other foot. 'One learns it from an early age, if one aspires to be a rake.' The second boot followed its partner to the floor. He glanced up, a hint of a smile in his eyes, but she could not respond to it. Silently he pushed aside the wet skirts and gently moved his hand up to remove the silk stocking. She noticed how his fingers trembled as he tugged at her garter, but they did not linger. As soon as the ribbon came loose he quickly stripped off her pink stockings. 'Can you stand?' he asked her gently. 'We need to remove your gown.'

Obedient to the pressure of his hand on her arm, she rose. 'I am afraid I have ruined the couch,' she murmured, looking down at the damp mark where she had been sitting.

'It makes no odds, there are plenty more in here. Turn around for me.'

Soon gown, stays and chemise were all removed and Carlotta was wrapped in the heavy brocade dressing gown. It was much too big for her and crumpled in thick folds around her feet.

Luke removed the remaining pins from her hair and spread it over her shoulders. He paused, a smile tugging at one corner of his mouth. 'You look a veritable urchin, Miss Rivington.'

For the first time that evening Carlotta managed a little smile.

'You are still shivering.' Luke pushed her gently down onto the rug. 'Sit there, the heat will soon warm you.'

She looked up at him. 'You will not leave me?'

He hesitated, then dropped down beside her. 'I am here as long as you need me.' He put his hands on her shoulders and, twisting her away from him, began to comb his fingers through her hair, lifting and separating the tresses so that they splayed across her back. Carlotta sighed. The combined effects of the fire and Luke's gentle caresses began to relieve the tension in her muscles. She could even think about the events of the evening.

'So Sir Gilbert was responsible for all the horrid things that have happened?'

'Yes. He attacked your father and sent his man to set fire to their house and to loosen the wheel on the gig. Reed confessed it to us when we went looking for you.'

She sighed. 'All because of a painting. And he was willing to—to kill rather than lose face?'

'Mattingwood lost what little fortune he had at the gaming tables and now exists on the goodwill of his fellows. To be pronounced a fraudster would ruin him.'

She began to shake again. 'D-despicable man.'

His hands rested on her shoulders. 'He is gone now, *cara*. You are safe.'

'I know it.' She dropped her cheek on his hand and rubbed it gently, closing her eyes. Luke's grip tightened. He was very close behind her, so close that when she leaned back she found herself resting against him, the ruffles of his shirt pressing on her hair. She felt rather than heard his ragged sigh.

'Carlotta.' His breath was warm on her cheek. 'Carlotta, I—what the devil is that noise?'

Carlotta, too, heard a commotion in the outer room—voices and swift, heavy footsteps, growing ever closer. The door flew open and she smothered a gasp. There in the doorway stood Daniel Woollatt.

Chapter Seventeen

'In heaven's name, what are you doing here?' demanded Luke, helping Carlotta to her feet.

Mr Woollatt pointed at Carlotta, a look of horror on his face. 'More to the point, my lord—why is Miss Rivington dressed in that—that—?'

'It is a gentleman's dressing gown,' explained Carlotta. 'My own clothes are too wet, you see.'

James slipped into the room, carrying a portmanteau. 'It is as I told you, Woollatt. Mattingwood tried to drown Miss Rivington.' He gave his brother an apologetic look. 'Woollatt arrived just as I got back, Luke. He insisted upon coming with me.'

Luke nodded and looked again at Mr Woollatt. 'I am sorry, then, that you had to return to such bad news.'

'I was never more shocked in my life,' said Mr Woollatt heavily. He was still staring at Carlotta. 'You came down here *alone*?'

Carlotta found herself blushing. 'It was very foolish of me, I know, but thankfully Mr Ainslowe and Lord Darvell arrived in time—'

'Ainslowe tells me you thought you were meeting Darvell here.'

'Yes, I had written a note, you see—'

'A note?' Even in the candlelight she could see the vein in

Woollatt's temple was standing out. He was clearly very annoyed. 'What in heaven's name possessed you to do such a thing? You are an unmarried lady, you should not be writing notes to a gentleman. One, moreover, of Lord Darvell's reputation.'

Carlotta blinked. 'It was very urgent; I needed to tell him—'

'You should have gone to your aunt and explained the situation. And then to compound your folly by stealing out to keep an assignation—!'

Carlotta stared at him. A sharp retort arose to her lips, but she felt the pressure of Luke's hand on her shoulder.

He said coldly, 'Surely at this stage you should be expressing your relief that Miss Rivington is safe.'

'Well, I am thankful for that, of course, but such unbecoming behaviour—I am deeply shocked.' He shook his head, a look of distaste twisting his countenance. 'Not only that—Ainslowe was obliged to tell me of…your parentage.'

Carlotta's head went up at that. 'Indeed?' And just what is wrong with my *parentage*?'

'I do not think you need me to tell you,' retorted Mr Woollatt. 'A runaway match, and to an artist, no less! I must say, madam, I think you have been less than honest with me.'

Luke took a step forward. 'Miss Riv—Miss Durini's lineage may be a little unusual, but it is perfectly respectable. Lord Broxted would not be sponsoring her if he was in any doubt of it.'

'I am well aware of that!' replied Mr Woollatt testily. 'But there is something repellent about the way this matter has been handled. What my mother will say when I tell her—and it will have to be explained to her—I dread to think.'

Carlotta heard Luke's angry hiss, saw his hands form themselves into fists and she quickly touched his arm, giving him the tiniest shake of her head.

'You are quite right, Mr Woollatt,' she said quietly, stepping forward. 'It would have been much better if I had been honest with you from the outset. I have no doubt that your mother would be most distressed to learn the truth about my—my family. Indeed, I am sure she would find such a connection most abhorrent. It is not to be thought of. Perhaps it would be best if you told her that it had all been a misunderstanding, that there is no engagement.' She drew the diamond ring from her finger and held it out to him.

There was a long silence. Carlotta knew that Luke, James and Mr Woollatt were staring at her and it took all her will-power to remain still, her arm outstretched. At last, with a little nod, Mr Woollatt reached out and took the ring. It was only then that Carlotta realised she had been holding her breath. Now she exhaled as quietly as she could, hoping it would not sound too much like a sigh of relief.

'Perhaps we were a little hasty,' muttered Mr Woollatt. 'But all is not lost, nothing has been announced yet. We will take a little time to consider.' He pursed his lips and looked thoughtful. 'Perhaps next Season I shall bring my mother to town and introduce you to her. Naturally, she will find it hard to forgive you for crying off, but once you are acquainted, and if you behave with becoming modesty, I have no doubt she will warm to you in time.'

She forced a smile and was grateful to be spared a reply when James stepped forward, saying in a hearty voice, 'Well, then, if that's settled I think we should all drive back to the house. I have dry clothes for you here in this bag, Miss Riv—I mean, Miss Durini.'

Luke took the portmanteau. 'You go on, James, and take Woollatt with you. Miss Durini is still very pale. I would not risk taking her into the night air just yet. You may send the carriage down later to collect us.'

A look passed between the two brothers; Carlotta saw it and

a little voice in her head urged her to protest, to say that she was perfectly well enough for the short journey to the house. But it was a very *little* voice and easily silenced. James was already at the door.

'Yes, of course. Come along, Woollatt. Come back to the Court with me. I have a fine cognac in my study that is just the thing for these occasions.' He ushered Woollatt out of the door before him.

'James!'

'Yes, Luke?'

'Do not rush to send the carriage back.'

James looked towards Carlotta.

She reached up to touch the dark locks curling over her shoulders. 'It would be most unwise for me to venture out of doors with my hair still wet.'

His knowing grin made her cheeks burn. 'As you wish, then.'

Carlotta did not move. She listened to the voices dying away, heard the outer door slam, then there was silence. At length Luke spoke to her.

'You are very pale.'

'Yes.'

'If I pull a chair closer to the fire, will you sit down?'

She nodded, and watched him drag a velvet-covered sofa to the very edge of the rug.

'This might help.' He went across to the side table and poured her a glass of wine from one of the open bottles. 'The servants will not come in until it is light. We may as well make use of what is here.' He came back and sat beside her, handing her the glass. 'Now, drink it.'

His arm was about her shoulders. It seemed the most natural thing in the world to lean back against him.

'Your hair would dry quicker if you were to kneel before the fire again.'

'But this is so much more comfortable.' She took a sip from the glass. The wine was dark and warm and tasted of berries. 'Do you think he will?'

'What?'

'Introduce me to his mama next Season.'

'Very likely, but you will be Lady Darvell by then.'

Carlotta was in the act of taking another sip of wine and choked. She was obliged to hand the glass to Darvell, who placed it carefully down on the floor beside the sofa.

'Are—are you asking me to marry you?' she asked when she could command her voice.

'No, my sweet life, I am informing you that we will be married, even if I have to drag you screaming to the altar.'

Her lips twitched. 'What about my—um—unfortunate birth?'

'There is nothing unfortunate about your birth. Your father is a great artist. I only hope he will think me worthy of his daughter. I have very little fortune, as you have reminded me on several occasions.'

She blushed at that. 'It was very bad of me to throw that up at you. I am ashamed of myself.'

His arm tightened around her. 'I had hurt you. I did not understand how much.'

'That day last summer…' She began to play with the cord of her dressing gown. 'Did you—were you going to propose to me?'

'Yes, until I heard Broxted offer to take you away with him. I thought you deserved a taste of society.'

A great wave of unhappiness rushed through her. She bowed her head. 'I was so miserable! I d-did not wish to go and live with my uncle. I—I thought you did not l-love me.'

With something very like a growl he gripped her shoulders, pulling her round to face him. 'Not love you—do you know what it cost me to leave Malberry that day? I felt as though I was cutting out my own heart!'

Carlotta looked up. His eyes scorched her; she trembled under the intensity of his look. She wanted to reach out to him, to pull him closer and feel his lips on hers but he continued to hold her at arm's length, to subject her to that burning gaze. 'I left Malberry and buried myself on my estates, taking charge of them as I should have done years ago. I wanted to be prepared, so that when Broxted brought you to town I would have something more to offer you than a mountain of debts. And I succeeded, too. Darvell Manor is beginning to pay its way, the land is in good heart, the tenants prospering—but all the time I was there I lived in dread that you might find someone else, that I would be too late.'

Carlotta blinked rapidly, determined not to cry. 'There was never anyone else,' she said simply. She reached up and gently touched his cheek. 'I have never loved anyone but you, Luke.'

He turned his face towards her hand, pressing his lips to the palm, then in one swift movement, he gathered her into his arms and kissed her.

All Carlotta's pent-up longing of the past twelve months was released. She flung her arms around his neck and kissed him back hungrily, responding to the demands of his mouth, her lips parting willingly to allow his tongue to explore ever deeper. Her body pressed itself against him and they slid from the sofa until they were kneeling together on the rug. Luke broke away, but only to ease her down on to her back, all the time holding her gaze, mesmerising, willing her to trust him. She answered him with a tremulous smile and he kissed her again, but this time it was slow and languorous, melting away the tensions in her body. His teeth grazed her bottom lip and she almost groaned at the intense, sweet desire that welled up inside her.

Luke tugged at the cord around her waist and the dressing gown fell free. She trembled as he touched her naked waist. Gently he moved his hand upwards, smoothing over her ribs and on until he was cupping her breast, which tightened beneath his fingers. His thumb began to circle the nipple, and a wave of pure heat began to build within her. Her bones seemed to melt as she arched her back, offering herself up to him. He kissed her chin, then her throat, his tongue leaving a burning line on her skin as it trailed downwards. His hand was still fondling one breast, and when his mouth fastened over the other she gasped at the unexpected surge of pleasure. His tongue circled the taut bud at its peak, causing the wave of heat that had been building inside her to grow stronger, threatening to overwhelm her. So intoxicating were the sensations he was awaking in her that as she felt his hand moving down over her belly she felt only growing excitement. Her eyes flew open as his fingers moved between her legs, easing her apart. She was very hot down there, and moist. Her body was pulsing, opening to receive him. She had never felt so out of control before, but there was no panic; Luke was holding her, his hand gently stroking her; and her body responded of its own accord to the rhythm of his caresses.

Sighing deeply, Carlotta opened her eyes for a moment. She looked up at the painted walls of the room. Suddenly the pictures made sense to her, the men and women touching each other, pleasuring each other. Her eyes dwelled on one particular couple: the woman was crouched between the man's legs, her head bowed over him while he lay with his head thrown back in ecstasy at her touch. Gently Carlotta pulled Luke's head from her breast. Immediately those pleasuring fingers on her body stilled and he looked at her, a question in his eyes.

'You are still dressed, sir.' Was this her voice she could hear? It was unfamiliar, deeper, richer. An exultant wave of wanton happiness bubbled up inside her. She tugged at his shirt, helping him to pull it over his head, then with eager hands she unbuttoned the fall flap of his breeches.

Luke gave a shaky laugh. 'Careful, sweetheart. There is no rush.'

Oh, but there is, she thought, her groin aching for him to touch her again with those magic fingers. As he slipped off the rest of his clothes she struggled free of the brocade dressing gown, wondering at her daring as she lay before him, naked. Luke was on his knees, staring down at her.

'Is—is anything wrong, my lord?' A little doubt shook her.

'Nothing is wrong, sweetheart. You are so very beautiful.'

She reached out for him, but he caught her hands.

'If you want me to stop, if you want to wait until our wedding night for our first full union, you must tell me now.' He added with an attempt at humour, 'I can cool off in the plunge pool.'

His voice was unsteady and Carlotta's heart swelled with love at his concern for her. She pulled one hand free and reached up to place her palm on his smooth cheek. 'You held back once before and I almost lost you,' she said softly.

Still he did not move. 'After this there will be no going back,' he warned her. 'You will be mine, body and soul.'

'And will that be the same for you, my lord?'

'I am already yours, Carlotta.'

His slow smile reassured her and, when she saw how aroused he was, her desire returned to fever pitch. She pulled him down to her and kissed him, but even as he leaned into her she twisted around, pushing him on to his back. The surprise in his eyes gave her another rush of pleasure. She began to kiss him, her hands caressing his body, then, remembering his effect on her, she began to work her way downwards, planting gentle kisses on his throat and the hard smooth skin of his chest. His long, slow sigh made her feel all-powerful. She revelled in the taste of his flesh, the enticing mixture of spicy, aromatic fragrance and clean male skin that inflamed her senses. She explored him with her hands and her eyes, marvelling at this male body that was as beautiful, exciting and strange to her as a foreign land. The crisp hair below his navel tickled her as she kissed his flat stomach while her hands continued to caress him. She heard Luke gasp. He gave a little groan and with an exultant laugh she glanced up again at the wall-painting. She ran her tongue around her lips. It was only fair that she should give Luke as much pleasure as he had given her.

Luke moaned softly as she applied her mouth to him. She heard his endearments, little words of instruction. Suddenly he was pulling her away, rolling her over on to her back. 'No more for me,' he murmured thickly. 'We will finish this together.'

Luke's mouth captured her lips again and once again his fingers slid down to find that magic spot. Her hips tilted up to meet him, welcoming his touch. He eased himself over her and she opened for him, eager now to receive him. She gave a little gasp as he entered her and he moved with slow, steady movements, stroking her gently. He watched her closely until she began to move with him. He restrained himself, curbing his own desires until she was gasping, her body arching, beyond her control. Carlotta threw back her head, her lips parted slightly as she clung to him, her fingers digging into his shoulders. Only then did Luke allow himself to give the final push, to drive into her, uttering her name as they clung together for a final moment of intense, shuddering ecstasy. They collapsed together on the rug, breathing heavily. The fire had died back to a golden, glowing mass, enveloping them in its comforting warmth. Luke rolled onto his back beside her. He reached for her hand, threading his fingers through hers.

'I never expected anything so wonderful,' he murmured.

'Was I…did I please you?'

He raised himself on one elbow and looked into her eyes, his own glowing. 'You were…magnificent.'

He kissed her, but when he broke away she chuckled. 'I followed the paintings.' She pointed to the walls.

'The devil you did!' Luke laughed and kissed her again. 'Perhaps your father will paint these scenes in our bedroom at Darvell Manor. Would you object to that?'

'If it is what you want, my lord.'

He ran a finger over her lips and trailed it gently down between her breasts. 'No, I want only you, night after night!' He grinned at her. 'We must be married by special licence, as soon as possible. I cannot bear to sleep alone after this.'

She touched his cheek. 'Nor I, my lord.'

He kissed her gently, his naked body hardening as it rested against hers. 'You see the effect you have on me?' he murmured, nibbling her ear. 'After tonight your aunt and uncle will keep you well away from me.'

She put her hand down to caress him and felt a soaring elation as he responded to her touch. She drew him closer. 'Then let us not waste a moment, my lord,' she whispered.

Chapter Eighteen

On a bright, spring morning, Lord Darvell's elegant travelling carriage swept through the gates of Malberry Court. Unable to contain herself, Carlotta leaned out of the window.

'We should be able to see the house soon… There it is! Can you see it, Luke?'

'I see something I like much better.' He caught her around the waist and pulled her back.

She collapsed onto his lap, laughing. 'Behave yourself, my lord.'

He kissed her, causing a bolt of excitement to shoot through her. Would she ever become immune to his touch? Carlotta hoped not.

'How can I behave myself, my lady, when you look so adorable?'

Carlotta settled herself back beside him and made her voice suitably severe. 'Well, you must try, Luke. Your brother will not think us respectable enough to be godparents for little James.'

Luke gave a mock scowl, but as the carriage pulled up at the steps of Malberry Court he jumped out and turned to help her alight, every inch the respectable husband, as James came hurrying out to meet them.

'You have made good time,' he said, gripping his brother's

hand. He turned to greet Carlotta, kissing her cheek and giving her an admiring glance. 'You are looking very well, my dear. Am I to take it my wicked brother is looking after you?'

'Alas, sir, he abuses me quite dreadfully.'

'Baggage!' Luke grinned. 'Tell me truthfully, James—does she look like a neglected wife?'

'No. In fact, you both look very pleased with yourselves! Have you been to town yet?'

'No. As you know we went to Rome directly after the wedding—my father-in-law wanted to show me off to all his relatives!'

'And why not?' declared Carlotta. 'He is very proud of his new son—a baron, no less!'

Luke grinned at her and kissed her hand. 'Since then we have been at Darvell Manor. I now take my responsibilities as a land-owner very seriously.'

'Aye, and about time, too! Come along in—Adele is in her room with the baby, but she has instructed me to bring you both to her.'

'How is she?' asked Carlotta as James led them through the hall.

'In good health. You will remember I was a trifle anxious when she decided she would not have a wet nurse for the baby, but you will see that they are both thriving.' He led them up the stairs and into the main bedchamber. 'Here you are, my love, I have brought them straight up to you, as you see—they have not even had the chance to put off their coats.'

Adele was reclining on a daybed, wearing a blue satin wrap and gently rocking the cradle at her side. She smiled and held out her hands to them.

'Carlotta, my love—and Luke! Come and see your little godson. Is he not beautiful?'

Luke glanced at the little bundle lying in the cradle and murmured indistinctly.

Carlotta met Adele's eyes and giggled. 'He is adorable,' she said, pushing Luke out of the way. 'I hope he is a good baby?'

'He sleeps a great deal, but when he is awake he is very demanding, just like his father,' replied Adele, her eyes twinkling. 'And everyone says he has the Ainslowe look.'

'Dashed if I can see it,' muttered James. 'We have had so many visitors I am beginning to wish we had turned the morning room into Adele's bedchamber; Lord and Lady Broxted called on us yesterday and Mr and Mrs Price the day before that. They are on their way to town to order Julia's bride clothes.'

'Ah, yes, she marries Viscount Fairbridge this summer.' Carlotta nodded. 'I am glad; I think they are well suited.' She paused. 'And what news of Mr Woollatt?'

Adele's eyes brimmed with merriment. 'My spies tell me that his mama has found him a very suitable bride—excellent breeding, reasonable fortune and from a *very* respectable family.'

'Sounds exceedingly dull,' said Luke. 'But then Woollatt is a very dull dog.' He pulled Carlotta into his arms. 'You are much better off with me, you know.'

Carlotta blushed, then giggled as James grimaced at this open display of affection. A snuffling cry from the cradle brought their attention back to the baby. Adele began to rock the cradle again and James moved over to gaze at his son.

'I was very much afraid I should not see this day,' he said, reaching down to stroke the sleeping baby's fat cheek. 'When the gig overturned, I was afraid I should lose you both.'

Adele reached out her hand, smiling fondly at him. 'You knew when we married that I come from tough yeoman stock, my love. It would take more than a little tumble to hurt me.'

'Nevertheless, I was never closer to doing a man harm than when I found out it was Reed who tampered with that wheel. I am glad he was sentenced to hard labour—any lesser punishment and I should have been tempted to take the law into my own hands.' He scowled at the memory.

'And Mattingwood—is he still awaiting transportation?' asked Luke. 'He was the bigger villain; Reed was working on his orders, after all.'

'He was transported for life soon after you left for the Continent.'

They were silent for a moment, then little James set up a cry and broke the spell. With infinite care, James lifted the baby and handed him to Adele, who rocked him gently in her arms until he settled back to sleep. James watched them for a few moments, then turned back to his brother.

'And is Durini to paint Darvell Manor for you?

'Devil a bit! He is far too busy. They have taken a house in Brighton for the summer; he is working at a certain royal palace at present.' His laughing eyes flickered towards Carlotta. 'However, he has promised me that he will paint our new bath-house. Which reminds me, James…we would like to make use of yours while we are here—I want to teach Carlotta to swim.'

It was said blandly, but Carlotta felt Adele's eyes upon her and could not prevent the blush stealing into her cheeks.

'What an excellent idea. Once the baby is weaned, I think we should do the same, James. I believe the exercise would be very beneficial.'

'Well, perhaps, perhaps,' said James, looking flustered. 'We shall have to wait and see.'

'You know, my love, I am quite as aware as Carlotta of the wall paintings in the bathhouse,' said Adele, choosing a bonbon from the little dish on the table beside her. 'We peeped into the warm room, you see, when we were walking in the grounds last summer.'

'You never told me that!'

'No, well, I thought you would be too shocked. However,

Carlotta is a married lady now, and Julia almost a wife, so I doubt if there is any harm done.'

'Quite the contrary,' murmured Luke, casting another wicked glance at Carlotta, who blushed to the roots of her hair. She was relieved when James suggested they should leave Adele to rest, and they were shown to their own guest room.

'James is quite the family man now,' observed Luke when they were alone. 'Marriage undoubtedly agrees with him.'

He watched Carlotta untie the ribbons of her bonnet and toss it aside, swiftly followed by her pelisse. As she stood with the light from the window behind her, he could see the curves of her body outlined through the thin muslin of her gown.

'And what do you think of the state, my lord, now that you have had several months to sample it?'

He held out his arms and immediately she walked into them.

'I think it agrees with me, too.' He put his arms around her. Looking down into the dark eyes that gazed so trustingly up into his own, he felt his heart tighten—she was so damned irresistible. 'No, it is not marriage,' he said slowly, 'it is *you* that agrees with me, *cara.*'

His mouth slid over hers and she responded immediately, her lips softening and her body leaning into him, arousing the desire that was never far away. He swept her up into his arms and carried her over to the bed.

'Luke! We have only just arrived.'

'No one will disturb us. I have locked the door.'

'But will not James be expecting us?' Her voice sounded husky, breathless—a sign that she wanted him, too.

'No, love. He was going back to sit with Adele. We need not appear again until the dinner hour.' He tugged gently at the ribbons securing her bodice. 'You will be wanting to change your gown…'

They undressed each other slowly, taking pleasure in arousing each other in the ways they had learned during the passionate days and nights since their marriage.

'With my body, I thee worship,' Luke murmured as they continued with their sensual rituals until they reached the final, fulfilling climax, clinging together as their passion spilled over, a great wave of blinding, gasping exhilaration that left them both exhausted.

The spring day was coming to a close, the light fading. Soon they would be summoned to the dinner table. Luke raised himself on one elbow and looked at Carlotta. She was curled on her side, her hand cradling her cheek. He leaned over and kissed her.

'It is time to get up, *cara*. Your maid will be banging on the door soon.'

A sleepy chuckle greeted his words. 'She knows better than that.' She sat up and reached for her wrap.

He heard her sigh. 'Carlotta? What is it?'

'I was thinking of Adele, and her fortune. I brought you so little…'

'You cannot call your uncle's ten thousand pounds a paltry sum!'

'No, but he insisted upon so much of it being tied up in settlements and jointures.'

'And quite rightly so. He is protecting you from the Wicked Baron.'

'Were you ever really wicked?'

He grinned and pulled her back on to the bed. 'No. I was more….wild. But I am tamed now.'

'Not completely, I hope.'

'No, love, not completely.'

She wound her arms about his neck, sighing again, but this

time with contentment. 'I am so fortunate, so—so blessed—to have a man like you, who loves me so much. It is the best feeling in the world to be so beloved.'

Luke's heart swelled at these words. He held her even tighter. 'And I intend that you shall continue to feel beloved,' he murmured as he prepared to kiss her again. 'For ever.'

* * * * *

HISTORICAL

Novels coming in September 2009

DEVILISH LORD, MYSTERIOUS MISS
Annie Burrows

The menacing Lord Matthison has the reputation of the devil, but secretly still yearns for his one true love, lost seven years ago. Cora Montague's body was never found, and when he encounters a fragile-looking woman, the image of his betrothed, Matthison is convinced Cora still lives. But what should he do to claim her…?

TO KISS A COUNT
Amanda McCabe

Leaving Sicily, Count di Fabrizzi and her heart behind her, Thalia Chase returns to England. She's shocked to see him again in Bath – with a suspected thief! The Count's dangerous mission doesn't leave room for beautiful Thalia. But what is a gentleman to do when a lady is so insistent on adventure, and so very passionate…?

THE EARL AND THE GOVERNESS
Sarah Elliott

Isabelle desperately needed the governess position William Stanton, Earl of Lennox offered her. However, working for the green-eyed Earl is more of a challenge than she expected! When their passion explodes in a bone-melting kiss, Isabelle knows she must leave. But the Earl has other plans for his innocent governess…

HISTORICAL

**Another exciting novel
available this month is:**

THE BRIGADIER'S DAUGHTER

Catherine March

From Lonely Miss to Daring Bride

It was an audacious plan – to marry her sister's bridegroom – and Miss Alexandra Packard was shocked at her own daring. Once she was married, the sensible, logical part of her urged her to speak up. The other part – the romantic, womanly, *lonely* part – kept her silent.

In truth, she did not want to stop being his wife. Indeed, she very much wanted to find out what it would be like to truly be Captain Reid Bowen's wife in *every* sense of the word…

MILLS & BOON

HIST0709 HB TBD

HISTORICAL

Another exciting novel available this month is:

HIS RUNAWAY MAIDEN
June Francis

A most tempting match…

Fleeing the clutches of her cruel stepmother, Rosamund Appleby dons a youth's disguise and heads for London…until she is halted in her tracks by Baron Alex Nilsson! Intrigued by this boy he suspects is really a well-born young lady, Alex seeks to protect her as they journey together.

But when Alex, who trusts no woman, finds himself hastily and conveniently married to beautiful, courageous Rosamund, he doesn't know which is more dangerous: the enemies plotting his downfall – or the seductive lure of a curvaceous woman in his bed…